BY A MOMENT

KEEPING SCORE

★ BOOK TWO ★

TAWDRA KANDLE

Hanging by a Moment

ISBN: 978-1-68230-405-1

Cover design by Robin Ludwig Design Inc.
www.gobookcoverdesign.com
Formatting: Champagne Formats

When life shatters, it helps to have friends. I don't know what I'd have done without Leo and Nate to comfort me, to hold me up and to keep me sane in face of sudden and terrible loss.

And if one of those friends happens to be the love of my life, the one guy I thought I'd never be close to again . . . I'm not going to complain. After all, in a vast sea of things that aren't fair, being with Leo again feels like the only shining beam of hope.

I know there aren't any guarantees for us. Leo's heading south to play football, rocking a full-ride at one of the top colleges in the nation. Meanwhile, all of my plans have fallen apart, and I have to figure out what comes next. Having Nate by my side is more important than I could have imagined.

The next four years were supposed to be the most exciting time of my life. Instead, they turn into a rollercoaster of uncertainty, complete with breathtaking highs and lows that threaten to break my heart.

In the end, the decisions we make now could change everything for the three of us, forever.

Other Books by the Author

Keeping Score

When We Were Us

Hanging By A Moment

Days of You and Me

The King Series

Fearless

Breathless

Restless

Endless

Crystal Cove Books

The Posse

The Plan

The Path

The Perfect Dish Series

Best Served Cold

Just Desserts

I Choose You

The One Trilogy

The Last One

The First One

The Only One

The Always Love Trilogy

Always for You

Always My Own

The Seredipity Duet

Undeniable

Unquenchable

Recipe for Death Series

Death Fricassee

Death A La Mode

This book is dedicated to my daddy, who shared with me his love of football, who taught me the all-important words GO ARMY, BEAT NAVY at a very early age, who watched college and professional football with me as long as I can remember, who never thought that teaching his daughters the ins and outs of the game was a trivial pursuit . . . and who, like Quinn's dad, left this earth far too soon.

I love you, Daddy, and I miss you all the time—but especially on Saturdays and Sundays from September through January.

This would be a great year for a little heavenly intervention with the Army team. Also, the Eagles could use a hand, too.

★ Prologue ★

"QUINN, CAN I ASK YOU SOMETHING?"

I rolled over onto my back to see Nate better. As usual when we studied together, he was sitting at my desk, but he'd turned in the chair to look down on me where I lay on the floor, my history notes spread in front of me.

I didn't answer him right away. Since that day about a year ago when I'd told Nate that Leo and I had ended our relationship, Nate hadn't mentioned anything about his own feelings for me. He'd done an excellent job of pulling back and being just who I needed—my best friend, with no hints of the crush he'd harbored for years. I'd been relieved, because I couldn't stand to lose another friend.

Narrowing my eyes now, I examined his face. He'd let his hair grow a little longer this year, and the dark brown waves skimmed his forehead, just above his wide blue eyes. The new meds he'd been on this year had helped him gain a little much-needed weight, and it showed in his cheeks. He didn't look heavy by any means, but the angular, almost-pointed look he'd had before had disappeared. The changes hadn't gone unnoticed by the other girls at school either; although Nate never gave any of them a second look, I knew more than one of our classmates wouldn't have minded if he had.

"Sure," I answered finally, my voice sounding a little tentative and suspicious even to my own ears.

Nate frowned. "I was hoping you'd say no."

A rusty and almost-unfamiliar bubble of laughter escaped my throat. "Then why did you ask me if you could ask me?"

He shrugged. "I guess I was thinking that just bringing—this—up gets me off the hook." He frowned, his forehead drawing together. "I think I did something wrong, and that you're going to be so pissed, you'll never talk to me again."

"Nate, seriously. I've known you since I was born. When have I ever stopped talking to you? Not even when you broke off Barbie's head."

"*That* was an accident. I was trying to pull on the stupid dress you always wanted on her, trying to help you out, and they never made the heads to stay on right."

I lifted one hand and waved it in the air between us. "Whatever. Just spit it out. What do you think you did?"

He looked downright miserable, his brow wrinkled and his eyes dark. "I don't think I did it. I know I did. At the time, it felt like the right thing, but now . . . I'm pretty sure it probably wasn't."

"Nate." I closed my eyes and sighed. "What is it? Tell me. I promise I won't be mad."

"I told Leo that he should break up with you."

The familiar stab of pain that hit whenever I heard his name silenced me for a moment. Nate mistook that for shock or anger, apparently, because he groaned and dropped his head into his hands.

"God, I knew I shouldn't have told you. I didn't do it because of—I did it for you. He was destroying you, Quinn. You were changing, and you were so unhappy. I was pissed. So the morning after you got drunk with the cheerleaders—"

"Yeah, thanks, I kind of remember that day. It stands out as being pretty shitty overall."

He went on as though I hadn't spoken. "That day, I went to his house and laid it out. I told him he was being selfish and stupid—and I guess I thought he might just, I don't know. Stop being an asshole to you. Man up."

I shook my head, rubbing it against the soft carpet. "No, you didn't. You wanted him to end things. That's why you did it."

"No, I—" Nate began to protest and then fell silent. "Maybe. But now I wonder. I thought you'd be happier. But you've changed even more, Quinn. You're not who you were before—before you and Leo."

"Before we were us." The tears were long gone. I'd cried a bucketful over Leo, and sometimes I still did, late at night. He'd left a T-shirt at my house, in my bedroom, on one of the many nights he'd snuck into my room after dark. I remembered that particular instance with perfect, painful clarity. We'd been apart from each other for four days because he'd gone with the football team on what they called a team-building trip, spending the night over in Philadelphia and listening to a bunch of coaches and former players from around the country speak. Before he'd gotten back, I'd gone to New York for two nights with my mom to see a play and visit her best friend from college, who worked at a news magazine in the city. We'd gotten home too late for Leo to risk coming over.

So when he finally did slip upstairs the next night, we were ravenous for each other. Leo had fallen on me with wild kisses, stripped off my clothes and made love to me with a brand-new abandon. We'd worked hard to keep quiet, giggling together when I had to turn up my television to muffle anything my parents might overhear.

Afterward, I'd lain in his arms, drowsy but not willing to let him go yet. I'd told him in whispers about the city, about how I was pretty sure my mother had taken me to make sure I remembered that I had goals and plans beyond just having a boyfriend. Leo, in turn, ran his fingers through my hair, touching his lips to my temple, my ear lobe and my neck as he murmured about football and how amazing it had been to hear his favorite players speak.

That night, he'd worn a long-sleeved button-up shirt over a gray T-shirt, and when he left, I teased him, refusing to give him the T-shirt.

"It smells like you. I want to sleep with it under my pillow." I'd buried my face in the soft material. "If I can't have you in my bed all night, at least leave me this."

Leo had smiled, his eyes softening the way they did when he looked at me. He'd kissed me hard. "If I can't stay in your bed all night, at least my shirt can hang around." And then he'd snuck out, creeping down the steps and out the back door. He knew which creaking boards to avoid from nearly eighteen years spent running around my house.

I'd lain in bed, listening, his shirt bunched up to my chin, and I'd drifted off to sleep, dreaming of a night when he didn't have to leave me . . .

A week after that horrible day when Leo had ended us, I'd found the T-shirt tucked under my bed. At first, I'd been tempted to cut it into tiny pieces or burn it, but then I'd lifted it to my nose, sniffing in his scent which still lingered. And I hadn't been able to do anything but stuff it under my pillow again.

So now when I was having a particularly hard day and found myself crying over Leo again, I pulled out the shirt and used it to blot my tears. It felt fitting, somehow.

Still lying on the floor, I opened my eyes, staring up into Nate's worried face. "I already knew, Nate. Or at least I suspected. Gia said something a while back about you being so angry that day, and I guess maybe I put two and two together."

"Why didn't you say something? I've been dying by inches for months, afraid you'd find out and freak at me."

I lifted one shoulder. "It didn't really matter, did it? At first I was a little annoyed. But then I thought . . . there had to be something else, right? I mean, you didn't hold a gun to Leo's head. You didn't blackmail him, did you? He had a choice. He didn't have to listen to you." I paused. "My dad said something to me a few months ago. I guess he'd been talking to Leo's father, and he says he thinks Leo's parents were worried about the two of us getting too serious too soon. Joe might have said something to Leo, too. Maybe he talked him into ending everything." I swallowed hard. "So you need to stop feeling guilty, because this wasn't your fault, Nate. I don't blame you."

He sighed, and his shoulders slumped. "You have no idea how scared I've been that you'd figure it out and be furious."

I rolled back over to my stomach, although I could still feel Nate's eyes on the back of my neck. "Nope. It's done. And even though . . ." My voice trailed away. "Even though it hurt, and even though I never would've ended things myself, maybe Leo's dad was right. We must not have been meant to be. If Leo really loved me—" An unexpected sob caught in my throat. "He wouldn't have listened to anyone. Not you, not his father—no one. It was just easier for him to break up with me than to figure out all the stuff happening between us. You know, like his partying and the football team . . . and what might've happened when we went to college. He chose all of that over me."

Nate didn't respond right away. I heard the squeak of my desk chair as he shifted, and I sensed that he was trying to decide whether or not to speak. When he did, his voice was cautious and tentative. "You've changed since you guys broke up. But so has Leo."

I forced a laugh. "Oh, yeah? Seems like he's still partying pretty hard. From what I hear, anyway." And I did hear. It was impossible *not* to know what the star of the school's football team did. Matt Lampert was the quarterback, and he was definitely popular in his own right. But there was just something about Leo, some kind of charisma, that made him stand head and shoulders above even Matt. Of course, from my point of view, it was easy to see who was hotter; Leo, with his wide gray eyes and light brown hair, his broad chest and long muscled legs . . . not to mention that ass . . .

I mentally shook myself. Wandering down that path wasn't healthy for me. Only heartache lay at the end.

"Yeah, he's still going to parties, but he isn't hooking up. Or it doesn't seem like he is. I never see him with any girls, and the cheerleaders are always whining about how he's not interested anymore."

I'd noticed the same thing, but I'd been afraid to acknowledge it, even in my own thoughts. "Maybe he's just being really discreet about his hook-ups." I glanced over my shoulder at Nate.

He smirked. "Yeah, 'cause *that* sounds like Leo."

I rubbed my eye. "You know what? I really don't want to talk about Leo anymore. I need to finish this reading, or I'm going to fail my midterms."

"Yeah, okay." The chair groaned again as Nate turned to face the desk. I'd just found my place in the book I was reading when he spoke again.

"Quinn, you want to go to prom with me?"

I was so surprised that the heavy textbook slid from my fingers. "Prom?"

"You know, it's that big dance for the upperclassmen. Rite of passage, all that stuff. We're supposed to spike the punch and maybe even join in a musical number where the whole class sings together."

"You've been watching *Grease* again, haven't you?"

He snorted. "No. I only ever watch with you."

"Whatever, dude." I kept my gaze glued to the page in front me, hoping I'd distracted Nate enough that he didn't realize I hadn't answered his question. I wasn't surprised he'd asked me; I'd been expecting it, actually. But I hadn't been expecting it tonight, in the context of this conversation. "Thanks, but no. I'm not going to prom. Matter of fact, I'm thinking of asking my parents if we can go down to the shore that weekend, so I don't have to deal with the whole thing." My mom and dad had finally bought the house at the Jersey shore that we'd rent-ed for a few weeks each summer during my childhood. They planned to spend more time there once I was away at college.

"You might regret not going. Someday." Nate was persistent, I'd give him that.

"Maybe." I pushed myself to sit up, stretching a little. "But I'm willing to take that risk. Hey, why don't you ask Gia? I don't think she's got a date yet." Our fiercely independent and strong-willed friend worked on the newspaper with me. Over the past year, she and Nate had gotten to be buddies; that was no easy thing, as Nate tended to be closed off to anyone outside our immediate circle. And since Leo and I had broken up, that circle had gotten considerably smaller.

Nate lifted his shoulder. "No, I don't think so. First of all, isn't she against proms on general principle? She'd probably want to go just to make fun of the whole thing. And if you're not going to go, I guess I won't either."

I felt a twinge of guilt, but I pushed it away. "Well, I think you should go. But if you don't, you can come down the shore with us. We'll drown our promless sorrows in pizza and saltwater taffy."

"Sounds like a plan." Nate stood up, pausing a minute to find his balance before he stepped away from the desk. "I guess I better head home. It's getting late."

"Okay." I rose, too, and grabbed my wallet from the bookshelf. "Let me find my keys."

I heard Nate's long exhale. "I wish you didn't have to drive me. It makes me feel—" He didn't finish, but I already knew what he meant. The weakness in his legs and hips was a little improved, but not enough for him to be medically cleared for a license. I knew it was an ongoing source of frustration for him.

"Nate. Honestly. Not being able to drive doesn't make you any less of a man in my eyes." I leaned in and kissed his cheek, glad that he'd topped me in height a few years back. "And I'm happy to give you a lift."

"Fine." He caught my arm before I could pull away completely, and for a moment, his bright blue eyes held mine. My heart thudded, but not in anticipation, unfortunately. Part of me wished I could feel something more than friendship for Nate, but I didn't. He was my beloved friend. The one I could talk to about anything, the boy I'd known as long as I'd been drawing breath. But there wasn't any desire there; his touch didn't make me tingle or want.

I didn't want to think about that other friend, the one I'd known just as many years. The one who, with a single glance, could make me melt with need. The one who'd broken my heart so badly, I didn't know if it would ever mend.

As if he could feel my thoughts stray toward Leo, Nate scowled and released my arm. Turning away from me, he opened the door and headed for the steps, which I knew he'd navigate slowly. I waited a few minutes before I followed him down.

★ One ★

Quinn

"HEY, HONEY, YOUR MOM JUST SWEET-TALKED ME into picking up dinner from Mandarin Inn tonight. You want your regular garlic chicken?"

"Hmmmm." I hummed under my breath, setting down the book was reading as my dad leaned through the doorway of my bedroom. "Yes, please. Oh, and can we get a side of fried won ton, please?"

"Sure. Anything for my high school graduate daughter." He winked. "Mom's calling it in, so by the time I get there, it should be ready. You hungry?"

I shrugged. "I guess. It's not like I've done anything today but lay around and read. Hard to work up an appetite doing that."

"Depends on what you're reading. For instance, in the book I'm reading, the main character keeps ordering Chinese food. I'm thinking maybe your mom somehow planted subliminal messages in it."

I smiled. "I wouldn't put it past her."

"Pesky woman." He smirked, because we both knew that my mother had him totally wrapped around her little finger. "Hey, you okay, hon? You know, I didn't want to say anything before, but shouldn't you be out raising hell, whooping it up now that you're done with school? Mom and I had this whole speech prepared about how you needed to think about your future before you got drunk and disorderly. We're disappointed that we haven't gotten to use it."

"Sorry about that." I picked up my book. "But it's not my scene. Plus, I'm not really in the celebrating mood. So I finished school. Big deal. It just means I get to go to another school for another four years. Maybe I'll be in more of a party mood after college graduation. Stay tuned."

Daddy grinned. "You can count on that, sweetheart. Nothing could keep me from being there the day you graduate from Evans, summa cum laude, valedictorian, the youngest hire at the . . ." He cast his eyes up. "*New York Times*."

Laughing, I shook my head. "Hold onto the dream. I'll just be happy if I make it through."

"You will, honey. You can do anything you decide you're going to do. Never forget that."

I waved my hand. "Sure, sure, sure. Go get my Chinese food, oh wise one. Now that you're talking about it, I'm starting to get hungry."

He leaned down to kiss my forehead. "Your wish, my command. Be right back, toots."

Listening to him clump down the steps as only a male could do, I smiled again. I heard him talk with my mom for a minute—probably making sure she'd called in our order and kissing her before he left—and then there was the jangle of keys and the slam of the front door.

I flipped over on my bed, rolling onto my stomach. I had what my mom called the post-graduation-let-down-blues; yesterday I'd capped off four stellar years of high school by showing up at the ceremony, pretending to toss my cap, and then hanging out at a backyard barbecue with my extended family, as well as my best friend Nate and his parents. It wasn't exactly a wild celebration, even after my great-aunt told us a story about being at Woodstock and demonstrated how she'd danced there.

I'd expected to feel different. I thought something might change. But no, it was just more of the same.

The high and low point of graduation had both come at the same time, when my mother and Sheri had insisted on posing Nate, Leo and me together for a picture. I hadn't been that close to Leo in a year. When he'd put one arm around me and pulled me tight up against his side, it had felt so painfully familiar that I'd had trouble breathing. Dizzy with want, I'd lost my balance and had to cling to Leo's arm briefly. I'd murmured an apology, and to my shock, he'd caught my eye and said softly, "Me, too."

If I were still the kind of girl who harbored hopes and dreams, I might've thought Leo meant something deeper by those two words. Since I wasn't, I'd tamped down any flare of optimism and turned away.

The summer stretched before me, feeling just as empty as the past year had. My mom and I were planning to stay down at the shore; since she worked exclusively on-line, designing and maintaining websites, she had the freedom to do that wherever she wanted. I'd scored a part-time job at an ice cream shop around the corner from our beach house. My dad would commute on weekends, apart from a few weeks of vacation from the pharmacy where he worked.

Nate would probably come visit with his parents. And maybe even Lisa and Joe would make their way down for a weekend; Lisa was feeling well enough now to make the hour-long drive. She was officially in remission from the leukemia that she'd been fighting for almost two years. It would be good for them all to be together again, I thought. As hard as I'd tried to avoid causing any tension between the three couples—my parents, Nate's and Leo's—after Leo and I broke up, I knew there was still some residual awkwardness. Which was a shame, of course, since they'd been all been friends for over eighteen years.

Shifting to my side, I closed my eyes, willing away the lingering residual pain that always came when Leo crossed my mind. It had to go away someday, I'd decided. And once I left town to start my new life up in New England, at Evans College, I'd be able to put behind me Leo and those shining months when we'd been us . . .

I must've dozed for a few minutes, because the next thing I knew, my mom's voice floated into my room.

"Quinn, sweetie, want to toss some paper plates and chopsticks on the table? Your dad should be home any time now." She paused, stopping in my doorway much as my father had a little bit before. "He must've run into someone and got talking. You know how he is."

"Oh, yeah. I know." I swung my legs off the bed. "Some little old lady comes up and says, 'Oh, Mr. Russell, I need to ask you a question about the cream you gave me last week . . .' And then one hour later, they're still talking."

"Meanwhile our Chinese food is getting cold." She shook her head. "Well, come on down and help me set up, so we can eat as soon as he gets here."

Mom and I didn't fuss; we were both still tired from the graduation party. A few random balloons floated around the house, looking lackluster and wan as the helium seeped out. The folding tables and chairs were propped against the side of the house out on the porch, and some crepe paper fluttered in the breeze.

I laid out leftover paper plates, bright purple with orange lettering spelling out GRADUATION in letters that were meant to look fun.

"Did we have any napkins left?" I called into the kitchen as I slouched against the back of a chair. "And can you bring out some serving spoons?"

"Sure." Mom sounded distracted, but I heard the silverware drawer rattle as she opened it. A few seconds later, she came into our small breakfast nook, holding a handful of spoons and frowning at the phone in her hand.

"What's wrong?" I took the spoons and set them in the middle of the table.

"Oh, nothing. I tried to call Daddy, just to hurry him along if he did get talking to someone. But it went right to voicemail."

"Huh." I slid out a chair and sat down. "It's probably dead. You know how he is. Always forgets to charge it."

"Yeah. Probably." Still, she gnawed at the corner of her lip. "But he knew how hungry I was. I don't think he'd dawdle. Not on purpose. I hope . . ." Her voice trailed off. "Oh, it's nothing."

"Hey, while we're waiting, want to help me pull down the last of that crepe paper? If it rains tonight, that's going to be a mess to clean up." I pointed out to the porch. "Daddy and I were going to do it later today, so if we take it down now, we can guilt him about it."

My mother smiled. "I like the way you think. Okay, you bring the ladder, and I'll get a trash bag."

We'd just about finished cleaning up when we both heard a car around the front of the house. Mom grinned, relief evident on her face.

"There he is." Stretching her arm long, she snagged the last scrap of crepe paper from the corner of the porch ceiling, crumbled it in one fist and tossed it across to me. She climbed down from the ladder, brushing her hands over her thighs. "Take that bag to the garage, will you, and I'll have everything set up to eat when you're done."

"Sure. Although I know you mean you want me out of the way while you give Daddy a little hell for making you worry."

My mother shook her finger at me. "You just go take care of that trash. I'll see to your father."

I laughed, tied up the bag and went through the back door of the garage, dropping the bag into one of the already-overflowing cans and cutting through to the kitchen. My stomach growled; I was hungrier than I'd thought.

"Hey, where are you guys?" I closed the door from the garage, glancing from the set table in the breakfast nook to the empty kitchen. I caught sight of my mom from the corner of my eye, standing in the front hallway. "Oh, geez, you two. I mean, he was only gone like an hour . . ."

I stopped speaking when I stepped into the hall. My mother was frozen, one hand to her throat. And in the open doorway, two men dressed in police uniforms shifted their gazes toward me.

They were both holding their hats in their hands. I didn't know why that struck me, but it did; I couldn't tear my eyes away the way they held the flat caps. One of them, who was a bit shorter than the other, was turning the hat in his hands, little by little.

The taller policeman cleared his throat. "Are you . . .?" He looked at my mom again, then back at me. "Uh, Bill Russell. Are you his, uh, daughter?"

I nodded, because my throat had sealed.

"Okay." The other man spoke now. "We—we're sorry to have to inform you that there was an accident. Mr. Russell was involved in a collision, and he suffered extensive, serious injuries." His eyes flashed toward my mother again. "You and your—uh, your mother? We'd like to drive you to the hospital right now."

"Is he all right? Daddy's okay, right?" My own voice sounded foreign to my ears.

The first officer's lips tightened. "The emergency medical technicians responded to the accident immediately and treated the victims on the scene. They transported Mr. Russell to the hospital, but unfortunately, his injuries were extensive, and he succumbed to them upon arrival."

"Succumbed?" I screeched. "Succumbed? You mean he's *dead*? Is that what you're saying? If that's what you mean, then why the fuck don't you just say it? Is he dead? Is my father dead?"

Their expressions didn't waver. The shorter policeman nodded. "I'm sorry. Yes, we're sorry to tell you that Mr. Russell was pronounced dead upon arrival, despite the best efforts of the doctors."

The taller man took a half-step forward. "Do you have family? Is there someone we can call for you, to meet us at the hospital?"

I started to shake my head. My family had all been here with us the day before, but I couldn't bear to think about calling them now, having to tell them—no. Instead I fumbled in the back pocket of my shorts, pulling out my phone.

"Lisa and Joe Taylor. Sheri and Mark Wellman. They're in my contacts." With shaking fingers, I punched in my security code and handed the phone to the closest man. "Call them. Lisa and Joe Taylor. Sheri and Mark Wellman."

My words, those names, finally penetrated my mother's stupor, and she moved, wrapping her arms around her middle and emitting a loud, high-pitched keening that I was certain I'd hear to the end of my days. I clapped both hands over my ears, curling onto myself and dropped to my knees, screwing shut my eyes and swan-diving into oblivion.

★ Two ★

Leo

"CAN'T YOU DRIVE THIS FUCKING CAR ANY fucking faster?" I hunched over, one hand braced on the dashboard, as though I could move us along the freeway.

"No, I can't. Or let me amend that. I *won't*. I'm going five miles over the speed limit. That's the best I can do."

I glowered at the guy behind the steering wheel, wishing like hell there'd been anyone but him sober enough to drive me home. His lips were pressed together and his jaw was tense, probably because I'd been repeating the same words more or less for the past thirty minutes.

He glanced in my direction and sighed, his mouth relaxing just a little. "Look, dude, I get it. You need to get home. But me breaking the law so we get stopped for a ticket, or worse, get into an accident, is only going to slow us down. So chill, okay? Put your head back and get some sleep. I got the address in my GPS, and I'll wake you up when we get there."

"I'm not going to sleep." I growled the words. "I can't. I—I just need to get to her." Shifting a little, I stared out the window, not even seeing the passing landscape. It was just trees and shit, the same areas I'd been driving past all my life. None of it mattered now; nothing else was important except getting to Quinn as fast as I could. I looked over at the driver again. "What was your name? Sorry. I know you told me. I wasn't really—it was a shock this morning. I'm still . . ." I ran my hand through my hair. "Processing."

"Tate Durham." He spoke with a kind of resigned exasperation, and I realized he must've given me this information more than once. "From Gatbury. I'm—"

"Yeah." I nodded. "That I remember. You played ball for Gatbury, you met Matt at that passing camp last summer, and you kept in touch. He invited you down to the shore this weekend because you're going to Carolina with us."

Tate cocked a finger at me. "Bingo. I guess you were listening."

"Kind of. It's coming back to me now."

"I'm surprised, actually. You were pretty much blotto from the time I got down there yesterday."

"Blotto? Who the hell says that? What're you, from the nineteen-forties?" My lips curled.

Tate didn't seem to be offended. "I was raised by my grandpa, and yeah, that's how he talks. Nothing wrong with a little retro slang, right? What would you rather I said? You were wasted? Drunk? Wrecked? Shit-faced? Bo—"

"Okay, I get it. Yeah, I was." I turned my attention to the window again.

"So, not to be insensitive or anything, but seeing as how

I'm your chauffeur just now, I'm going to let my curiosity get the best of me and ask. Who exactly died?"

Pain crashed over me again. "My girlfriend's dad. He—" I choked a little as my throat tightened. "I was really close to him. I've known him my whole life."

"Your girlfriend?" Tate frowned. "So that wasn't the blonde in bed with you this morning, I'm guessing?"

Shit. "No. I don't even know who she was. Quinn is—well, it's complicated. She's not technically my girlfriend. Not anymore." But calling her that had happened without me even thinking about it. In my mind, Quinn was still mine, even though it had been over a year since we'd been together. "And just for the record, the chick in my bed? I don't know how she got there, but nothing went down between us. I was alone in the bed when I passed out. That much I remember. She must've come in some time after I fell asleep."

"Hey, none of my business." Tate lifted one hand off the steering wheel and held it up. "I was just clarifying. So—Quinn, is it? She used to be your girlfriend?"

"Yeah. We've known each other our whole lives. Us, and Nate, our other friend. Our families are, you know, really close. If any one of us kids yelled, 'Mom!' growing up, all three of the mothers answered." I managed a smile, remembering. "So losing Bill—it's like losing my dad, in a way. I can't believe he's gone. And I can't imagine how Quinn is going to deal with it."

"You and Quinn are friends, but you also dated?" Tate slid a glance my way. "That must've been interesting."

"It's always been Quinn for me." The truth rose easily to the surface, circumventing the muck and confusion of the last year so neatly that it felt simple again. "I knew it, but I never felt like I was good enough for her. Quinn has this . . . this rightness about her. Like she knows what's good and she knows the way she should go, and she does it. She stands up for people who can't stand up for themselves. Injustice—it just infuriates her. And she was never shy about pointing it out, either, even when it made her look bad." I remembered her frequent run-ins with the cheerleaders, who'd resented Quinn for writing articles about the privileges they received at school. "Quinn sees the good in people. I guess I was always afraid if I got too close, she'd see there wasn't that much worthwhile in me."

"That's deep, man." Tate flicked the turn signal and eased into the passing lane. I wasn't sure if it was my imagination or not, but it felt as though he'd picked up a little speed. "What changed?"

"I'd like to say it was me, but it was more like I gave up fighting how I felt. Gave in." The memory of my lips on Quinn's was almost palpable.

"Uh huh. So why aren't you still together? Why were you down at the shore getting drunk and groping other girls?"

That was the million-dollar question. "Because I listened to bad advice from people who meant well. My dad asked me if I knew what it was going to be like, trying to have a long-distance relationship while I was focused on football in college. And our friend Nate convinced me that I was hurting Quinn by being with her. That I was changing her. I couldn't deal with it. Plus, my mom was sick—" I broke off. "Those are all excuses. Truth is, I was stupid and scared. I gave up Quinn, and it just about killed me."

"Huh." Tate nodded. "I'm not an expert on relationships.

Hell, I've never had one. But aren't high school hook-ups supposed to have a short shelf-life? Isn't that typical?"

"Maybe, but Quinn's not typical. And this wasn't a hook-up. It felt like it should've lasted forever." I rubbed at my eyes. "I know that sounds lame. Sorry."

"Actually, it doesn't. It sounds kind of perfect." Tate shrugged. "But then, I guess I'm not your average guy."

I wasn't sure what to make of that, but I was saved from having to reply by the smooth automated GPS voice instructing us to take the next exit.

Within a few moments, Tate was pulling up to the curb in front of the Russell house. I saw my mom's car in the driveway, parked behind Nate's parents' van and the compact Quinn and her mother shared. For one fleeting moment, I wondered if Bill's sedan was parked in the garage . . . and then I remembered. No, Bill's car was gone, just as Bill was. Reality smacked me across the face once again.

"You okay, Leo?" Tate studied me, his face somber. "You ready to deal with this? It's not going to be easy."

I exhaled and closed my eyes, thinking how different this guy was from most of my friends. On my way out the door at the beach house, I'd tripped over Matt Lampert's feet in my hurry. The guy I'd thought of as my closest friend for the past few years had blinked up at me in confusion.

"Dude, where you goin'?" He'd slurred the words, as though he was still wasted. Which maybe he was.

I'd paused. "I'm going home, Matt. Quinn—Quinn's dad. He was killed. My mom was trying to get in touch with me, and I guess she finally called on your phone, and—" I'd shaken my head. "Never mind. I gotta get home."

"Dead? Ser'usly?" Matt had struggled to sit up. "Dude, that sucks."

Anger had swelled in my chest. "No, *dude*, it doesn't suck. Dropping your phone into the toilet sucks. Missing a pass sucks. A man died. A man I loved like my own father, *Quinn's* father, is dead. This is tragedy, Matt. It's real life. God, sometimes you make me sick."

I'd seen the recoil of surprise on his face, but I hadn't taken the time to say anything else. I'd stalked out of the house without another word.

Now, though, I could almost feel Tate's empathy, his understanding. I was suddenly ridiculously grateful that this stranger was the guy who'd driven me home.

"Yeah. I know. I'd give just about anything not to have to go in, but you know . . . I have to. Me sitting out here isn't going to change anything, is it?"

He shook his head. "Doesn't seem likely. You need help with anything?"

"No, but thanks." I hadn't bothered to pack up my bag before leaving the shore house. Matt would get my shit and bring it home, or he wouldn't—I didn't really care. "Listen, Tate—thank you. For doing this." I leaned up and dug into my back pocket for my wallet. "Let me give you gas money."

Tate put out his hand to stop me. "Nope. I don't want it. Listen, I'm glad I could help you out. I'm sorry we met under these circumstances, but at least I could do this for you." He twisted his hand around, presenting it to me to shake. "If there's anything I can do, anything else, call me, okay?" He'd given me his phone number to text to my mom, so she'd be able to get in touch with us on our way home, since my phone had been charging as we drove. "Otherwise, guess I'll see you in a month or so down south."

"You know it." I opened my door and swung my legs out. "Thanks again, Tate. I mean it."

In one movement that was as fluid as I could manage, I swung out of the car, slammed the door and made my way to the front door. Quinn's front door.

I didn't knock or ring the doorbell. I never had; Nate, Quinn and I had grown up going in and out of each other's houses as easily as our own homes. I paused only a beat before I turned the knob, my stomach churning.

The front hall of the Russells' home led into a formal living room, which I couldn't remember us ever using. But today, everyone was sitting there: my dad was the first person I saw, slumped in a deep green wing chair. On the sofa, my mother and Sheri, Nate's mom, flanked Carrie, who seemed to have shrunk in the less-than-forty-eight hours since I'd seen her last.

Quinn's mom wore yoga pants and a huge sweatshirt. As I stepped into the hallway, I recognized the shirt as one of Bill's. Her hands were lost in the sleeves. Her sleek black hair, always so neat and styled, was tousled and held back from her face by a clip. She didn't look up or even react when my mother cried out my name and stood, her arms reaching for me.

"Oh, my God, Leo. Thank God you're here. You have no idea—" She bit her lip, casting a glance down at Carrie. "We were worried."

"I'm sorry." The response was automatic. I knelt in front of Quinn's mother and laid my hand on hers, which lay loosely in her lap. "Carrie, God, I'm sorry. I wish . . ." I stopped at that point, because there wasn't any reason to go on. Nothing I could say would change the horrible reality of the situation, and Carrie wasn't hearing me, anyway. She stared down at the carpet, her lips slightly parted and her eyes glassy.

Next to her, Sheri sighed, the softest breath fanning Carrie's hair. I looked at her and then at my mother.

"Where's Quinn?"

My mother didn't hesitate. "She's upstairs. In her room. She hasn't slept or eaten since—well, since yesterday."

"And Nate?" The last thing I wanted to do was get into a knock-down, drag-out—figuratively speaking, since I'd never hit Nate—with the guy who made up the third part of our trio. Not today. Not in front of Quinn. But I knew, too, that no matter what, Nate wouldn't be pleased to see me.

"I sent him home. Mark just drove him there." Sheri met my eyes, hers full of understanding. "He hadn't slept, either, and I convinced him that Quinn wouldn't go to sleep as long as he was here."

"Okay." I turned to the steps, taking them two at a time. None of the parents tried to stop me.

The last time I'd been in Quinn's bedroom, I'd snuck upstairs with her after Carrie and Bill had gone to bed. We did that sometimes, when we hadn't had a chance to be alone together for a while. Climbing the steps with her hand in mine had felt, to me, like a preview of the future, a tempting glimpse of our eventual life together. Since she didn't want to make her parents suspicious, Quinn would stick to her normal bedtime routine, and I'd lay in her bed, listening to her brushing her teeth in the nearby bathroom. And then she'd come back into the bedroom, smiling the way she only did for me, close the door behind her and crawl onto the bed, her eyes bright with desire.

I paused outside her door now and gave myself a little shake. Now was not the time to let these memories interfere with comforting Quinn. Or whatever it was I was going to do once I opened the door.

Turning the knob, I stepped into the room, my eyes going to Quinn right away. She was curled up in the center of her bed, but she wasn't lying down. She was sitting up, back ramrod stiff and her arms wrapped about her legs as she stared straight ahead.

At the sound of the door, she glanced up and froze. For a second, I thought she wasn't going to react at all, that she was going to ignore me and pretend I wasn't there. And then her face contorted into rage and her hands fisted.

"What the *hell* are you doing here? Get out." She hissed the words at me, rising up onto her knees.

I swallowed over the lump in my throat. "Quinn. Mia. Baby, I'm so—"

"Shut up. *Shut up*. Get out of here. I don't want you. I don't need you."

I chanced a step closer to the bed. "Quinn, come on. Let me . . . let me help you."

"Help me? Are you fucking kidding? Just how the hell are you going to help me, Leo? You going to bring my father back to life? You going to reverse time so he doesn't get into the car to go get us dinner last night? Or maybe you're going to make it so he leaves a little later, or a little sooner, just enough of a difference so that the truck that hit him is already through the intersection before he gets there? If you can make anything like that happen, then I'm willing to listen. If you can't, get the fuck out of my room and leave me alone."

"God, don't you think I wish I could change it? If I could do it, I'd make sure nothing happened to your dad. I'd give anything to keep him from being in that accident. Don't you know, Mia, there's nothing in the world I wouldn't do to keep you from being hurt?"

She sank back to sit on the bed, snorting. "Oh, really? Beg to differ, Leo. I happen to have a pretty good memory, and the day you decided I was in the way of your precious football career? Yeah, I remember that day. You sure as hell didn't mind hurting me then."

I ventured nearer to her, moving until the front of my legs hit the edge of the mattress. "I didn't break up with you because of my football career. I did it because—because I was already hurting you. I was forcing you to become someone you're not, and I was afraid you'd give up what was important to you because you loved me."

"Break my heart then, or break my heart later. That was the choice, huh?" Quinn rolled her eyes. "Did it ever occur to you to actually talk to me about it? Did you think maybe if we'd discussed it, like we used to do everything, we could come up with a solution that didn't fucking tear me apart?"

I shook my head. "No. Because I know you, Mia. Everything you do is for other people. You'd have sacrificed for me and never even blinked. You would've chosen me over you, and I couldn't let you do that."

"You took away my choice. You walked away, turned your back on me, like I didn't mean anything to you." Tears filled her eyes and spilled over, rolling down her pale cheeks. "Like

I meant nothing."

I dropped to my knees next to the bed and reached out my hand to find one of hers. "You are everything to me, Mia. You always have been. I was stupid and scared, and I listened—" I shook my head. I wasn't going to blame anyone else for my own idiocy. "I regretted it every minute of every day."

"Then why didn't you do something about it? I didn't exactly disappear. Day after day, you walked right past me like I wasn't there." She dropped her forehead down to her knees, but she didn't pull away her hand from mine.

I gripped her fingers a little tighter. "Because for once in my life, I was trying to do the right thing. To do something for you, even though it was killing me."

Her shoulders shook. "He said . . . my dad . . . he said I'd probably find out someday you had a reason I couldn't understand now." Her words were barely discernible, gasped out between sobs. "He always told me . . . it was more than I thought."

I closed my eyes, choking back my own tears. "God, Quinn. I'm sorry. I'm sorry for everything." I lifted her hand to my mouth and kissed her knuckles. When her fingers tightened around mine, I took a chance and climbed onto the bed, crawling to her. "Baby, let me hold you."

She hesitated, and for a minute, I thought she was going to push me away. And then she lifted her tear-streaked face to me, and her full bottom lip trembled. Sliding her hand free, she touched the side of my face before moving her fingers to my neck and curling them around, bringing me close to her.

"Leo, I don't know . . . I don't know how to breathe anymore. I don't know how to keep going on." She bridged the short distance between our mouths, so that when she spoke again, her lips moved against mine.

"Love me again, Leo. Show me how to keep living. Make all the hurt go away."

She didn't have to ask me twice. I circled her waist with both my arms and tugged her against me, dragging her into my lap. Feeling her there again felt so right, as though I were re-attaching a limb I'd chopped off over a year ago. Her body shuddered, and I held her tighter.

"It's okay, Mia. It's going to be all right."

She shook her head, her dark curls swirling around us both. "No. Nothing is ever going to be the same. I can't—he's gone. I'll never see him again. I'll never hear him laugh or call me kiddo or tell me how good his cooking is—God."

A fresh bout of tears erupted, and I wanted to cry with her. "I know. He was the best." I stroked her hair back from her face. "Do you remember, when we were kids and we couldn't wait for something to happen, and it felt like it was taking forever, he'd say, 'Oh, you can—'"

"'—stand on your head for that long!'" Quinn gave a half-laugh that morphed into a sob. "And I used to tell him I couldn't stand on my head at all."

"Your dad was always the first to come play with us if we were tossing the football around. Or the first one to volunteer to drive us to the park, when we were really little." I swallowed. "I probably shouldn't tell you this, but he said he was going to come see me play at Carolina."

She lifted her face to look up at me. "I know. I overheard him talking to my mom about it. He said he wasn't going to mention it to me, but he just couldn't imagine not going down to see one of your games." Her fingers twisted into the collar of my T-shirt, damp with her tears. "He loved you, Leo."

"Yeah." I nodded and buried my face in her hair, breathing deep to inhale her intoxicating scent as much as to stave off my own crying.

"Leo." Her breath swept across the skin of my neck. "I don't know how I'm going to live without my dad. I don't know what I'm going to do."

"Mia." I tipped her chin up so that I could stare down into her eyes. "You don't have to do it alone. And we'll take it all one step at a time. I'll be with you all the way."

She blinked once, so slowly that I thought she might be falling asleep. And then she leaned closer again, whispering so softly that I had to focus to hear her.

"Make me forget. For just a little bit. Help me to feel better."

Before I could figure out what she meant, Quinn kissed me, open-mouthed and hard. There was nothing uncertain about her; on her lips I felt desire and desperation. Her hands tightened on the back of my neck.

I knew that a stand-up guy, someone here to comfort his friend, would not take advantage of the fact that said friend was currently thrusting her tongue into his mouth, with her boobs, boobs that he'd been dying to touch again for over a year, teasing against his chest. He would not be getting hard and horny as hell, and he'd just hold her, so that nothing happened that she might regret.

I was not that guy.

With a sound that was combination groan and growl, I raked my fingers through her hair, holding her head in place.

As hard as she'd been pressing her mouth to mine, I kissed her even deeper, angling her body closer against me.

"God, I've missed your hands." She covered my fingers, still deep in her hair, with her own hands. "Missed them on me. Missed you touching me." Shifting, she wriggled one leg between us and swung it around until she straddled me. "Missed feeling you against me."

My aching cock was lined up perfectly with the heat between her legs. When she shifted to take advantage of the angle, I wanted to cry again, but this time with want. With her gaze glued to my face, Quinn began moving up and down, grinding herself against me with agonizing slowness. Madness bubbled up within me, and fumbling with the hem of her T-shirt, I shoved my hands underneath. Finesse and care be damned—I just had to touch her.

Rational thought fled completely when I realized she wasn't wearing a bra. The weight of her tits in my palms turned me ravenous. With my hand still under her shirt, I snaked it around to spread my fingers over her back, holding her steady as I pushed the cotton material out of my way and bared those gorgeous breasts to me.

Quinn's breath quickened, and she arched her back, presenting the rosy-tipped peaks to me. They were practically begging for my attention, and I wasn't going to deny them—or myself. I closed my lips over one, sucking it into my mouth hard until Quinn moaned.

"Too hard?" I skimmed my lips down the slope of her boob.

"No. Never too hard." She guided my head to the other nipple, cupping my cheek in her hand. "Just having your mouth on me again is—oh, my God."

Her last words were a gasp as I caught the other stiff tip between my teeth, letting my tongue tease it. I wanted to spend hours just worshipping her tits. I could've done it, if I weren't afraid the real world might intrude eventually.

But Quinn had other ideas, anyway. She slipped one hand between us, stroking my dick over the fly of my shorts. I was painfully hard, so aroused that I wasn't sure I wouldn't come right there and embarrass myself.

"Mia. Baby." I sat up a little, brushing her hair away from her eyes. "Are you sure you want to do this? I mean . . . I want you. But if you—you know, I can wait."

She shook her head. "Maybe you can. And good for you. But I can't." Rising up on her knees, she peeled off the yoga pants, fumbling a little to balance as she kicked them away. My mouth went dry and my heart nearly stopped when I realized she wasn't wearing any underwear beneath them.

Grasping one of my hands, she brought it between her legs, pressing my fingers into her folds. "Can you feel how wet I am? How much I want you? I've been dying by degrees for months, Leo. The rest of the world is falling apart around me. Let me have this. Let me have you."

There was no fucking way in any world that I could have denied her. I kept my fingers on her slick core, watching her face in almost-drugged need as I plunged two fingers inside her.

Quinn whimpered a little. Her eyes drooped to half-closed, and her mouth fell open. I could tell that every ounce of her focus was on the spot where my hand worked her. I fell backwards onto the mattress so that I could watch her come apart.

With one fluid movement, she pulled her T-shirt over her head. I lay there for a minute, just taking her in: her arms and shoulders were tanned and toned, her stomach the same golden color and taut. Two pale triangles surrounded her breasts, where her bathing suit had covered them. I'd never seen anything so beautiful, so breath-taking, in all my life.

She was panting now in time with the motion of my fingers, her chest rising and falling rapidly. I let her ride my hand for a few minutes before I pressed my thumb against her clit.

With a sharp cry, she froze, bending her back and throwing back her head, coming against my relentless fingers, her tight channel squeezing them. I stayed with her until she began to squirm away, falling next to me on the bed.

"Leo." Her voice was muffled against my chest. I drew her close to me, and she wrapped both arms around my waist, nuzzling her face into my neck.

"I got you, baby. I got you. I'm never going to let go."

Her breath warmed me, even as one hand slid under my shirt. "I think you have too many clothes on. I'm lying here buck-ass naked, and you're still completely dressed."

I rubbed small circles on her back. "It's okay, Mia. I don't have to—it's enough to be here for you. Why don't you try to sleep now?" I thought of our parents sitting downstairs, and the fact that sooner or later, Nate was going to come back.

"I can't. Not yet." Her fingers traced my nipples, and even though I would've sworn it was impossible, my cock got even harder. *Damn.*

"You could try." Being noble wasn't easy, but for Quinn—I'd be fucking Sir Galahad. Or wait—was I thinking of Lancelot? I couldn't remember. All the blood in my body was heading away from my brain.

"Or . . ." She walked her fingers down my stomach to the button at the waistband of my shorts. "I could do . . . this."

She popped the button and then slowly, slowly tugged down the zipper. I could almost feel her fingers on me. Almost, but not quite.

"You're killing me." I ground out the words between clenched teeth.

"Am I?" Quinn flattened her hand against the muscle at the top of my thigh. "I don't want that. Maybe I should do . . . this then."

She twisted her wrist and suddenly her fingers closed around my cock, over my boxers. I sucked in a breath and screwed my eyes shut, thinking of anything I could to distract myself from the pleasure. *Cold toilet seats. Snails. Aunt Snook's gelatin molds.*

"Okay." I spoke out and opened my eyes to Quinn watching me, her head cocked. "Sorry. I had to dial it back before I spewed all over you." I touched her cheek. "Proceed. I'm good now."

"Glad to hear it." She moved faster than I expected, given how relaxed she'd seemed. Before I could say anything, her mouth was on me, only the thin cotton of my boxers between her sweet and wicked lips and my dick.

"Aw, fuck, babe. Ohhhh . . ." I watched as her head bobbed up and down, thoroughly wetting the cloth that covered me. Shooting me a quick and speculative glance, she paused, stretched the elastic around my jutting cock and shimmied the underwear down my legs.

"That's better, isn't it?" This time, the wet heat of her mouth encircled my erection with no barriers between us.

"Well, it sure as hell isn't worse." I loved the feeling of her sucking on me, but I also knew I wouldn't be able to hang in there very long. Not today.

Quinn rose up over me, as though she'd heard my thoughts. "I need you inside me. Having you in my mouth is incredible, but—I need you."

Straddling me again, she took me in one hand, rubbing the head of my dick against her swollen sex. I wanted nothing more than to pull her down onto me, impaling her on my cock, but I hesitated for a minute.

"Quinn, I don't have a condom with me. Do you?"

With wide eyes, she shook her head. "No. I never—we never kept them in here, in case my mom went looking for something in my room." The tip of her tongue darted out to wet her lips. "You don't have one in your pants? In your wallet?"

I tried to push myself up a little bit. "No. I haven't carried one with me since we—since you and me." I stroked the side of her cheek. "I haven't been with anyone else, Mia. I couldn't. It never felt right after us. I only ever wanted you."

She stared into my eyes. "Really?"

"Really truly."

I watched her chest rise and fall, and I sensed she was struggling to make sense of everything. I wondered if she trusted me.

"I haven't, either. But I'm still on the pill." She bent, touching her lips to mine. "I don't want to wait another minute, Leo. I need you, right now."

With those words, she lifted up again and sank down on me, slowly easing me into her until we were as close as possible. I canted my hips, trying to hit the right spot inside her, remembering with perfect clarity what she liked. I palmed her tits, pinching both nipples between my fingers and thumbs.

I didn't have any idea what I'd done to deserve this—to earn the chance to be back inside the girl I'd loved and wanted for so long. I was fairly sure I didn't deserve it. But I was here again, and damned if I wasn't going to hold on tight.

"Oh." Quinn breathed out and moved her hips in a circle. She'd found what she'd been looking for, the perfect position and motion. Her eyes fell closed again, her lips pressed together, and her forehead wrinkled a little as she concentrated on the pleasure.

When she moaned again, I dropped one hand to the place where we were connected, and the next time she lifted up, I pressed my fingers against her clit.

The force of her sudden orgasm stole the last shred of my control, and I growled out her name as I thrust upward, holding Quinn's hips until the most intense, mind-blowing pleasure flooded into me, stiffening my body into one convulsing muscle.

It took me more than a few minutes to come back to myself. The world and the sky had exploded around us, and my vision had gone black. I blinked, trying to catch my breath.

Quinn slid into my arms, and as I gradually recovered, I realized that her body was shaking again.

"God, Leo. Oh, my God. My father . . ." She wept into my shoulder, her tears soaking my skin as she let go and cried with abandon. "He's gone. He's never coming back. It . . . hurts. So fucking much. Oh, my God."

I couldn't do anything but stroke her hair and murmur quiet, meaningless words into her ear. I couldn't undo this one; I couldn't make it better. This heartbreak was real, the grief was intense, and the loss was forever. All I could do was hold her and promise over and over that I was never going to leave her. Not again.

Slowly, the sobs shaking her body lessened. Her tears subsided, and her breath slowed. And eventually, finally, she slept in my arms.

When I was certain that she was deeply asleep, I risked shifting a little to pull a blanket from the end of her bed up over us. I had a hunch that one parent or another would sneak up to check on things pretty soon, and none of us was ready to deal with Quinn and me, naked together in her bed. Not yet.

I eased my phone from my back pocket and typed a text to my mother with one thumb.

She's asleep. Don't let anyone come up here. We're okay.

I knew my mom might have a million questions for me afterward, but I also knew that for now, she'd respect my request. And with that assurance, with Quinn's comforting warmth on top of me, I let my eyes drift shut and slipped into a deep and healing sleep.

★ Three ★

Nate

MY STOMACH GROWLED, AND THAT WAS WHAT woke me up. I couldn't remember when I'd last eaten. We'd been just about to sit down to dinner the night before, when my mom had gotten the frantic telephone call from Lisa Taylor. I'd been in the kitchen already, pouring a glass of lemonade, and I'd glanced over at my mother's face when I heard her voice.

"Oh, my God. No. *No*. Lisa—what—oh, my God. Okay. Yes, I'll head over now. Yeah. No, I know. I just can't—yes. I'll see you there."

My dad had just come inside with a plate of burgers he'd been grilling outside. He was whistling, I remembered now. We'd had a relaxed Saturday after the excitement of graduation and the party over at Quinn's house. That was my parents' usual MO: they worried that too much fuss or out-of-the-ordinary activity would wear me out, make me more susceptible to getting sick. So a busy day was always followed by one at home.

My mother had turned around, and my father saw her face. He'd stopped whistling, slid the plate onto the counter and gripped my mom's arms.

"What is it?"

Her eyes had flickered to me. "It's Bill. That was Lisa, and she said the police called her from Carrie's house. Bill was—he was in an accident, and oh my God, Mark. He was killed. Bill's dead."

I'd heard what she said, and I was dizzy. Bill? Quinn's dad? He couldn't be dead. I'd just seen him yesterday. I'd sat with him for a while at the party, and he'd talked to me about some of the new medications the doctors had me taking. As a pharmacist, he was always interested in my treatment. But then, typical of Bill, he'd also asked me what I wanted to do in college. I'd told him that I had thought about majoring in history and philosophy, with the possibility of teaching after graduation.

"You'd be a great teacher, Nate." He'd smiled. "You have more insight and maturity than guys twice your age. I can definitely see you doing that."

"We've got to go over to the house." My mother was speaking again, staring at the phone in her hand as though it had some answers she couldn't quite comprehend. "Lisa and Joe are driving Carrie to the hospital. She has to . . . identify him. And she doesn't want Quinn there, of course. I said we'd go wait with her. God. Oh, my God, Mark, what're we going to do?"

My father was shaken. He looked blankly at my mother. "I guess—I'll just cover up the burgers and put them away.

Right? Or should I take them with us? Maybe Quinn will want something . . ."

"God, Mark. No. She isn't going to want to eat. Just put the fucking hamburgers down and come on. We need to get there now. Lisa doesn't want to leave her alone. She said Quinn's in shock."

It was the first time I'd ever heard my mother drop the F-bomb, but she didn't seem to notice, or if she did, she didn't care. I followed both of my parents into the garage, and in silence, we all got into the car. My dad drove the familiar route slowly.

"For God's sake, we need to get there today," my mom snapped.

"Yeah, but we want to get there in one piece. Not going to do anyone any good if we end up speeding and get into an accident, too." My dad's voice was tense, and whether it was his tone or what he said, my mother began to cry, loud, heaving sobs.

My dad gripped the wheel tighter and swore under his breath. And I just sat there, still moving on automatic pilot, wondering what the hell I was going to say to Quinn when I saw her.

Carrie, Lisa and Joe were just coming out the front door as we pulled up into the driveway. My mom sprang from the car and met them, wrapping Carrie into a tight hug while Dad and I straggled behind her.

After a few moments, Joe steered Carrie toward his car, which was parked in front of the house. Lisa paused to speak to us.

"Quinn's in the kitchen. She hasn't said a word since we

got here. They're both—God, they're both in shock. The police were still here when we arrived." She closed her eyes and swallowed. "Just see if maybe you can get Quinn to—I don't know. Talk. Or eat. I don't know."

My mother nodded. "We'll take care of her. Are you sure you're okay to go to the hospital with Carrie?"

"Yes. Joe and I will take care of that, and then we'll bring her back, and we can figure out what happens next." Lisa shook her head. "Of all of us . . . you know, I never thought we'd be helping them plan Bill's funeral. Mine, maybe. But Bill . . ." She glanced over her shoulder. "I need to go so we can get this over with. I'll text when we're on our way back."

We stood there, the three of us, watching Lisa trudge across the grass to the car where Joe and Carrie waited. For the first time in my memory, I was dreading going into Quinn's house. I didn't know what to expect; Quinn had always been the strong one of us, the one who made everything better. Sure, over the last year, when she was getting over Leo, she'd been a little quieter. A little more reserved. But I always knew I could depend on her strength.

Now it was my turn to be strong for her. I wasn't sure if I knew how to do it, and once we opened the front door and went into the house, I was even less certain.

Quinn huddled in a chair at the kitchen table, hugging her legs to her chest. My mother sat down next to her and pulled her into a hug.

"Quinn . . . sweetie. Oh, honey. I'm so sorry."

I watched Quinn's expression, and although she didn't fight my mother's embrace, her face remained blank. Immobile. She didn't react or respond, and after a few minutes, my mom released her and sat back.

My dad and I pulled out chairs and sat down, too. For a long stretch, we stayed there, staring at each other, at the floor, at the walls . . . anything but at Quinn, whose eyes never moved from the center of the table.

"He was bringing us Chinese food. But I could have gone. Or maybe if I had talked to him a little longer. Or not so long. If he hadn't been in that place right then . . . he'd be okay." She lifted her gaze to my face. "Maybe it's not even him, you know? The police said we had to identify him. Mom could get there, and maybe he'll just be sitting there, talking about the accident and how he needs to get home. But they got mixed up and thought it was him. That happens, right? It could."

My mother pressed her lips together. "Quinn, honey, I wish I could tell you that might happen, but it sounds like . . . the police don't notify the family if they're not sure."

"If they're so sure, then why did they make Mom go and look?" She shook her head, and I recognized the stubborn look in her eye. It was the same expression she wore when she was trying to talk me into doing something I didn't want to do. "It just doesn't make any sense. Dad's a careful driver. You know that, Mark. Right? How could he get into an accident?"

"He probably didn't do anything, Quinn. Sometimes things happen, and we can't figure out why. I know it's hard."

"It's stupid. And I'm not going to believe it until—until my mom gets back here." She crossed her arms over her chest and retreated back into herself. For the next forty-five minutes, silence reigned in the kitchen, only broken when the front door opened again, and Carrie returned with Lisa and Joe.

Their eyes were red, and I could tell that Lisa, in particular, was shaking. But Carrie looked eerily like her daughter. She walked into the living room, that room that they almost never used, and sat down on the sofa, pulling a pillow over her stomach and holding it tight. Lisa came into the kitchen and began making coffee. I noticed she kept looking at her phone, and it occurred to me that no one had mentioned Leo. I wondered if he was out partying with his football buddies.

Quinn rose abruptly, her chair scraping on the tiled kitchen floor. She stalked into the front hallway and stood in the arched opening to the living room, hands on her hips.

"Well?" Her voice was rough. "Was it him? Or did they make a mistake?"

Carrie lifted her eyes. "Yes. It was him."

For a few tense beats, none of us moved. And then Quinn dropped her arms to dangle at her sides. She moved into the living room and sat down in one of the overstuffed wing chairs.

Over the course of that horrible, endless night, my mother and Lisa took turns making coffee, pouring it and passing it around. Joe offered to go get food, but Carrie flipped out, absolutely refusing to let him go, and of course, we all understood why. The last time a man had left her house to bring back dinner, he'd ended up in the morgue.

Just before midnight, a couple of people from the Russells' church came to the house carrying bags of rolls, platters of lunch meat and a few random casseroles and cakes. They didn't say much, but they set out the food and made us all eat. All of us, that was, except for Quinn, who stubbornly refused to even try a bite.

Carrie, exhausted from bouts of crying, nodded off some time in the early hours of the morning, her head resting on my mother's shoulder. Lisa curled up in the opposite corner of the sofa and dozed, and Joe stretched out on the carpeted floor. After a few minutes, he began to snore softly. My dad slept in his chair.

But Quinn didn't close her eyes. She shifted now and again, but she didn't speak, and she didn't cry. When I tried to talk to her, she frowned at me as though I were speaking in a foreign language and didn't answer me.

By the time the sun rose, I could barely keep my dry eyes open. Every time I blinked, it felt like sandpaper scraping over my eyeballs. My mother, who'd been putting away a few things in the kitchen, touched my shoulder.

"Nate. You need to go home and get some sleep. Dad'll drive you. He should sleep some, too, in his own bed instead of that chair."

I shook my head. "I don't want to leave Quinn." I knew it was idiotic. I wasn't doing her any good, but the idea of not being with her made me panic.

"I think maybe if you go get some sleep, she might, too. Just a few hours, honey. C'mon. I can't have you getting sick. I can't deal with it."

That was what finally got to me. I nodded reluctantly and stood up. Quinn glanced at me without even a flicker of interest in her eyes.

"I'm just going home for a little bit. I'm going to get some sleep, and you should, too."

"Nate's right, Quinn. Why don't you go lie down, sweetie?" Lisa rubbed Quinn's back. "I'll get you tucked in. Come on."

As I left the house, the last thing I saw was Quinn dragging her feet as Lisa led her up the stairs. I hoped she could sleep.

At home, I was afraid I was too keyed up to drop off, but my body must've had other thoughts, since I was sound asleep the minute my head hit the pillow. I only woke up when hunger gripped me.

I checked my phone now, surprised to see it was early afternoon. No wonder I was starving; I hadn't eaten much of the food at Quinn's house the night before, so it had been nearly twenty-four hours since my last meal. I got up slowly, stretching my legs the way I always had to before I could trust my weight to them. Moving fast, leaping out of bed the way other kids did—that had never been an option for me. Instead, I did some deep-breathing, trying to be patient with my sub-standard body while my mind raced ahead.

I knew Lisa had been trying to find Leo last night. She'd muttered something to Joe about him not answering his phone, and her expression had been a mix of worry and mad. I wondered if she'd reached him, and then I wondered if he'd come home. I couldn't imagine that he wouldn't.

The last year had been tough on all of us, but I'd been surprised at how much guilt and regret I'd suffered. Seeing Quinn in pain was hard. Knowing I'd had a part in making her hurt was excruciating. I'd managed to survive by telling myself that it had been for her own good, that I'd been thinking of her future.

It didn't help much.

Since the day that Leo had broken up with her, Quinn had never looked at him. It was as if he had simply ceased to exist. I never caught her eyes sliding his way, never found her gaze lingering on his departing back. But Leo was a different story. When Quinn didn't realize it, he watched her almost hungrily. During assemblies, when we were all together in the gym, he always took advantage of the crowd to keep his eyes glued on her. There wasn't any doubt in my mind that he missed her.

And on graduation—God, had that been only the day before yesterday? I'd known that Leo was dangerously close to breaking. When Carrie and my mom had insisted on taking pictures, he hadn't hesitated to pull Quinn tight against his side, and I hadn't missed the way he'd murmured to her. I was sure Quinn had heard it, too. Doom struck me deep in the stomach, the sense that Leo wasn't going to be able to stay away from Quinn much longer. He was going to crack, and if Quinn took him back—well, that meant I'd return to being just Nate, the other friend.

I sighed as I finally shuffled out of my bedroom and made my way to the kitchen. My dad was sitting at the table, staring into a half-drunk cup of coffee. He looked up at me and attempted a smile.

"Hey, bud. You get a little rest?"

"Yeah. I pretty much passed out. How about you?"

He nodded. "Yeah. But then I woke up and your mom wasn't next to me, so I couldn't sleep anymore." He pointed to the cup. "Tried to make some coffee, but I don't like mine the way I like hers."

"We should go back over there. Mom and Lisa are probably tired, and they need someone else to take over so they can rest. And Quinn might need me."

My father sat back in his chair. "Mom texted me just before you woke up. Leo got to the house a few hours ago."

I dropped into a chair. "Shit. I was afraid of that."

"Nate." His voice was mildly chastising.

"I'm an adult now, a high school graduate. I can curse if I want to."

"I wasn't talking about the cussing. Hell, son, say anything you want today. I was referring to what you said about Leo."

"What about it?" Yeah, I sounded surly, almost like a petulant child. I didn't give one single fuck.

"He's here for Quinn. He's helping. Mom said she's finally getting some sleep."

I wanted to growl, but instead I just nodded. "Good. She needed it."

"And Nate, we've talked about this before." My father paused, and I could sense his struggle, the fight between wanting to support and encourage me and needing me to understand the truth. "Quinn and Leo were apart for a year. And unless I'm mistaken, you told Quinn how you feel about her, and yet . . . nothing happened. It isn't meant to be. So if Leo is the person who's going to help Quinn get through the worst day of her life, you need to stand back and let him do it."

"I know that." I leaned my forehead on my hand, slumping forward. "I do know it, Dad. I'm not getting in the way of anything between them. But I don't have to like it."

"That's true." He laid a hand on my shoulder. "Okay. Let's get ourselves together and go."

When we walked into Quinn's house an hour later, it seemed

as though time had stood still. Carrie was still curled on the sofa, with my mom's arm around her shoulder. Joe came out of the kitchen, carrying a slab of lasagna on a paper plate.

"Hey. You two get some shut-eye?"

My dad gave Joe one of those manly half-hugs, clapping him on the back. "Yeah, a little. You've got to be exhausted."

"I conked out for quite a while on the floor." He lowered his voice and leaned toward us. "The funeral director's on his way over. He's been calling since this morning, but Carrie said she wasn't ready to talk to him yet. I finally just told him to come. So I'm not sure what she's going to do when he gets here."

My dad blew out a long sigh. "Okay. Well, we'll try to keep it low-key and hope for the best. Did Bill—does anyone know what he wanted?"

Joe shrugged. "I don't know. Maybe we can try to get some idea from Carrie . . ." He and my father both stepped into the living room, talking quietly.

I took advantage of the fact that all the parents were preoccupied and began climbing the steps, hoping no one would notice and try to stop me. I knew Quinn had to be upstairs in her room, and if Leo was here, he was with her.

Hesitating outside the door, I knocked softly and then turned the knob, not sure what to expect and dreading what I might see.

Leo sat on the end of the bed, and he looked up when the door opened. He was wearing shorts but no shirt, and his hair was messed up, as though he'd just slid out from under the covers. Holding up a finger to his lips, he glanced back over his shoulder to where Quinn lay sleeping.

She was on her stomach, with her hair half-covering the side of her face. A sheet had been tugged up nearly to her shoulders, but I could tell she wasn't wearing a shirt or bra even before I caught sight of her yoga pants, turned inside-out, hanging off the side of the bed.

Leo stood up and motioned me back. I moved out of his way, and he stepped into the hall, closing the door behind him carefully.

I waited for him to start in on me for disturbing them, but to my surprise, Leo wrapped one arm around me in a tight hug.

"Nate." His voice broke. "I still can't believe it. How can this be happening?"

For the first time in many years, I let my resentment of Leo slip away and pounded him on the back. "I know. It's like a nightmare."

We both pulled back, and I jerked my head toward the bedroom. "How's she doing?"

Leo lifted one shoulder. "Man, I don't know. She was mad, and then she was crying, and then after . . ." His voice trailed off, and he cleared his throat. "Well, she just really broke down, and once that happened, she fell asleep. I didn't want to move and risk waking her up, but she's still pretty deep." He leaned against the wall, rubbing his forehead. "I don't want to leave her alone, though. I promised I'd stay."

"Okay." I nodded. "Do you need anything? Want me to bring you up some food?" I'd eaten a leftover burger at home before we'd come back over, and my stomach had finally stopped growling.

"Thanks, but I'll wait until Quinn's ready to eat." He studied me for a minute, his face inscrutable. "Nate, about what happened before . . . last year—"

I held up my hand. "We don't have to talk about it now. I know I fucked up. I didn't have any right to come between you and Quinn, and—I don't have an excuse, except that I thought I was doing the right thing at the time."

"You weren't wrong." He leveled his gaze at me. "I was being an asshole, and if you hadn't said it—well, I don't know what might've happened. As it was, breaking up with Quinn—it opened my eyes to how I was screwing up stuff." He braced one hand against the door jamb. "I'm smarter now, though, Nate. Smart enough to know I'm better with Quinn than I am without."

"I'm not going to get in the way. Definitely not now." I paused as I heard a commotion downstairs, and the front door open. *Must be the guy from the funeral home.*

"I appreciate it." He tilted his neck, cracking it. "I better go back in there. What's going on downstairs?"

"Funeral guy just got here, I guess. Carrie's got to make some decisions. God, this sucks."

Leo winced a little. "It's just surreal. I keep waiting for someone to tell me it's all been some sick joke."

"Can you imagine what it would be like? Losing your father?" We both were quiet for a minute, thinking of horrible possibilities.

"I had to think about losing my mom last year, and that was shit I wouldn't wish on my worst enemy. So no, I can't even wrap my mind around having a parent gone, just like that." He closed his eyes, letting out a long breath. "We're both going to have to watch Quinn for a while, make sure she's really okay. She puts up a good front, but she's hurting."

"We can do that. It'll be like when we were little. Remember when Quinn went through that phase when she cried whenever her mom left? And you and I used to do silly crap to distract her."

Leo smiled. "I'd forgotten that. She was a mess."

"Yeah, she was." I smiled a little, too, remembering. "There's no reason we can't do the same thing now. We'll get her through this, right?"

"We will." Leo held out a hand to me, his eyes sober. "The trio. Together again."

★ Four ★

Quinn

THE SEVEN DAYS AFTER MY FATHER DIED WERE A BLUR of numbness. Later, I would look back and not remember much more than a few minutes here and there.

People came to the house. My mother's family as well as my father's, people I hadn't seen in years, arrived in town. They didn't stay with us—except for my mother's sister, who did—but it seemed there were always at least three or four people at the house. And they all wanted to talk to me, or hug me, or feed me.

All I wanted was to be left alone. Well, alone with Leo, that was.

He never left me during that week, unless it was for brief snatches of time when he had to run home for more clothes, and even then, he made sure Nate was with me. The two most important guys in my life seemed to have come to some sort of meeting of the minds, and they were more at ease with each other than I'd seen them in years.

The three of us hid out in my room as much as we could. When I had to go downstairs and be sociable, Leo held my hand in his and sat next to me the whole time. He was fiercely protective, cutting off anyone who veered into anything too deep or painful. And he took care of my mom, too, frequently sending her upstairs to rest when she began to look overwhelmed.

Every night, when I climbed into bed, Leo was with me. That first evening, after he'd come back to me, my mother had been too upset to notice him climbing the steps with his arm around my shoulders, but Lisa had seen us and called to her son.

Leo had paused without turning around. "What, Mom?"

"Do you think this is a good idea?" Lisa's voice was even. I'd never known her to get rattled with any of her sons, and tonight was no exception.

"Yeah, actually, I think it is." He shifted on the step, sliding his hand down to grip mine. "Quinn needs me. I'm not leaving her alone." There was steel in his tone, and his mom must've heard it, too. She nodded, though I heard her sigh.

"All right." Lisa glanced at me, and her eyes softened. "Dad and I are going to head home in a few minutes. If you need anything, Quinn, you call me."

"I will." I wanted to tell her how much I appreciated everything she'd done over the past twenty-four hours since the unthinkable had happened, but I was too tired and my brain was too sluggish to form the words. I squeezed Leo's hand and leaned into him. "Thank you, Lisa."

As if she understood, she smiled a little. "I'll see you tomorrow."

I wasn't sure I'd be able to sleep again after I'd stayed in bed through most of the afternoon, but the minute Leo had slid under the covers, wrapped his arms around me and pulled me into his chest, I'd dropped off again into a blessedly dreamless slumber.

After that, we fell into the same rhythm. I was pretty sure my mother eventually noticed Leo coming out of my bedroom in the morning, but she didn't say anything to me. But then again, that week we were all just trying to survive. We didn't have the strength or the will for anything else.

To be honest, I wasn't too worried about my mother realizing that Leo and I were sleeping together, because that was all we were doing. After that first day, I didn't want anything from Leo but his warm body and the knowledge that he was there for me. I couldn't think of sex; it was as if part of my brain had been clicked off.

Leo never pushed me. He kissed me softly on the lips each night and each morning, and he touched me all the time, but never in a way that was meant to tantalize. We didn't have deep talks about the future or the past, and I was grateful for that, too. He let me be, without pressure or expectations.

When the three of us were alone together, the boys were able to distract me now and then, mostly with silly guy stuff. The part of me that was still aware loved seeing the two of them relaxed with each other again. They teased, gently, and Nate made Leo fall off the bed laughing at his imitation of my uncle. It was just like old times.

For a solid week, we lived in a sort of limbo where I had the boys with me almost constantly. We didn't talk about the outside world or anything else. It was an awful, horrible time, and yet it was somehow sweet, too. Special and set-aside, days when I didn't think about anything I couldn't handle.

Other friends came to see me, too, of course. Gia had actually stopped by that first day, shortly after Leo had arrived, but I'd been asleep. She came back the next day, hugged me and cried with me, too. I was struck again by the fact that this girl who'd started out as just someone I knew from the newspaper staff had become my best girlfriend, the one person who listened to me talk about Leo and Nate and somehow understood all that insanity.

Jake Donavon, who'd been editor-in-chief of the paper during my junior year, visited one day that week, too. I hadn't seen him since he'd been home from college over Christmas break, and I appreciated him taking time to see me.

To my utter amazement, quite a few of the guys from Leo's team also showed up at the house. Beau and Dylan brought their girlfriends along, and even Brent, who'd never quite trusted me, stopped by for an hour. I'd noticed, though, that the team's quarterback, Matt Lampert, Leo's best friend outside of Nate and me, was conspicuously absent. He'd never liked me, although we'd had an uneasy truce for a little while when Leo and I were together.

A week after my father was killed, we all gathered at the Methodist church for his funeral. I sat in the front row next to my mother, with Leo on my other side. I'd insisted he sit with us, and who was going to tell me no? Nate was next to him, and I could feel the strength flowing to me from both of them.

Lisa and Joe sat behind us, with their older sons, Simon and Danny, and with Sheri and Mark. Lisa patted my shoulder now and then and offered my mother tissues, which she took and crumpled up in her hand.

I never had any memory of the service itself. All I remembered was the color of the carpet in the church—a deep red—and the comfort of my hand inside Leo's. He never let go.

Mom and I didn't cry during the service. We made it through, and afterwards, we did a hell of a lot of nodding in response to kind, well-meaning words from people who had no fucking clue what to say to two women who had just lost their husband and father, respectively.

After the service, about half the crowd came back to the house, where someone—I never really knew who—had organized food to feed everyone. It was nearly three hours before the last guest finally walked out the front door, leaving my mother and me alone with Lisa and Joe, Sheri and Mark, and the boys.

My mom stood in the front hallway and turned in a slow circle, as though seeing it for the first time.

"I can't believe it's all over." She sounded detached and exhausted.

"Carrie, why don't you go upstairs and change, maybe take a bath. Lay down and rest. We'll finish cleaning up down here, and then we'll go. Unless you need something else."

Mom shook her head. "No, you've all—you've been incredible. I don't know what Quinn and I would've done without you."

"We're family." Sheri folded my mother into a hug. "We do for each other. How many times have you guys kept us sane when Nate was in the hospital?"

"And who brought my family meals and sat with me

during chemo?" Lisa grinned. "We do have the best times, don't we?"

"Let's maybe find another way to bond, shall we?" Mom sighed. "All week, I kept thinking, *we just have to get through this, get through to the funeral.* I only thought about holding it all together until today. But now that it's all done . . . I'm terrified. What comes next? Everyone's gone. It's time to get back to normal. Only problem is, I don't know what normal looks like anymore."

"Babe, you awake?" Leo's voice was low and husky, murmuring against my ear.

I snuggled a little closer to him. "Mmmmm. Kind of." My bedroom was dark except for the faint glow of the streetlight just outside. Tonight, for the first time all week, I hadn't dropped right off to sleep after I'd laid my head on Leo's broad chest.

"I talked to my mom a little bit tonight before they all left." His fingers moved in small circles on my upper arm. "She didn't push, but she suggested I give you and your mother some space tomorrow. She said you two need to talk about some stuff and make decisions."

Panic welled up inside me, and it was on the tip of my tongue to argue. But I knew deep down that Leo couldn't stay glued to my side forever. We both had to figure out what was going to come next for us, just like my mom and I had to do the same.

"Yeah." I swallowed hard. "She's probably right." I turned a little, resting my chin on Leo's sternum, staring up into his face. "But don't go far, okay? I'm not sure I'm ready to go cold turkey on my Leo addiction."

He brushed his hand over my hair. "If it'll make you feel better, I'll sit in the car outside, just in case you need me."

I sniffed. "You don't have to do that. Maybe after breakfast, you could just go home for a little bit."

"That works." He crunched up, bending so that his lips could reach the top of my head. "Hey, Mia? We haven't really talked about anything serious yet. I mean, about us. But I wanted to say this now, before anything goes any further."

Trepidation gripped my gut. "I'm not sure I'm ready to deal with this."

"Babe, no." Leo slid me off him, rolling to lay on his side so that our faces were close together. "Nothing bad. I just wanted to say . . . I love you, Mia. I didn't say it to you last week. I hoped you understood it, but I thought I better be clear. I love you. I loved you before, and I never stopped."

I traced his jaw with one finger. "I love you, too, Leo. Still. Always. Forever."

He released a breath as though he'd been holding it. "Okay. Good."

I frowned. "Did you doubt that I did? That I do?"

"No, not really." He nuzzled my neck. "But I wasn't sure if you were ready to deal with me again. I know you needed me this week, but I was afraid once things started to settle down, you'd think that maybe I wasn't worth the effort."

Following my finger with my lips, I kissed his chin. "You're worth everything, Leo. And I hate that it took my dad—what happened, I mean, to get us back together, but I'm not going to have any regrets anymore. Loving you is part of me, and so are you. I wouldn't have made it through this week without you." I paused, enjoying the feel of the late-night scruff on his neck. "That first day, before you got here, I wanted to die, too. It hurt so bad, and I felt like nothing was ever going to be right again. But then you came to me, and I'll never forget that you were here for me."

"I always will be." He tipped up my chin and kissed my lips, softly. "Nothing in my life works without you."

"Then I guess we need to make sure we stick together." I leaned forward to deepen our kiss. "Hey, Leo?"

"Hmmm?" He was focused on my mouth, tracing the seam of my lips with the tip of his tongue.

"Make love to me, please?" I pressed my body closer to his, just to bring home my point.

Leo drew back a little, his eyes filled with concern. "Are you sure you want that, Mia? We don't have to do anything. Trust me, just holding you every night has been like heaven on earth for me. We don't have to do anything more than that."

"We might not have to, but I'm telling you . . . I need you. I want you to take my mind off everything."

"I'm never going to deny you, babe." His arms slid around me, and his hands cupped my ass. "But I could just make you feel good. We don't have to . . . you know."

"Engage in full sexual intercourse?" I whispered, teasing, just in case my mom happened to have woken up and was wandering past my bedroom door. "But I want to."

Leo rolled to his back, flinging his arms on either side of him. "Fine. Have at me, woman. I'm not going to stop you. Do what you must."

Smiling a little, I sprawled over his body, desire surging when I felt his erection hard between my legs. "Gladly."

"So what now?"

My mom and I sat at the kitchen table, alone with each other for the first time in over a week. She'd showered and put on jeans and a T-shirt, but I could tell that after yesterday, the effort to do even these most basic things had tired her. Her always-bright eyes were dim, with deep shadows beneath them. I wondered how well she'd been sleeping these nights while I was finding comfort in Leo's arms.

I sighed and shifted in my chair, not sure how to answer her question. I was eighteen years old and a brand-new high school graduate. My parents had always taught me to be independent and to think for myself, but somewhere deep inside, I'd counted on not having to be an adult for a while longer. I was heading to college in the fall, true, but my parents were paying for what my grant didn't provide, and I'd known they'd have my back over those four years.

But now, my mother was looking at me as if I might have answers to questions she didn't know how to ask.

"Well . . ." I tried to think about what my dad would say. "I guess we need to figure out first things first, right? Like the house. Can we afford to keep it, or do we have to move?"

My mom nodded. "We don't have to make any decisions about the house right away. Dad and I both have—well, had—life insurance that pays off the mortgage in the event of a death." She gripped the edge of the table. "I remember when we got it. It sounded so ridiculous, to think that either one of us would die before we'd finished paying for this house."

I covered her hand with mine. "It *is* ridiculous. It's ridiculous that Dad is gone. But I'm glad you guys did that, because I'm not sure I could handle leaving the house yet." I paused. "What about the beach house?"

"We should be able to hold onto that, too. I make enough to cover those payments, and there will be some other insurance money, too." She seemed to want to say something else, and I watched her struggle to couch her words. "Uncle Doug mentioned something to me. He said we may want to think about suing the other driver in the accident. It's not going to bring Daddy back to us, but it could help with your college, or maybe your first house someday."

I frowned. "What do you think about that?"

Mom sighed. "I really don't know. Honestly, I don't want to think about it right now. Maybe down the road, but at this minute, I can only deal with putting one foot in front of the other, you know? I'm still trying to wrap my mind around this reality. Every morning, I wake up and hope it was a nightmare. I need to focus on some more positive stuff for the future. I can't deal with it yet."

"Then let's table it for now." I gnawed on the inside of my lip. What I wanted to bring up next wasn't going to be easy, I knew. "About college, Mom. I've been thinking."

She cocked an eyebrow at me. "Yes?" Her tone was one of both trepidation and challenge.

"I think I'm not going to go to Evans."

"Bullshit." Her answer came so swiftly that I knew she'd been expecting this.

"No, listen, Mom. I'm serious. I'm not saying I won't go to college, but I don't want to go to Evans."

"You don't want to go to the college you've been dreaming about for two years? The college your dad was so excited for you to attend?"

I shrugged. "Maybe that's part of it. Maybe I don't want to go to Evans without Daddy here to cheer me on." Tears filled my eyes as I remembered his last words to me, about being in the front row of my college graduation.

My mother glanced away from me. We both knew tears were contagious. "So, what's your plan? Ditch college altogether?"

"Of course not." I took a deep breath. "I was thinking about going to Birch instead."

"Birch? Really?" She sat back in her chair, considering. "You were accepted there. They were one of your back-up schools, though. Why would you want to give up the journalism program at Evans for Birch?"

"For a few reasons." I'd actually been thinking about this quite a bit in the last two days. "First of all, Gia mentioned something to me the other day about a brand-new program Birch is offering this year. It's not pure journalism; it's more like a combo of social media, digital marketing and journalism, all wrapped up together. I think it sounds amazing."

"All right." My mother nodded. "That's one reason. What's another?"

I scrunched down in my chair a little. "I don't want to go that far from you. Birch is just fifteen minutes away."

"Quinn. Really, I'm going to be okay. I'm not going to have you staying home and throwing away your future because you feel like you need to babysit me."

"It's not you." I pulled my feet onto the chair with me and hugged my legs. "I'm not ready to leave you, Mommy. I don't want to go away. I don't want to be that far from you."

For a long moment, she didn't answer. Her eyes rested on my face, conflicted and thoughtful.

Finally, she smiled a little. "Okay. We'll need to figure out how this is going to work, but if you're sure it's what you want, we'll talk to some people over at Birch and see what we can do."

"Thank you." I leaned over and wrapped my arms around her. "Thank you so much."

"And speaking of things we need to talk about . . . don't think I haven't noticed that Leo's pretty much moved into your bedroom."

I was sure my cheeks were flaming as I sat back. "He was just here to take care of me." I fiddled with the hem of my tank top. "I wouldn't have been able to sleep without him here."

"I take it the two of you are back together now?"

"Yes." I knew I sounded definitive. "I know all the reasons we won't work, but I also know I can't give him up again, Mom. We'll figure it all out."

The corner of my mother's lips tugged up into something resembling a smile. "I'm sure you will."

We were both quiet for a few minutes, and then she spoke again, in measured words. "I'm not going to tell you Leo can't sleep in your room, Quinn. After this week, it sounds like that would be closing the barn door after the horse ran amok. But please, sweetie . . . be careful. And I'm not just talking sex."

When I started to interrupt, my mom held up her hand. "No, hear me out. You're eighteen years old, Quinn. I can't make your decisions for you. I love Leo, and I'm grateful that he's been so supportive this week. But he's heading down to Carolina in about a month, and you'll be starting a new life, too. It's going to be tough on both of you."

I'd already expected this cautionary chat, so I only nodded. "I know, Mom. We're being smart, and we'll get through college. We can handle the long-distance thing." I smiled at her. "Leo and I are meant to be together. And nothing's going to be in the way of that this time."

★ Five ★

Leo

The day we graduated from high school, I'd been sure the summer that lay ahead would be full of two things: getting wasted and hanging with Matt, my best bud. It turned out I was wrong on both counts.

Thank you, sweet baby Jesus.

Instead, I didn't lose a single minute of my last summer of freedom. I didn't get drunk even once; I stuck to a beer or two if I was hanging out on a warm evening. And I hardly saw Matt at all, because almost all of my waking hours were spent with Quinn.

Of course, a lot of my *non*-waking hours were also spent with her. What can I say? Life was damn good.

It wasn't all laughs and sunshine, sure. We were all still grieving, missing Bill, and Quinn struggled to figure out what was coming next for her. I argued with her about giving up Evans, because I knew how much she'd wanted to go to college up there, but her rationale for choosing Birch instead made sense. She and her mom had compromised: Quinn would attend Birch, but she was going to live on campus, not at home, even though we all lived about fifteen minutes from the college. Her friend Gia was doing the same thing; she was the youngest in a large family, and Quinn told me that Gia's mom was going to sell their house as soon as the summer ended and Gia had moved into the dorms.

Nate was also going to Birch. A year ago, that might've made me uneasy, knowing that Nate would've done anything to come between Quinn and me, but now, I was grateful that he was going to be there for her when I couldn't be. I knew the transition wasn't going to be easy, and having her friends nearby would help.

For a nanosecond, I'd considered throwing away my full ride to Carolina University, seeing if I could get into Birch, so I could be close to my girl. But she nipped that idea in the bud, nailing me with one of her serious, determined-Quinn looks, the one she thought made her look fierce, but which was really only totally adorable and made me want to kiss her nose.

"*You* are going to Carolina, where you are going to kick some serious ass on the football field. And then you're to win the championship game, and when you're a senior, you'll get the Heisman. And you'll be number one draft pick that year for the NFL. Got it?"

"Hey, dream a little bigger, babe, why don't you?" I flicked her on the chin. "No pressure on me or anything, right?"

"Nope." She was sitting on the swing at the park, *our* park, the place where we'd finally admitted to each other how we felt. I stood behind her, giving pushes, and now I gripped both chains and pulled back until her head was level with mine.

"You know I'm doing it for you, right? For us. So that when we get to that place, that done with college place, I can give you the kind of life you deserve."

Something like doubt flickered in her eyes. "I know that football is part of you, as much a part of you as your gray eyes."

I shook my head. "My eyes aren't gray. They're blue. Light and boring blue."

Quinn smiled. "When you're this close to me, and you're just about to kiss me senseless, they're gray. And trust me, I should know. I'm the one looking at them."

"Right. Anyway, the point is, I'm not choosing football over you. I want you to understand that."

"And I want *you* to understand two things. First of all, you don't have to be ashamed of loving the game. I get it. It really is part of the whole Leo package."

I wiggled my eyebrows at her. "And what a package it is."

She sighed, rolling her eyes, and went on speaking as if I hadn't. "And second, you don't have to do anything to give me the life I deserve. All I will ever want is you, whether you're the most celebrated tight end in the league—"

"And what a tight end it is, too."

"—or if you're sweeping out the locker room after the game. You're still the one I want, no matter what you do. So yes, I tease about you winning championships and trophies, but in the end, all that means shit to me. I only want it for you, because I see how talented and amazing you are."

I hiked her up a little, firming up my hold on the chains, and took advantage of our position to kiss her senseless, as she put it. Hey, it sounded like a good idea. Her mouth opened to me, as it always did, warm and welcoming, and I teased with just the tip of my tongue. Quinn leaned back against me, the hint of a moan escaping from her throat.

"If it weren't broad daylight, I'd suggest we test this swing. See if it could hold us both." I whispered the words against her lips.

"I *am* a swing sex virgin." She twisted a little and lifted one hand to the back of my neck. "Maybe we should come back when it's dark and try it out."

"It just so happens that I, too, am a swing sex virgin." I nuzzled her neck, kissing just under her ear lobe. "We'd be on level ground. So to speak."

She giggled and kissed my jaw. "Hey, Leo?"

"Hmmm?"

"Did you know my mom drove into the city today with your mom, for her check-up?"

A smile began to spread across my face. "I did not know that. I knew my mom had a check-up, but I didn't realize Carrie was going with her."

"She did. And do you further know that means my house is empty for at least the next three hours, since they're having lunch afterwards?" Her eyes met mine, sparkling.

"Are you suggesting something wicked, Ms. Russell?"

"Only if having hot and wild sex with your girlfriend is wicked, Mr. Taylor." She batted her eyelashes at me, and I wrapped one arm around her waist, holding her tight to me as I let go of the swing.

"Why the hell are we wasting time here, then?" I palmed her ass, fitting her to me more securely. "We may not be able to have swing sex right now, but I'll bet you a second orgasm I can make you scream my name before we're in your bed for five minutes."

She grinned. "Let me get this straight. You make me scream your name—which implies a first orgasm—and then I get a second? Or you do?"

"Who cares? I figure we're both winners, either way."

"Agreed. Race you to my bedroom."

I was scheduled to report to Carolina the last day of July. Having a shorter summer made me acutely aware of the passing of each moment, and I didn't want to waste a single one.

Not long before Bill's death, Quinn's parents had bought the beach house where they'd spent summers almost as long as I'd known them. Quinn had been meant to work down at the shore that summer, but she'd changed those plans after her father died. I'd given up most of my clients at the lawn service my brothers and I had run for years, so I was free to spend a day here or there with Quinn at the beach.

It was Carrie's idea that we all spend my last week of summer at the beach house. I had mixed feelings about it; being down the shore would be fun, and in a lot of ways, it would be like old times: my mom and Sheri would be with us all week, and Mark and my dad would come down for the weekend. Days of sun and sand, nights on the boardwalk—I knew it would be good for Quinn.

On the other hand, there wasn't going to be much privacy with six to eight of us under one roof, and I was about to leave for a college ten hours away from my girlfriend. I wasn't going to be able to see her until September at the earliest, since she'd be starting classes right around the time of our first game; I wouldn't be able to come up and visit her until after the season was over. We'd talked about Quinn making a weekend trip down for a game, but nothing had been firmed up yet.

All of which to say, I'd been hoping to spend my last week at home making up for the time I was about to lose with her.

Explaining this to Quinn's mom—or mine—wasn't going to fly, I knew. So I swallowed my disappointment and told myself I was just damned lucky to have her back at all. I was also fortunate that her mom had looked the other way so much already this summer, giving us most nights together. I didn't have any reason to complain, but I was greedy for my girl.

We'd been at the shore for three days when Gia drove down to spend the day. I knew Quinn and Nate had gotten to be close with her during senior year, when I wasn't part of their lives. Gia still treated me a little stiffly, as though she hadn't yet made up her mind whether or not to trust me.

But she'd been fairly relaxed all that day, and it made me happy to see Quinn laughing and joking with her friend. She was getting better, recovering from her dad's death, but it was a slow and painstaking process. There were still mornings when I awoke to find her sobbing in my arms and times that I saw her staring at nothing, pain in her eyes. I walked a fine line between distracting her when I could and listening to her when she wanted to talk it out. Being a guy, I really just wanted to fix it for her—make the hurt go away, bring back her ready laughter and the way she used to exude joy.

My mom and I had discussed Quinn one day, sitting at the breakfast table on one of the rare mornings I woke up at home.

"You can't make this better, Leo." Mom shook her head, but there was compassion in her eyes. "You can't do or say anything that'll make the pain less, or make it go away faster. This kind of grief—it's like a physical injury. Quinn has to go through the whole process, and you can't do it for her."

"So what *can* I do?" I scooped scrambled eggs onto my toast and took a bite. "There's got to be something, right?" I swallowed the eggs. "What did Dad do for you when Gramps died?" I remembered, vaguely, when my mom's dad had passed away. I had been eight years old, and all of us boys had been mystified by our normally happy-go-lucky, laid-back mother having crying fits and hiding in her bedroom for hours on end.

"He didn't do anything. He was just there for me. When I cried, he held me. When I needed to talk it out, he listened. And when I wanted to forget about everything for a while, he did everything he could to distract me."

I nodded. "That's what I've been trying to do for Quinn. But it doesn't feel like enough."

"Of course it doesn't. You're a male, honey. You want her to just be over it already, because it stresses you out when Quinn's hurting. But no matter how much you love her, you're not going to be able to take away this grief. If you want to be a real man, though, you won't walk away from it, or pretend it's not happening. Every minute you're standing up with her, or helping to hold her up, you're being who she needs." My mother set down her coffee cup and reached across the table to pat my arm. "I'm proud of you, Leo. Most boys your age would freak out and turn tail in a situation like this."

"Yeah, well . . . I already did that once. I guess maybe I learned my lesson."

She laughed. "I doubt it. Like I said, you're a man." Standing up, she snagged my plate and headed for the dishwasher. "Have I mentioned that I wouldn't be your age again for all the tea in China?"

I rolled my eyes. "Thanks."

Now, sitting on the beach listening to Gia and Quinn laugh and chatter, I remembered my mom's advice. Maybe there were a few things I couldn't give to my girl, maybe I couldn't be here all the time, but there were others who could give them to her and be here for her.

"Hot today." Nate dropped a folding chair next to me, leaning carefully to make sure it was stable before he sank down. He wore a baseball cap low over his eyes, the brim almost hitting the top of his dark sunglasses. Any kind of temperature extreme was risky for Nate, so he took precautions, protecting himself from the sun as much as he could.

"Yeah, well . . . it's summer, dude. And you're out here in the middle of the day."

"I know. But it sucks to be the only one hanging out inside, when the rest of you are on the beach." He grimaced. "Plus if I had to listen to our mothers talk about hot flashes any longer, I was afraid I was going to start growing boobs."

I laughed. "Too much estrogen, huh? I don't blame you for that. But I'm glad your mom and mine are down here with Carrie this week. It's been good for her." I lowered my voice. "Good for Quinn, too, to have you around, and Gia here today. It's too bad Jake couldn't make it." Quinn's former editor-in-chief at the school paper had remained a good friend, and I was secure enough in her love for me that I didn't mind that. Although they'd dated for a while during our junior year, it had never been serious. His summer internship at our county newspaper had kept him from visiting this week.

Nate watched the girls, and his face softened. "Yeah. It's nice to see Quinn relax. Gia's good for her, even though it's weird to think about her having a friend who's a girl. I'm still getting used to that, and it's been over a year."

I cocked an eyebrow at him. "Why is it weird?"

"I don't know. I guess I'm just used to her being fine with only you and me. She never hung out with girls when we were growing up."

"True." I smiled as Gia leaned over to whisper something in Quinn's ear and pointed to a guy walking by in the surf. Quinn fell back on the blanket, convulsing in laughter. "Maybe that wasn't such a good thing." I settled back in my chair and pushed my sunglasses over my eyes. "Nate, when I'm away, you'll watch out for her, right? You'll make sure she doesn't feel alone or lonely?"

The chair creaked as he shifted. "Of course. I'll keep my eye on everything. She's going to be okay, though. Quinn's tough."

"She still cries sometimes." I spoke softly.

"Of course she does. She just lost her father. She's going to keep on crying a lot. But I'll sit with her when she does, and Gia and I'll both keep her busy."

I sighed. "I was mad at first that she decided not to go to Evans, but I'm really glad she's going to be at Birch with you two. I won't worry so much."

"Yep. We'll take care of her." He stared straight ahead.

"And you don't have to worry at all, Leo. Not about anything. I know what I did before was wrong, getting between you two. I won't say or do anything again."

"I trust you, Nate." And it was true. I did. "And even more than that, I trust Quinn. Things are different now. I know what it's like to lose her, and I know I can't handle that. So I'm sure as hell not going to screw it up."

"It's not going to be easy." Nate's voice was mild. "But I guess you both know that."

"We do. But we're going to make it work." I was beginning to feel antsy, so I pushed up from my chair and stretched, then leaned down to sprinkle a little sand into the enticing curve of Quinn's back. "Hey, gorgeous. Want to go for a walk with me?"

She rolled onto her side and shaded her eyes with one hand. "Did you just put sand on me, Leo Taylor? Do you know it sticks to the sunscreen? It's a pain in the ass to get off."

I reached down and grabbed her hand, tugging upward. "It just means longer in the shower, babe." With a leer, I added, "I'm more than happy to help you wash off those hard-to-reach places."

"You're a degenerate." Her cheeks were flushed, though, and I knew she was turned on, too.

"And you love me for it." I pulled harder, and Quinn stumbled to her feet, landing smack against my chest, just as I'd hoped. She was wearing a black bikini that set off her tanned skin and showed off her curves. Her body was utter perfection: long slim legs, flat stomach and rounded hips . . . an ass that was just right for grabbing, and those tits? Well, when they were on display in the two triangles that made up her bathing suit top, my dick was in perpetual state of arousal.

And now, with that luscious body pressed against me? God help me. If our friends weren't right there, I might've tossed her back onto the beach blanket and figured out a way to get us both off without anyone guessing what we were doing.

As it was, I had an idea of how to get her alone, in a less public setting.

"C'mon. I need to move around a little, or I'm going to get stiff."

She tipped her head back to see me and smirked. "I think maybe you already are. Stiff, that is." She murmured the words so that I was the only one who could hear them.

I leaned my forehead against hers and whispered back. "Can you blame me, when you're bouncing around in those little scraps of fabric? You're killing me, woman."

Quinn winked. "That's the idea, right?" She bent to retrieve my T-shirt, which she'd been using as a bathing suit cover-up, and dropped it over her head. I helped her pull her arms through.

She freed her pony tail from the neck of the shirt and nudged Gia with her toe. "You okay to hang with Nate while the Neanderthal drags me along the sand?"

Gia grinned, her eyebrows arched. "Hoping to find a cave for your woman, Leo?"

I mock-scowled and pounded my chest. "Make cave for woman. Have big fun."

Quinn shook her head, but I saw the smile playing on her lips. "What can I say? He's unenlightened, but he's mine. Let's walk, big guy."

We made our way down to the ocean's edge before we began heading along the beach, our joined hands swinging between us. Quinn was silent, but she seemed content, stopping now and then to examine a shell and skirting the occasional washed-up jellyfish.

"Mia." I squeezed her hand. "Are you going to be okay when I leave on Sunday?"

She didn't answer me right away, but her mouth tightened a little. "I don't want to think about it. I'm going to miss you like crazy, and it's going to suck and it's going to hurt." She took a deep breath. "But I'm going to be all right."

Our steps slowed, and Quinn turned a little to face me. "Last year, when you broke up with me, I thought I was going to die. I felt like you'd cut out my heart. But I decided that I had to keep going on. To do that, I had to pretend that you didn't exist anymore."

I felt an iron band of guilt and regret constrict around my chest. "God, I'm sorry, Mia. If I could do things over—"

"But we can't, and everything happens for a reason. I've got to believe that." She moved closer to me, so that her boobs teased against my chest. "I only mentioned last year because at least now, this time, I can still talk to you. We can text and video chat, and I'm going to visit you. Even though I won't be able to kiss you and touch you every day, I'll still know you're with me. And you love me. So . . . will I be happy? Not really. But am I going to be okay? Yes, I am." She punctuated her words with a single hard kiss on my mouth.

I pulled her tighter. "I wish we were past this already. I wish we were on the other side of four years of college, and beyond the good-byes. I hate this, us being separated."

"I hate it, too. But then, I've hated a lot of stuff that's happened lately. It doesn't seem to make much of a difference."

"We're going to do everything we can to make it work. I'll do anything, Mia. Anything and everything for you."

"I know." She twined her fingers at the back of my neck. "I trust you, Leo."

"Do you?" I raised my eyebrows. "Because if you do . . . I have an idea."

"Oh, no." Her eyes went wide, but I didn't miss the spark of interest there, too. "What kind of idea?"

"The best kind." I slid my hand down to take hers and began moving up the beach, away from the water. "I don't know if you've noticed, but time alone has been kind of scarce this week."

One side of her mouth quirked up into a smile. "Maybe I have. Kind of hard for you to sneak into my room when I'm sharing with my mom."

"Right, and since I'm in the same room with Nate, I don't think he'd appreciate us using my bed."

"Yeah. He's been so much better this summer, but I think that might be pushing things."

"True. So . . ." I led her around the dunes, through a break in the sea grass, and under the boardwalk. "I remembered this place. We came down here one time with your mom and dad, remember? For your birthday one year, I think. Your parents let you bring Nate and me, and we were on this beach instead of the one right in front of the house. We were playing hide and seek, and it was Nate's turn to be It. You and I hid right . . ." I pulled her under with me, into the shadows. "Here."

"I remember." A genuine Quinn smile lit up her face, and seeing it made my heart falter. She hadn't smiled like this for too long. Her eyes were filled with delight as she glanced around the small alcove. "Nate found us, but not right away. You and I sat in here for a while, and we talked. Like, really talked. I think maybe that was around the time I began to fall in love with you."

I wrapped my arms around her waist. "Really? Way back then? I was such a little jerk."

She laughed. "You were not. You were adorable." She traced my jaw with the tip of one finger. "So when did you know you loved me?"

"I've always known I loved you. As long as I can remember." I spoke without having to think about it, because the words were true. "But I knew I was in love with you . . . in middle school. We were over at Nate's, and I said something, probably some stupid joke, and you laughed. Like, really laughed, threw back your head, and I remember thinking, *God, Mia's so beautiful*. I wanted to be near you more then, but I was kind of dating Sarah. And I knew how Nate felt about you." I shrugged. "I was an idiot fourteen-year old. How I felt about you was confusing and kind of scary. But the longer I pushed you away, the harder I fell."

Quinn sighed. "And yet here we are."

"Yeah. In spite of ourselves." I skimmed her hair away from her face, combing my fingers through the strands. She shivered and pressed against me, grinning when my body responded.

"And here I thought this walk was supposed to help you from getting *stiff*." She ground her pelvis into mine.

"Mia." I groaned her name. "I hope you know what you're starting here."

"Oh, like you just brought me under here to reminisce." She rose on her tip-toes to kiss me, her mouth opened as her tongue sought mine. "This has make-out spot written all over it."

"Mia Quinn, you're a vixen." I dropped my hands to her ass, slipping my fingers under the material of her bathing suit bottoms. "As if I would think such a thing."

"Ha! As if you *wouldn't*." Her hands left my neck and roamed down my back, tracing the lines of muscle. "It is really private under here. I mean, I can hear people, but I don't think anyone would notice us."

"I think you're right." I ventured one finger a little further, parting her folds, nudging her legs a little further apart. "God, babe. You feel so fucking good."

She hummed, letting her head drop back. "*You* make me feel so fucking good."

Since Quinn rarely dropped an F-bomb on me except when she was really revved up, I knew she was right there with me. I shifted, moving my hand to go under the front of her bathing suit for better access.

"Turnabout is fair game, right?" She eased down the elastic of my trunks and grasped my cock.

"Feels damn fair to me," I muttered, my eyes dropping half-way shut with pleasure. "Are we doing this?"

She paused. "Aren't we? Why else would you bring me under here? To talk politics?"

"Oh, absolutely not." I palmed one of her boobs, brushing my thumb over her nipple through the slippery cloth. "I didn't bring you under here to talk at all." I covered her lips with mine and kissed her, stroking my tongue over the inside of her mouth.

Quinn moaned, and her hand on my dick picked up speed. She had the perfect pressure, the exact right moves . . . and when she slid her fingers down to cup my balls, I was pretty sure my eyes rolled back in my head.

Above us, footsteps suddenly sounded, and muted voices floated overhead. I hesitated, lifting my face away from Quinn's for a minute to see if she was going to be spooked.

But she only smiled at me. "It's wild, isn't it? They're right above us, and they have no idea we're here, with your fingers inside me and my hand on your cock."

"Wild." I found her clit with my thumb and pressed, thrilling to the sound of her quick intake of breath. "You coming against my hand right now? Right this very fucking second? Even wilder."

Without breaking my movement, I plunged two fingers within her, picking up speed. Quinn let go of my dick, using both hands to grasp my shoulders, holding on for dear life. Her mouth fell open and her breath came in little pants. I watched her face in fascination, and the hottest, most erotic moment of my life was seeing her fall apart while my fingers drove her out of her fucking mind.

When she began to come down from the crest, I yanked down her bathing suit bottoms, gripped my dick and slid into her in one fluid movement. Quinn cried out, riding me. I was fairly sure that her fingers were going to leave marks on my shoulders, but I didn't care at all. Her tight channel was still contracting from her last orgasm, and standing here, feeling her grind on me, I knew I wasn't going to last long.

I fumbled with her top, pulling down the triangles of

cloth that covered her beautiful tits until her nipples were free. Bending to capture one tempting pink peak with my mouth wasn't easy, but God, was it worth it. I sucked hard, scraping my teeth over her.

"Harder." She half-growled the word through clenched teeth. "Do it harder. Take me harder."

I obeyed, rolling one nipple between my finger and thumb and then, when Quinn began to groan, dropped both hands to her hips and began to pump into her faster, rougher.

Quinn began to make little cries, and I knew she was close. I let myself go, digging my fingers into her ass and roaring as I came hard, erupting deep within her.

For the space of several beats, we stood clinging to each other, trying to breathe. In the silence, we heard the shuffle of feet on the boardwalk above us, and a woman's voice.

"What was *that*?" She sounded suspicious and faintly alarmed. "Did you hear that, Ed? It sounded like . . . like someone, uh, in pain, maybe."

Quinn's eyes went huge. "She heard us!" she whispered. "What're we going to do?"

"Shhhh." I put one finger to her lips, trying not to laugh. "Just wait."

"Ahh . . ." A man—Ed, I assumed—cleared his throat. "Ah, Frannie, I think it was just kids. Down on the beach, I mean."

"But it sounded like it came from right under us." Frannie was persistent, that was for sure. "Should we check?"

"You know how sound travels on the beach, hon. Come on, let's set down these chairs. My back is killing me. What did you pack in this beach bag, anyway?"

Frannie and Ed's feet tromped over our heads, down the

steps and away, and in my arms, Quinn shook in a fit of giggles.

"Oh, my God, Leo." She buried her face in my chest. "What if Ed had said they should look under here?"

I shrugged. "I think Ed knew the score. I think he had our backs." I smirked. "So to speak. He wasn't going to let her find us."

"Lucky us." Quinn rested her cheek against my chest, her warm breath fanning out over my skin.

"Yeah, I'd say lucky us. Or at least lucky me." I stroked her hair. "That was the most . . . damn, babe. You were fucking hot. If this is our last time together until you come see me at Carolina, we went out on top, for sure."

"Hey." She stroked my cheek. "We're not going out at all. This was one step, one small good-bye before we don't have to say good-bye ever again. Right? That's the plan."

"That's the plan, Mia." I brushed a kiss over her lips. "Doesn't make it easier. Doesn't mean it doesn't feel like that path isn't way too fucking long right now. Doesn't mean I don't wish it could be different, and the good-byes were over forever."

"They will be, baby." Quinn framed my face with her hands, and her green eyes were serene and certain. "One day, one day soon, all the good-byes will be in our past. And then you'll be stuck with me forever."

I leaned my forehead against hers. "I hope that's a promise."

★ Six ★

Nate

"It's got to be tough."

I was zoning, so when Gia spoke as she dropped into the chair that Leo had just vacated, I was startled. She settled herself down, stretching her legs out in front of her.

"I'm sorry, what's tough?" I glanced at her sideways.

"That. Them." Gia nodded toward Quinn and Leo, who were walking at the edge of the ocean, holding hands and looking like an advertisement for the perfect summer. "Seeing them together. It can't be easy for you."

"Why would you say that?" I let my hand trail through the warm sand next to me, drawing designs.

"Oh, come on, Nate. I know how you feel about Quinn."

That stung a little. I knew Gia and Quinn were friends, and I wasn't dumb; I realized girls talked to other girls, and there was a fairly high likelihood that they talked about boys. But I'd never really considered that Quinn would share anything with Gia about me. About us.

As if there were an us, which of course there wasn't. Not beyond the friends us, anyway.

"Did she say something about me and—her? To you?"

Gia hesitated and then shook her head. "Not in so many words."

"What's that supposed to mean?" One thing I'd learned about Gia early on in our acquaintance: like me, she was honest to a brutal fault. She wouldn't sugarcoat things when it came to Quinn.

"It means that she didn't so much share it with me as I asked. Not that it was much of a secret, Nate. Not to anyone who spends any amount of time with the two of you."

I frowned. "Why did you ask?"

Gia was silent for a minute. "If I tell you, do you promise not to laugh?"

Now I was curious. "Yeah. As much as I can, anyway." Honesty was a trait I could appreciate in others mostly because it had always been a part of me, too. I'd try not to laugh, but I couldn't swear it wouldn't happen.

"Okay, that's all I can ask of you." Gia stared straight out into the waves, and the tip of her tongue darted out to lick her bottom lip. I realized she was nervous about whatever she was about to say. "Last fall, I kind of had . . . a crush on you. And I asked Quinn if there was something between you two. She got uncomfortable, said that there wasn't anything on her side, but . . . like I said, not so many words, but I got the picture." Gia finally glanced my way and glared at me. "You said you wouldn't laugh."

"I said I'd try not to. And I'm not laughing at you. I'm

laughing at the idea of you having a crush on me."

Now temper flared in her eyes. "Why? You don't think someone like me could have those kind of feelings?"

"What? No." I scowled. "I don't even know what you mean by that. I don't think someone like you would be interested in a guy like me."

"Oh, really? You're crazy then."

I snorted. "What would make you—you know. I mean, God. Look at me." I pointed to my legs, covered in the lightest-weight sweatpants my mom could find. No way was I wearing a bathing suit and exposing my legs in public, but I couldn't handle jeans in the heat. This was the best compromise, but damn, I hated it. Hated that I had to compromise in the first place. Hated that I couldn't run down the beach like all the other guys who took for granted what they could do. And now Gia was claiming that she was interested in me? Yeah, I found it a little hard to believe.

"Why was I interested in you? God, Nate. First of all, the hotness of you." She pointed at me. "You must not look in the mirror very often. You're a hottie, dude."

I felt my face getting warm, and this time it had nothing to do with the sun. "You're crazy."

"I'm not, but if I am, I'm not alone. Didn't you know how many girls were hung up on you in school?"

"Oh, yeah, the school gimp, the one all the other guys tease and harass. Yeah, I'm a real prize." Sarcasm dripped from my words.

"Okay, Nate, I get it. You're talking about one part of you. I'm saying, some people see more than that. Some people see your gorgeous eyes, your hair, the way you're built . . ." She paused. "And it's not just your looks, bud. When I got to know you, I liked you even more. You're a genuinely decent guy, and let me tell you, that's rare. You're not a douchebag. So yeah, I got a little moony-eyed over you. But I saw how it was. And I wasn't going to get between you and Quinn."

I wasn't sure how to respond to all of this. Gia had become a good friend, someone who I felt comfortable with—not quite the same as Quinn and Leo, but close. Still, I wasn't interested in her as a girlfriend. There was only one girl in the world for me, and she'd just strolled off down the beach with my other best friend.

"Which brings us back to my main point." Gia dug her heels into the sand, making twin trenches. "Quinn and Leo. That can't be easy for you."

I lifted one shoulder. "It wasn't before. Now . . . after everything Quinn's gone through, I'm just glad to see her happy, you know? Or at least as happy as she can be right now. If Leo brings her comfort, or a little peace, I'm fine with that." I took a deep breath, wincing a little at the twinge of discomfort. "It wasn't like she's ever going to see me like that, anyway. It's always been Leo for Quinn."

"And it's always been Quinn for you." Gia nodded. "I'm sorry, Nate. If you ever need someone to vent to, or a shoulder—I'm here for you." She grinned and winked at me. "And don't worry, I'm not going to try to jump your bones. I got over you last year. Now I'm okay with being your friend."

"Thanks, Gia." In a rare—for me—gesture of affection, I reached over and laid my hand on her arm. "I'm glad we're friends. I don't get to know people easily, but you're worth the effort."

"Nate Wellman, that may be the sweetest thing anyone's ever said to me." She covered my hand with hers and gave it a little squeeze. "Can I admit without it sounding creepy that if I'd known how awesome your mom is, I might've tried harder to get your attention? You seem like you have a very cool family. You're lucky."

I nodded. "I guess. But I'm an only child. I always thought maybe sisters or brothers might be cool."

"I guess the grass is always greener, but siblings can be overrated. Believe me, being the youngest of six has definite drawbacks." She grimaced, and I remembered that Quinn had mentioned Gia's parents had been divorced for a long time and still battled over the last kid left at home—that would be Gia.

"You're not close to your sisters and brother?"

Gia sighed. "Not very. They all fled the family home as soon as they could, and that left me to deal with the parentals. I thought it would get better once my mom and dad finally called it quits, but then they decided I was the monkey in the middle. The only time my mom noticed me was when my dad wanted me, and then she pitched a fit." She reached down and scooped up a handful of sand. "She's close to my older sisters. And she likes my brother's wife."

"I'm sorry." Gia was always so bright and brash, I'd never stopped to wonder what she was like, deep down.

"Oh, you know. It is what it is. I'm glad to be going to college and getting away from all of them."

"All the way at Birch?" I teased. The college Quinn, Gia and I were going to attend was only about ten miles from our town.

"My father lives in New York. My mother's selling our house in the fall and moving up to Trenton to be closer to my oldest sister and her kids. So yeah, Birch is going to be perfect."

"I can't wait." It was true. I'd fought long and hard to get my parents to agree that I could live on campus. My favorite long-time doctor had had my back on the issue, and I'd had to make a number of concessions: I'd be living in a handicap-accessible room, so that I didn't wear myself out climbing steps. I'd take the campus car service, designed specifically for students like me, to get to classes more than a few steps from my dorm. And I'd keep up with my regular doctors' appointments, check in with my parents frequently, and avoid tiring myself.

Even so, I was starving for any taste of freedom. Move-in day was circled on my mental calendar, and I was counting the days.

"Yeah, I feel the same. I don't know how psyched Quinn is, though. Leaving her mom could be rough." Gia stretched and yawned. "Not to mention Leo being down at Carolina. We're going to have to pay attention to her, you know? Make sure she doesn't get too down. Keep her busy." She leaned up, slid her dark sunglasses down her nose a little and regarded me over the top of them. "You with me?"

I smiled. "Sure. Operation Distract Quinn is a go."

"Awesome." She pushed her glasses up again and sat back in her chair. "And I'll do my best to keep my dirty thoughts about your hot bod to myself, 'kay?"

I made some sort of sound in my throat, a noise between choking and groaning. Gia laughed and kicked up her feet.

"Oh, this is going to be fun."

Leo left early on Sunday morning. He'd packed up all his stuff for college before we'd come down to the shore, and his dad brought it down on Friday night, so Leo could stay with us until the last minute. And by us, of course, I meant Quinn. The closer we got to Leo's departure time, the more they clung to each other and the more desperate Quinn's smiles became.

On that last morning, we all stood outside in the muggy, hazy air, everyone making uncomfortable small talk and stupid jokes as the clock ticked on.

Finally, Joe clapped a hand on his son's shoulder. "You better get on the road, bud. Long drive ahead of you. And what time are you supposed to meet Tate?" Leo was sharing the drive with another Carolina freshman football player, this one from Gatbury, the next town over from us. He'd met Tate Durham over the summer, through Leo's friend Matt Lampert, and they'd hit it off. Tate was one of the few decent football guys I'd met, and I noticed he seemed to have a good influence on Leo.

"We're meeting at exit two at nine o'clock." Leo blew out a long breath. "Yeah, I need to get going." He hugged my mom and Carrie, and then he and my dad thumped each other on the backs, joking about man-hugs.

When he got to me, he paused a minute and then wrapped one arm around my shoulder, drawing me close.

"Watch out for our girl, okay? Don't let her get too sad.

Make her laugh." His voice was low and thick with emotion.

"I got this, Leo. Don't worry." I pulled back a little and looked him in the eye.

"Yeah, you got it. I know." He managed a smile. "Thanks, Nate."

We all stepped back a little as he and his mom said good-bye. Lisa held her son's face in her hands, speaking some kind of wisdom meant only for his ears. Leo enveloped his mother in a tight embrace, and even I got a little choked up.

That left only Quinn. My mother cleared her throat and began to shepherd all of us back into the house.

"Okay, people, let's give them some privacy. Let's get breakfast started. Who's going to be my sous chef today?"

We straggled through the front door. When I glanced back before I stepped inside, I saw Quinn wrapped in Leo's arms, both of them rocking a little as she shook. I felt kind of like a voyeur and turned my head quickly.

"God, shouldn't this be easier? He's the third kid. I should've rolled over in bed, blown him a kiss and gone back to sleep." Lisa blew her nose and wiped at her eyes. "This is ridiculous."

"But he's your baby." Carrie rubbed her back, reaching for her own tissue. "I mean, he's not even my kid by blood, and I'm welling up here."

"Thanks for not laughing at me." Lisa hooked an arm around my mom's neck and another around Carrie's. "I don't know what I'd do without my girlfriends."

"We keep each other sane. Or mostly sane." My mom reached for the coffee pot. "Speaking of sanity, who needs a cup of caffeine?"

I wandered into the living room and leaned against the back of the sofa, watching the front door. My dad and Joe casually debated driving routes to Carolina as they set the table for breakfast. We were all pretending that everything was okay, that Quinn's heart wasn't breaking again just beyond the door.

When she came back inside, I didn't make a move toward her; she'd need a little space, I knew. Her eyes were slightly red, but she smiled at me.

"I want to go out to the beach before breakfast. Want to come with me? It's pretty cool still."

"Sure." I didn't hesitate. "Let's go."

When Carrie and Bill had first begun renting this house, back when all of us kids were pretty little, they'd had the thoughtful foresight to make sure there was a ramp leading down to the beach, for when I came to visit. I had happy memories of running down that wooden slope with my walker to the sound of Leo and Quinn's laughter and my mom's worried shrieks.

Good times.

Today, though, Quinn and I both walked slowly down the ramp. Right before we reached the sand, Quinn paused and kicked off her sandals, leaving them at the edge of the wood. She took my arm, as if she needed me to steady her, although I knew it was more likely the other way around.

"Chilly this morning." Quinn looked out over the pounding surf.

"Damp," I corrected. "The sun will burn off the mist, and then it'll be blistering by noon time."

"Probably." We reached the wet part of the sand, and

Quinn stopped walking. "Will you be happy to go home today?"

I shrugged. "I guess. My mom keeps saying we need to do college shopping, but I'm not sure what she expects me to need. I've got clothes, they'll give me a bed and a desk, and I'll buy books and shit once I get there."

Quinn laughed. "Typical guy. You need sheets, doofus, and towels and all that. That's what your mother means."

"Whatever." I bumped my shoulder against hers, smirking. "Hey, you okay?"

She was quiet for a few minutes, her gaze focused far out at the horizon. "I think so. I know this is how it's got to be, for now. Leo has to be at Carolina, playing football, and I have to be up here with my mom."

"Yeah. Doesn't make it easy, though."

Quinn flashed me a smile of gratitude. "No, it doesn't. I want to make this work, though. I know it was kind of weird to other people, probably, that Leo and I ended up back together so fast after my dad . . ." She stopped and took a deep breath. "But it felt right. It felt like something clicked. Something changed. Leo's been a different person this summer, don't you think?"

As much as I hated to admit it, I had to nod in agreement. "I overheard my parents talking about him. My dad said Leo's grown up a little. Maybe the year that you two were apart taught him something."

"Maybe it was good for *both* of us." Quinn sighed and laid her head on my shoulder. "I think we see things a little clearer now. And we realize how important our relationship is, and how quickly stupid stuff can mess it up."

"That's good, I guess." I ventured one arm around her, holding her loosely to my side. I knew this was nothing but friendship, nothing but Quinn being her usual affectionate self, but I was going to enjoy it anyway. "So you think everything's going to be different this time? You and Leo are going to be able to deal with the distance thing, and being apart for four years?" Privately, I had my doubts. I couldn't imagine being away from Quinn for four months, let alone four years; I'd been silently dreading our separation for college when she'd been planning to go to Evans.

I expected her to jump to assure me that she and Leo were going to be fine, that they'd come out on the other side of these college years even stronger. Instead, she frowned, her forehead furrowing.

"I . . . I hope so." She answered me slowly. "You know, a year ago—or maybe a year and a half ago—I had this crazy belief that everything turns out well. If I did the right things, worked hard, all that shit, my life would be the way I wanted it. I thought my parents would both be there when I graduated college, when I got married, and when I had kids. I really believed that Leo and I were going to be together forever, no matter what, because that's what's meant to be. But now, I know that nothing's guaranteed. Nothing's promised to any of us. My dad isn't going to be there to walk me down the aisle. And as much as I want to believe that Leo and I are going to work this time, I know the odds are against us." She shook her head, and her hair rubbed against my chin. "I guess I learned this summer that there isn't any sure thing. Not even our next breaths."

I shifted my weight, giving one leg a little break. Standing for long periods wasn't easy for me, but there was no way I was going to suggest we move on now. Not when I had Quinn in my arms, even if it was only a friendly embrace. Her chest rose and fell against mine, and her hair blew up into my face. I breathed in her scent and struggled with how to respond to what she'd said.

"I think I've always known that," I said at last. "At least, since I was about ten. I overheard a doctor talking about how long I might have to live, and I realized I didn't have the same life expectancy as you and Leo."

"God, Nate." Quinn turned to look up at me, dismay on her face. "You never told us about that."

I lifted one shoulder. "What did it matter? Nothing any of us could do, really. But I think I decided then that I don't have time for bullshit, you know? Small talk, telling white lies, not being honest with people about how I feel . . . not being real. Life's too short for us to be phony or waste time, right? Anyway, that's what I took away from it. Appreciate every day and keep it real."

Quinn rubbed my arm with her cheek. "Sometimes I forget how smart you are, Nate. Yeah, you're right. Appreciate and keep it real." She swiped at her eyes with her fingers and then rose to kiss my cheek. "Thank you for being my best friend. I know I leaned on Leo this summer, but I don't know what I would've done without you. And I'm so glad we're going to be together this year." She snaked her arms around my chest and squeezed. "Don't leave me, Nate, okay? Promise. I need you."

I was used to the feeling of my chest constricting, of not being able to breathe. It was part of my condition, and it happened on an all-too-regular basis. But this time, standing here now, my breath was catching and my heart was pounding for an entirely different reason.

"I won't, Quinn. I promise. I will always be here for you, no matter what."

★ Seven ★

Quinn

Freshman Year
August

"ARE YOU SURE YOU DON'T WANT ME TO DRIVE OVER with you?" My mother gnawed on the corner of her lip, a habit I'd noticed had become more pronounced in the last few months.

"It's not that I don't want you to be there, Mom." I rubbed her arm and smiled. "It's just that it doesn't make any sense. You have the meeting with the estate attorney, and there's nothing for you to do at the college. Gia and I are driving over together, Nate's already there, and we're just going to bring in my clothes and stuff. Unpack. You can come over tomorrow, for the parent crap."

"Nice language, Quinn." She rolled her eyes, but her voice was mild. "But all the other parents will probably be there. I don't want you to feel like an orphan."

"I'm not an orphan. Just fatherless." I tried to keep it light, but my mother winced.

"I'm still not sure you're doing the right thing, though. Daddy wanted you to go to Evans. He was so excited about it."

"Yeah, well . . . that was before. We've been over this, Mom. I'm happy about my decision. Birch is an excellent college, and I can be with Gia and Nate."

"You're sure you're not just staying because you're worried about me?" She narrowed her eyes, suspicious.

"Absolutely not. I'm completely selfish." I winked. "I'm not ready to be that far from you yet, but that's for me, not you." I paused. "Do you think I'm being a baby? Do you think Daddy would be ashamed of me?"

"Oh, sweetie, of course not." My mother pulled me into a hug. "Don't be silly. I'm thrilled you're going to be just a few minutes down the street from me. But I don't want you to look back and have regrets."

"Nope. No regrets." I leveled a look at her. "Right? We're not living that way." My phone buzzed, and I glanced down at the screen. "Oh, that's Gia, wondering where I am. Okay, I need to go, but call me when you're done with the meeting. And I'll see you tomorrow for brunch and stupid orientation."

"It's not stupid, but yes, I'll be there. Send me a picture of your room tonight."

I opened my car door and climbed in. "Mom, you'll see it tomorrow." When she only cocked her head at me, I sighed. "Right. I'll send it. Love you, Mommy."

"Love you, too, sweetheart. Be safe."

I focused on starting up the car and backing carefully out of the driveway, ignoring the lump in my throat. Unfortunately, I made the mistake of glancing at my rearview as I pulled away. Mom stood alone in the driveway, her hand to her mouth, and I knew she was fighting the same tears I was. Resisting the urge to stop the car and run back to hug her one more time, I steeled myself to turn the corner.

But once I was out of her sight, I burst into ugly crying.

"What's wrong?" Gia's concern was etched into her face and voice as she opened the passenger-side door. "Are you okay?"

I shook my head and sniffled. "Leaving Mom—was hard."

"Oh, Quinn." She rested her arm on the seat of the car. "What can I do?"

"Toss your bags in the trunk and let's get moving. I just need to stop thinking and get there."

She smiled at me. "You got it."

I popped the trunk and watched as Gia maneuvered her bags around mine in the back of the car. I hadn't packed too much, but the trunk wasn't very big. When Mom and I had picked out a used car for me, we'd been focused on reliability and price, not trunk space.

Finally, she slammed it shut and came back around to slide into her seat. "Okay, we're golden. Ready to become two official college students?"

"Sure." I shot her a smile. "It's got to be better than high school, right?"

"Fingers crossed." Gia fiddled with her seat belt. "So was your mom emotional?"

"We both were, but we were also both pretending it wasn't a big deal." I braked at a stop light and then turned onto the main road that would take us to Gatbury. "Where was your mother?"

She shrugged. "We had a good-bye breakfast, and then she went to see my sister and the grandkids in Princeton. The whole leaving-for-college deal isn't a big thing for her when it comes to the sixth kid."

"Still. I'm sorry, G." I couldn't imagine my mother not caring enough to hang around for my college departure. She'd hated missing move-in, even when I'd insisted I was okay with it.

"It's fine. And my dad texted this morning that he'd be in town in October and hoped to see me then. At least he remembered I was leaving today." Gia's parents had divorced ten years before, and the split had been far from amicable. I knew my friend had frequently felt as though she was the rope in an endless game of tug-of-war. Lately, though, it seemed both her dad and mom had better things to do than to pay attention to their youngest offspring.

My phone, resting on the console between us, buzzed an alert that I had a new text message. "Speaking of texting . . . can you look at that, please? It's probably my mom, checking to see if we got there okay. You know, because I've been gone for about fifteen minutes."

Gia scanned the screen. "Oooooh, it's the Lion. And God, who knew he had such a dirty mind?"

My face felt as though it turned five shades of red. "Gia! Give it to me." I kept my eyes on the road and one hand on the wheel as I attempted to snag my phone back.

"Settle down. I'm just teasing you. He says, 'Happy move in day, Mia! Call me when you're settled. Practice til five. Love you, baby.' Awwww . . . how sweet."

I relaxed and turned my attention back to driving. "He *is* sweet. And he probably sent that during a break in practice. They're really working them hard, and he says it's damn hot down there."

"I bet." Gia stretched her arms. "When are you planning to go visit him?"

"Three weeks. Two days." I grinned sideways at her. "Six hours."

"Not that you're counting or anything."

"Not much." I slowed to make the turn into the college's main gate. "Actually, I was going to ask if you wanted to ride down with me. We could do the whole road-trip deal. You know, mix tapes and junk food and sleeping in rest areas?"

Gia grinned. "I'm so in. But can we update that description to be playlists instead of mix tapes? Since your car doesn't even have a tape player?"

I lifted one shoulder. "Well, it won't sound as poetic, but sure." I peered out the windshield as we reached an intersection. "Can you check and see where we go from here? See, this is good practice for you being my navigator."

She pointed to the left. "The sign says this way to Gibbons Hall. How was that?"

"You'll do." I steered us around a bend, down a dip in the road and then back up to a tall brick building with a large wooden sign on the outside, proclaiming it to be Gibbons Hall. There was a loading area on the side and a parking lot across the street. Since we didn't have too much to tote and the loading spot was pretty crowded, I chose the lot. "Here we are. Home sweet home-away-from-home."

"Looks like it."

We both climbed out and hoisted bags onto our shoulders. "Let's take your stuff up first, and then we'll check out my room. Okay?"

Gia smiled. "Thanks. How did you know I didn't want to go up and meet my roommate by myself?"

I bumped my shoulder against hers as we crossed the street to the dorm. "Because I don't want to do it alone either."

Just inside the double doors at the front of Gibbons, a long table was set up, manned by a bunch of people behind laptops. A line of freshmen waited to pick up their keys. Gia and I stood in the back of the queue until it was our turn.

As it turned out, Gia was on the fourth floor, and I was in a room on the second story. We climbed up the steps to her room first, stepping around knots of people chatting in the hallway and parents carrying up boxes.

"Do you think we're doing something wrong, that we don't have more shit with us?" Gia eyed up a guy carrying a stack of milk crates overflowing with books. "Some of these people look like they're moving in forever."

I shrugged. "We have the advantage of knowing home is less than fifteen minutes away. Anything we might need, we can get pretty fast."

"I guess so. Oh, here's my room."

We stopped outside a door that was closed, and Gia fumbled with her key. Casting me a here-goes-nothing look, she unlocked it and pushed it open.

The room was shadowed and bare, with two beds, each pushed up against an opposite wall. A set of dressers abutted each bed, and desks with matching chairs were next to them.

"Well, it's . . . basic." I stepped into the room and searched for a light switch. "But about what I expected."

"Yeah. Let's drop the bags. We'll put the sheets on my bed, and then we can go check out your space." She deposited one suitcase on the floor by the left-side bed. "Hope Ellie the roommate is okay with me choosing my side."

We worked together, with me making up the bed while Gia unpacked her clothes and dumped them into the dresser drawers. I noticed Gia glancing over her shoulder every time we heard voices outside in the hall, but by the time we'd finished, there was still no sign of the roommate.

"Okay, then." She scanned the room. "I'll put up some posters and pictures later. Let's head down to the second floor and see if your roommate is here yet."

I picked up one of my duffel bags. "If you want to wait up here in case Ellie shows up, I'm okay. I promise."

"Nah. I want to see who the housing department stuck you with. And Nate should be around somewhere, right? Wonder how he's making out."

"He texted this morning that his mom and dad were driving him over, if I wanted to ride with them." I flashed a half-smile at Gia. "I was glad you and I had already made plans. I love the Wellmans, but it would have felt weird to come here with them. Like some kind of bizarro-world version of my own family, you know?"

Gia nodded. "Still, I'm sure he's going to want to see where you are."

"He won't be able to navigate those steps very easily. They put him in a handicap-accessible room, you know. So he'll be on the first floor over at Liddleton. I have a feeling we're going to be hanging out there more than here."

"Maybe he'll end up making a whole new group of friends and forgetting all about us." Gia winked at me. "Remember all those stupid videos the guidance counselors made us sit through last year? 'Going to College is A Brand New World.'"

"Yeah." I smirked. "But the people who made those movies didn't know Nate. He's got quirks and faults, but he's loyal. He'd never turn his back on us."

We made it down to the second floor and counted off the numbers until we reached the room I'd been assigned. Unlike Gia's door, mine was ajar, although I didn't hear any noise from inside. I hoped like crazy that I wasn't going to walk in on a happy family, all helping their college freshman to organize her new room. I wasn't sure I could take too much family vibe today.

But when I peered inside, there was only one person there, a girl. One side of the room was clearly claimed; one bed was made, one dresser moved and one desk already stacked with books, while on the other side, nothing had been touched.

The girl sitting on the edge of the made-up bed was beautiful. Not just your typical, run-of-the-mill college pretty, but catch-your-breath-and-turn-to-stare gorgeous. She was probably about as tall as I was, I thought, although it was hard to be sure before she stood up. One long tanned leg was folded beneath her, while the other was bent, her foot resting on the mattress as she stroked color on her toenail.

The door creaked a little as I pushed it open further, and she looked up, brushing back a curtain of long white-blonde hair. Huge blue eyes regarded me with interest.

"You must be the roommate." With measured movements, she replaced the nail polish brush, screwing it back onto the bottle. She untwisted her leg and dropped both feet to the floor, then stretched her arms over her head languidly as she rose. "Nice to meet you. I'm Zelda Porter."

I took a few steps forward. "Quinn Russell." Hooking a thumb over my shoulder, I added, "And this is my friend, Gia Capri."

"Hey." Zelda nodded. "So I got here super early and set up my stuff on this side. I hope that's okay."

"Sure." I dropped one of my bags near the foot of the empty bed. "I'm not fussy about what side of the room I have."

"Cool. Please tell me you're from a big family, and you're used to having a roommate. 'Cause I'm an only child, and I don't know shit about sharing."

I shook my head. "Sorry, I'm an only, too."

"But she's really easy to be around." Gia leaped to my defense. "Quinn's one of the nicest people I know. She's patient, and she's funny, and she—"

"Gia." I rolled my eyes at her. "Seriously. I don't need you to testify for me." When I saw her expression shift to hurt, I added hastily, "But thanks. It's nice to know my fan club has my back."

"I'm sure we'll get along great." Zelda lay back on her bed, carefully crossing her bare feet at the ankle, mindful of the still-wet polish. "But I do have to ask—what did you do to get me as a roommate? I was pretty sure I was going to end up with some loser, given the situation."

"What situation?" I sat down on a corner of the mattress that was apparently mine.

Zelda flicked an assessing glance at me. "I had a roommate. Or I had someone who was assigned to be my roommate, more accurately. She decided that we weren't a good fit anymore." The corner of her mouth twisted up a little.

"Uh huh." I resisted the urge to look at Gia, who'd never been known for her poker face. "Did you . . . um, disagree?"

"You might say that." She lifted her foot again, examining the line of her polished big toe. "I fucked her boyfriend, and she disagreed with my rationale for doing it."

Gia sucked in a quick breath, and I was pretty sure my mouth sagged open. "Oh."

Zelda sighed and set her mouth in a firm line. "Here's the thing you need to know about me. I like boys. Men. And I like sex. I don't do relationships." She fingered the small charm that hung from a thin silver chain around her neck. "The girl I was supposed to room with—she lives up by Trenton. Since I'm from Lancaster, not too far away, she invited me to come up for a weekend this summer, so we could get to know each other. I did, and we got along great." She paused. "Until she caught me riding her boyfriend's cock in his Jeep, while it was parked in her driveway."

"Holy God." Gia muttered behind me, and I couldn't blame her.

"Listen." Zelda leaned forward, her eyes fastened on me. "I just told you the thing you have to know about me is that I like men and I like sex. Both true. But you also need to know, I'm not a poacher. I don't steal boyfriends."

"All evidence to the contrary." Gia murmured words again, but if Zelda heard her, she didn't acknowledge it.

"That guy—my would-be roommate's boyfriend—he came on to *me*. He made it clear in a hundred different ways that he wanted me. He made the move. Did I say no? I didn't.

Should I have?" She hesitated. "Maybe. But I'll tell you something. I wasn't the first girl he cheated with. Far from it. I'm just the one he got caught fucking."

"And that makes you . . . what? The hero of the story?" This chick was hitting me where I was vulnerable, I knew. A long-distance relationship was trying under the best of conditions. But having a boyfriend who attracted attention wherever he went, who was part of a popular college football team and probably had girls throwing themselves at him every day and night . . . that definitely added an element of unease. The idea that there might be someone like Zelda down at Carolina, willing to sleep with any guy—yeah, that was unsettling.

"No, I never said I was a hero. But I'm not exactly the villain, either. I didn't so much as flirt with that son of a bitch. All I did was fail to say no when he made the offer." She stood up again and put her hands on her hips. "By the look on your face, I'm going to assume you've got a boyfriend, and now you're wondering if he's going to be safe around me."

"I do have a boyfriend. But he's never screwed around on me. I trust him." I took a deep breath. "As far as trusting you—as long as you don't give me any reason not to, I will. You didn't have to tell me what happened with the girl who was supposed to be your roommate. But you were honest with me, and that counts."

She nodded. "Thanks. I appreciate that." Her lips curved into a half-smile. "So I'm guessing you didn't have the same experience I did. How'd you end up here, with me?"

I unzipped the bag at my feet. "I had a late change of plans, and so everyone had already been assigned roommates before I signed up for housing. I was supposed to go to another college, and I changed my mind at the beginning of the summer."

"Oh, yeah? What, did you decide to follow your boyfriend to Birch?"

"Nope. My boyfriend's not here." I pulled out a framed picture and held it out to Zelda. "He goes to Carolina University."

She took the photo and examined it carefully. "Damn. He's a cutie." She gave it back to me, smirking. "Don't worry, doll. That's as close to a flirt as I'll get. So if your man's down south, how'd you wind up here?"

The pain slid through me like a ghost, chill and full of dread. "I was supposed to go to Evans. It's a small college up in New England."

Zelda lifted one slim shoulder. "Never heard of it."

"Yeah, well, it's pretty well-known for its English and creative writing majors. And it's one of the few schools left that still offers a decent journalism program."

"Ah, that's your deal, huh? You're a writer?"

"It's what I want to be." I turned the suitcase onto the bed, dumping out my clothes.

"No, you're already a wonderful writer." Gia reached down, picked up one of my T-shirts from the pile and began folding it. "College is just a formality."

I snorted. "Well, four years is a hell of a formality." I caught Zelda's eye. "What's your major? Or don't you know?"

For the first time since we'd come into the room, she seemed a little less sure of herself. "Ah, I'm studying plant sciences."

"That sounds interesting." I cocked my head. "What do you plan to do with that after graduation?"

Zelda smiled. "Hopefully, I'll get to join a team working on reclaiming ecosystems that have been destroyed, either by man or by nature turning on itself. But we'll see. There are a ton of different opportunities in the field."

"Very cool. How did you—" My phone buzzed in the back pocket of my shorts, and I pulled it out, scanning the screen. "Oh, Nate's downstairs. He wants us to go over to lunch with him. Gia, could you grab those other two bags from the backseat of my car? I need to get the yogurt in the fridge before we go." I glanced over my shoulder. "We do have a fridge, right? I ordered one of the minis."

"Yeah, it's under the window." Zelda pointed. "I put some bottles of water in it. I hope that's okay."

"It's fine. I figured we'd share it." I opened a drawer of the wood-veneer dresser and dropped a pile of T-shirts into it.

"I'll get the perishables and tell Nate we'll be right down." Gia held out her hands for my car keys, which I dug out of my pocket.

"Thanks, G." I waited until she had disappeared through the open door and down the hallway before I spoke again, in a lower voice. "Sorry. She means well. She's kind of become my personal cheerleader the last few months."

Zelda raised one eyebrow. "Yeah, she was fast to leap to your defense. She's very . . . loyal."

"Gia's protective of me." I zipped the suitcase again and pressed it flat. I focused on the bag and tried to keep my voice matter-of-fact. "My dad died two months ago. It was very sudden. So all of my friends kind of watch out for me now."

"Oh, my God." The shocked sympathy was the part I hated the most. "I'm so sorry."

"Thanks." I still didn't quite understand why I responded that way. *Thanks* for apologizing that my father was dead? Social convention was so odd. "Anyway, that's why I'm here instead of at Evans. I live in Eatonboro, and this way, I can still be close to my mom."

"Why aren't you living at home? I mean, not that I don't want you for a roommate, but Eatonboro is practically walking distance, right? I passed it on my way here."

"This was a compromise." I smiled. "My mother didn't want me giving up the college experience, but I didn't want to be three hours away from her. So this way, we both feel better."

"And that's how you got saddled with me, huh? Why didn't you try to share a room with your friend? Gia, right?"

"Yes, Gia." I closed the drawer and leaned against it. "We had to kind of pull some strings for me to get in here, as it was. I'd turned them down, and then I had to schmooze a lot of people to switch that around. My mom says we played the dead daddy card, and she's right."

Zelda winced a little. "That's kind of cynical, isn't it?"

"I guess. My parents and I have always been a little, um, irreverent. Sorry if it comes off . . . flippant. It's not that I look at it that way." I stared out the window, not seeing the bright green leaves on the oak just beyond the glass. "I miss my dad more than I can tell you. Every day, I wake up and for a few minutes, I can pretend he's still alive. I can fool myself that the accident never happened. But it did, and my mother says life has to go on for us. So sometimes we border on the inappropriate, but it's just our way of coping." I drew in a deep breath and let it out. "Anyway, we had some connections in admissions here, and I'd already gotten into Birch as a back-up college. I was grateful they let me in so late in the game, though, and I didn't want to push my luck by demanding my choice of roommate, too, you know? Plus, I think it's good to expand my horizons. Gia's two floors up from us, and that's probably close enough."

"Got it." Zelda grinned, and I was struck again by how gorgeous she was. "So who's this Nate? If he's not your boyfriend, is he fair game for me? And is he hot?"

I hesitated, biting the corner of my lip. "Nate's my best friend. He's wonderful, but he doesn't have much experience with women."

Her eyes sparkled. "Ooooh, an innocent for me to corrupt?"

"No." There was a little more emphasis in my voice than I meant there to be. "It's not like that. He . . ." I wasn't sure how to explain Nate to someone like Zelda, but I had to say something before she met him. "He was sick a lot as we were growing up. He's got a degenerative muscle disease, and he's—he's different."

Zelda studied me. "So you're saying hands off."

"Well, no. I'm just saying—don't come on too strong, okay? Nate doesn't have a real radar when it comes to girls, and it takes him a long time to make new friends. He's known Gia for over a year, and he's only now starting to trust her. Maybe don't steamroll him."

She laughed. "Wow, I really made a first impression on you, didn't I? Don't worry, doll. I know how to play it cool. And trust me, if someone I respect tells me to keep away, I do it."

Gia came in with two canvas bags over her shoulders.

"Here we go. I don't think it all has to go in the fridge, does it?"

I unhooked one bag from her arm. "No, just the yogurt and the cheese." I smiled at Zelda. "I'm addicted to crackers and cheese. It's my go-to snack."

"As addictions go, there are worse." She slid her hands into the pockets of her shorts, watching me.

"Nate's waiting for us. I told him we'd be right down." Gia set the other bag on top of the mini-fridge.

"I'm ready." I closed the refrigerator door and turned to Zelda. "Want to come with? You can meet Nate."

She met my gaze steadily. "You sure you want me?"

I didn't hesitate. "Of course. Isn't that how roommates get to know each other?"

"Okay." She spread her hands in front of her. "Let's mambo."

As we closed the door behind us, locking it with the key on the cord I'd looped around my wrist, I slid Zelda a sideways glance. "You said you'd listen if someone you respected asked you to stay away from a guy. Do you respect me?"

She shrugged. "I don't know you yet, but for the time being, I'll give you the benefit of the doubt."

"Thanks for that." I sighed and nudged Gia with my elbow. "Okay, let's go."

Nate was sprawled on a bench outside the front door of our dorm. As we approached him, I tried to see my friend as a stranger might: a typical college guy, long legs stretched out on the pavement, his brown hair a little too long over his eyes. He wasn't muscled or broad the way some of the boys passing us were, and unlike most of them, Nate wore jeans. He was self-conscious about the way his legs looked in shorts and never went out in public with them on.

He flipped up his sunglasses when I was within a few feet of him, and the practiced, almost-cool move took me by surprise. Sometimes I forgot that Nate wasn't still the awkward kid I'd known all my life. A knot of girls passing us stared in his direction, and one of them giggled, her eyes going wide. Yeah, Nate was definitely going to have his share of admirers at college.

He didn't give them any attention at all, though. His gaze was on me, his eyes searching, checking to make sure I was okay, the same way he'd been doing for the last few months. I knew it was because he cared for me, but I was suddenly tired of being the one who worried everyone.

"How's the room?" He glanced at Zelda, but again, he didn't react to her.

"It's good so far." I forced a smile. "Basic dorm. You know. Oh, and this is Zelda. She's the lucky girl who gets to share a room with me for the very first time in my life."

"Hey, it's a reciprocal deal. You're my first, too." She winked at me and held out a hand. "Nate, right? Nice to meet you."

He hesitated only a beat before he took the offered hand. "Yeah. Good to meet you, too."

I plopped down on the wooden bench next to him. "So how about yours? How's the roommate?"

Nate straightened. "Uh, so far, so good." He fiddled with some chipping paint on the seat. "He's actually a football player."

"Seriously?" I frowned. "I thought you were in a, uh . . ." I paused. "Like, an accessible room." I didn't use the word *hand-*

icap, but it hung out there anyway.

"I am." Nate's voice was mild, as it always was. There were things he was sensitive about, like the way his legs looked or when he was awkward getting up or down. Things I was used to ignoring or pretending didn't exist. But accommodations made for his limitations had never fazed him. "I should've said he used to be a football player. I guess he played for Franklin Township. He was a year ahead of us, but he took a bad hit on the field during a game when he was a senior. Like, a seriously-bad, life-threatening hit."

"Oh, God, I think I remember that." Gia leaned on the back of the bench. "It happened early in the season, before we played them. I heard it was horrible. Like, people on the sidelines could hear . . ." She trailed off, biting her lip as she glanced at me. "Anyway."

"He's paralyzed, in a wheel chair. He's not real talkative, but he was civil." Nate exhaled. "I think maybe he was a little surprised that I could walk. The housing people told him he'd be rooming with someone like him."

"What's his name?" I'd always gone to our high school football games, but I hadn't paid much attention to players on the other teams, at least not until I'd started dating Leo.

"Eli. Eli Tucker, but he said everyone calls him Tuck."

Zelda was standing next to me, and I think I was the only one who heard her sharp intake of breath. I swiveled my head to look up at her, but her face had frozen into inexpression.

"Eli Tucker? From Franklin Township?" She tilted her head and spoke with measured indifference. "Huh. I think I met him once."

When I raised an eyebrow, she added, "A long time ago,

though. I doubt he'd remember me." She straightened a little, as though stiffening her spine, and rubbed her stomach. "Are we going to eat or what? I'm starving."

"Sure." I pushed up off the bench and began heading for the brick path I was pretty sure led toward the student life center. "Let's go."

I motioned for Zelda to walk with me, as Gia joined us, giving Nate the privacy to maneuver to his feet. We didn't move very fast, and within a few minutes, he came up alongside me.

"So . . . Zelda and Quinn. I guess you two ended up rooming together because you've both got weird names at the end of the alphabet?" Nate cocked his head at me, smiling.

I cast Gia a warning look. I wasn't going to share the more colorful parts of my new roommate's story with Nate. Not yet, anyway. As protective of me as he was, he'd flip out for sure.

"I don't know." Zelda answered before I could. "I'm thinking it was because we're both hot chicks who aren't going to take shit from anyone." She smirked at me, bumping her shoulder against mine, and I grinned in return.

"I think I like your reasoning."

Nate rolled his eyes. "It's going to be an interesting year."

★ Eight ★

Leo

Freshman Year
September

One of the first things I'd discovered about college was that locker rooms were pretty much the same. Oh, the lockers were a little nicer at Carolina, sure—but the smell and the noises were both exactly the same. So was the vibe, the mood and attitudes.

"Hey, Taylor. Looked great out there tonight." Thom Wilkens, the QB and team captain, paused behind me and punched me in the arm. "Keep up the good work, and you might see more play time during the games."

"Thanks." I grinned. "I know I've got a lot to live up to."

Thom shrugged. "Yeah, I hear that. Being the quarterback who comes in after Drake Stamos, the guy who led us to a national championship? Not fun. I'm constantly feeling like those shoes are way too fucking big. We're a young team, and we're all figuring this shit out. So you need anything, you come to me, yeah?"

"Got it." I nodded as Thom made his way toward his own locker, stopping here and there to drop encouragement to other players. Dude was new to leadership, but he was doing a terrific job.

"Fucking asshole." Next to me, Matt slammed his locker and fisted his towel. "He acts like such a big fucking deal. Who the hell does he think he is?"

"Shut up." I glanced over his shoulder, hoping Thom hadn't heard him. "What the hell's your problem?"

Matt scowled. "It's not my problem, dude. It's that guy, who thinks he's some fucking bigshot because everyone says he's the second coming. He's a fucking sophomore. A year older than us. Why does that make him so amazing?"

"Matt." I grabbed his arm. "You've got to keep your voice down. I don't know what Thom did to you, but—"

"Oh, he's *Thom* now, is he? Your new buddy? Yeah, you'd like him, because he's stroking your dick, huh? And you're sucking up so you get to play in another game."

I bit down the anger rising up in my chest. "You're a fucking idiot, you know that, Lampert? You've been acting like a jerk for the last month. What's wrong with you?"

"Guess I'm just not a *team player*." Matt pivoted and stalked off toward the showers without giving me so much as a backward look.

"Someone didn't take his happy pills today." Tate came over to the bench, drying off his hair. "What's going on?"

"Wish I knew." I closed my locker. "I don't have the time or energy to deal with his shit right now, though. I've got to hit the showers."

"Yeah?" Tate raised one eyebrow. "You got plans tonight?"

I grinned at him. "Oh, yeah. My girl's gonna be here in about an hour. I got plans on top of plans."

"Hey, that's great. You haven't seen her since you came down, have you?"

"Nope." I hadn't let myself think about this weekend too much today, since I'd had a full schedule of classes and then practice to get through. But now, with all that behind me, a kind of jubilee made me want to dance or shout or something. I couldn't wait to see Quinn, to hold her . . . to talk to her in person.

"So what's on the agenda?" Tate pulled on his jeans.

I shot him a look full of meaning, and he rolled his eyes. "Okay, bro, I get it. But seriously, you've got to get out of the sack at some point, right? I mean, you're planning to show up for the game Saturday, right?"

"Yeah, of course. And I can't do anything too wild tomorrow night, since we've got curfew, but we're going to get some dinner tonight, and I don't have class tomorrow, so I figured I'd show them around the campus."

"Them? You got more than one woman coming down?"

"Actually, I do. Quinn's friend Gia rode with her, so she didn't have to make the trip on her own." I studied Tate, my eyes narrowing. "So what're you doing tonight, Durham? Want to come along?" Since that awful day when Tate had driven me home from the shore, we'd kept in touch and even hung out a little over the summer. We'd driven down to Carolina together and gotten to be friends in the past month. I liked Tate; he was steady and even-tempered, likable and friendly.

He didn't have the same hair-trigger hot temper that Matt did. He also wasn't a partier, and it was gratifying to have a friend like him, who understood that I didn't want to get wasted every weekend. That I had different priorities now.

He considered as he shook out a Henley and slid his arms into the sleeves. "You're not setting me up with the extra chick, right? I mean, thanks, but I'm really not looking to date. Or for a relationship. I'm not in a place where I feel like I can commit to that." His expression was serious, and I knew he was speaking the truth. Tons of girls had offered themselves to him since we'd been here, but he'd explained to me that he needed to focus on classes and football right now. Girls were a distraction he couldn't afford.

"No, I just figured it might be fun. And maybe Gia wouldn't feel like a third wheel."

Tate nodded. "Okay, I guess I'm in."

"Awesome. I'm thinking Moonie's at seven."

"I'll be there."

"Be where?" Matt was back, shaking his wet hair like a dog just out of the bath.

"Yo! Watch it." I shoved his shoulder. "That was a really fast shower. Did you even use soap, Matt? Do I need to start checking behind your ears, like your grandma?"

"Bite me, Taylor. I shower faster than you because I don't shave my legs and pits like the ladies and you do."

"Yeah, whatever. You're just jealous because I'm so much prettier than you."

"In your dreams, boy. In your dreams. So where are you going with Durham?"

Tate shot me an apologetic glance and waved. "See you

tonight, Leo. Later, Matt."

I sighed and wrapped the towel around my waist. "I need to hit the showers, bro."

"Sure. Fine. After you tell me what's going on and why you're hiding something from me."

"I'm not hiding anything from you." That wasn't exactly a lie. I just hadn't gone out of my way to let Matt know what was going on. "You know Quinn's coming down this weekend. Remember? You promised to make yourself scarce tonight and Saturday night."

"Yeah, yeah, yeah. I remember. So why is Durham going out with you guys tonight? Three's a crowd, right?"

"Gia's driving down with Quinn. I thought it would be nice for her to meet someone down here, too. Nothing big, just hanging out."

"Why'd you ask him and not me?" Matt dropped his towel and reached into his locker for pants.

I looked longingly toward the showers again. Quinn was going to be here any time now. She and Gia were checking in at a local motel and then coming over to my dorm. I wanted to be there when she arrived. But Matt seemed like he might be genuinely hurt that I'd ignored him in favor of Tate.

"Well, Matt, for one, you don't like Quinn. I didn't figure you'd want to come out with us."

Matt straightened up and stared at me, his eyes wide. "I don't not like Quinn. Why would you think that?"

"Oh, let's see. Maybe it's all the times you told me you didn't like her, or how you treated her like shit when we were dating in high school. And how you stayed away all summer, when I was with Quinn. And how you didn't even bother to show up to pay your respects when her dad died. Rest of the team came by. But not you. Not my so-called best friend."

Matt frowned. "That was in high school. And this summer—I figured she needed you, so I stayed out of the way. I don't do funerals or death. You know that."

"Yeah." Matt's upbringing hadn't made it easy for him to deal with loss or disappointment. I understood it, but I didn't have to like it.

"Anyway, it doesn't mean I don't like Quinn. You're my bro. If you like her, I'm okay with her, too. Right?"

"I don't just like her, Matt. I love her. Quinn's my girl. She's around for good."

His lips twitched. "Right. Then you should let me come tonight, so I can get used to it."

I heaved a breath and ran a hand through my sweat-damp hair. I could argue with Matt for another hour and not change his mind. It was easier to just make it easy on myself and give in.

"Fine. You can come with us tonight."

A smile lit up his face, and I felt guilty that I'd been trying to avoid including him. "Cool. So who's the chick coming down with the Quinnster?"

And just like that, the guilt was gone. "Don't call her that. You know she hates it. Oh, and it's Gia who drove down with her."

At his blank look, I added, "Gia Capri? One of Quinn's friends? Worked on the newspaper with her? Was in our class? Graduated with us, like, three months ago?"

He shook his head. "Name doesn't ring a bell. Is she hot?"

I hesitated. "Uh, she's cute. Petite—"

"Petite? What the hell does that mean? She's short?"

"Well, she's . . . petite. You know, yeah, a little short." Inspiration struck. "Like Mila Kunis."

Matt perked up. "Nice tits?"

"Mila Kunis? Uh—"

He shook his head, impatience on his face. "No, idiot. This chick. Quinnst—Quinn's friend. Does she have nice tits?"

I counted to ten under my breath. "I'm not going to answer that question, bud. You can wait and see for yourself." When he began to smile, I hurried to clarify that. "But don't say anything about her tits to her. Or to Quinn. Or to me, in front of the girls. Got it? Are we clear? And I am serious as fuck about this, Matt. I haven't seen my girl in six weeks, and I'll be damned if I'm going to let you screw it up."

"Fine. I got it. Geez. When did you get to be such whipped wussy, Taylor? You used to be fun."

I shot him a one-fingered salute and headed for the showers. "I'm still fun. I'm just fun with the sexiest, most beautiful girl in the world. And if you get in the way of my fun tonight, I swear I'll cut off your fucking balls."

Somehow, even with all the delays in the locker room, I made it back to the dorm before Quinn and Gia arrived. She'd texted me that they had checked into the motel and were getting changed before coming over.

Just knowing she was close drove me out of my mind. I wanted to jump into my car and drive over there, plans be damned. If it weren't for Gia being at the motel with her, I might've done just that. But if I was in motel room with Quinn, I didn't want a third person there with us.

My phone buzzed, and I jumped to check it.

On our way. <3

Okay. If they'd left the motel, they'd be at Bratton, my dorm, in about ten minutes. I'd add five more minutes for parking and getting inside and upstairs.

Twenty minutes. I could wait that long.

Probably.

Matt had disappeared from the locker room by the time I'd finished my shower. I'd texted him that if he was serious about coming out with us, he had to be in our room by seven, or we'd leave without him.

At two minutes before seven, he strolled in and glanced around.

"Where are they?"

"Almost here." My knee jiggled with nerves. "Should arrive in about . . ." I checked my phone again. God, was time going backward? "Ten minutes."

"Uh huh. What's going on with your leg there?" He pointed to my bouncing knee.

"Oh, nervous energy, I guess."

He smirked, raising one eyebrow, but I ignored him. Clearly he had no idea that if I stopped my leg jiggling, I'd end up pacing the floor, wearing out our carpet.

Finally, I couldn't take it anymore. "I'm going downstairs, so they don't have any trouble finding us." I stood up and almost sprinted to the door.

"Should I come down, too?" Matt turned in his desk chair.

"No." I pointed at him. "You stay here. We'll come up."

"Okay, boss." Matt nodded. "Whatever you say."

I jogged down the three flights of steps and burst through the doors. A group of girls stood in the lobby, and a couple of them called out to me. I smiled but didn't respond. I had a more important goal.

Outside the early fall air was still warm. I'd already fallen in love with nights in the south; the sky was like velvet, and it seemed like there were more stars than I'd ever seen up north. I stood in the shadows, listening to the sounds of people coming and going. It was still early enough that some students were on their way back from the dining hall, while others were probably heading to the library or to evening lectures. I felt sorry for every one of them who wasn't me tonight.

I heard her voice before I could actually see her. She was saying something to Gia, and then they both laughed. I couldn't stand still one more second.

Rounding the hedge that lined the pathway in front of the building, I stepped onto the bricks and scanned the few people walking until I saw her. Our eyes met at the same time, and then she gave a cry and took off toward me.

I used to think those scenes in movies where two characters ran in slow motion into each other's arms were ridiculously corny. Who did that? Apparently the answer was me, because there we were, and I had zero regrets.

And then Quinn was in my arms, and I didn't care about any other fucking thing in the world.

"Leo." She was crying, trying to touch my face and kiss me and hug me all at once while her words ran together. "My God, what're you doing down here? I couldn't believe it, when

I looked up and saw it was you . . . I'm so glad to see you."

Glad didn't even begin to cover it. I ran my hands over her hair, down her back and drew her as close to me as possible before I did what I'd wanted to do most and claimed her mouth.

She tasted just like always—that mix of mint and Quinn that drove me wild. My tongue stroked deep within her, tangling with hers, and my lips were relentless.

"Mia, I can't believe you're finally here. God, you have no idea. It felt like this day was never going to end." I kissed her again, hard. "And now that you're here, I don't want it to end. I love you, baby. I've missed you so much."

She half-laughed, half-sobbed. "I missed you, too. Video chatting sucks."

I swept my thumbs over her cheekbones. "Why the tears, babe?" Quinn had cried a lot this summer, but as a rule, she wasn't a weeper.

"Happy tears." She twined her arms around my neck. "Only happy tears this time." Her boobs pressed against me, and her hips canted into mine. And all I wanted was her.

My dick was hard and straining, and one part of my mind began trying to figure out how fast I could get inside her, even though I knew it wasn't an option yet. First came dinner, where I'd have to act like a reasonable human being, especially since Gia—

For the first time since I'd caught sight of my girl, I remembered that other people existed in the world. Lifting my eyes, I found Gia, leaning against a tree, trying to look unobtrusive.

"Hey, Gia." Sliding my hand down Quinn's arm, I held

firm to her hand and offered the other to her friend. "Thanks so much for coming down. How was the trip?"

Both the girls laughed. "Long and uneventful, except for us being silly, of course. Oh, and arguing over music."

I grinned at them. "Well, I'm glad you're both here." Tucking Quinn against my side, I nodded toward the dorm. "Want to come up and see my room? And then I figured we'd grab some dinner at this place off-campus. If that sounds okay."

"As long as I'm with you, I don't care what we do." She smiled up at me.

"Then you're in luck, baby, because everything I have planned for this weekend is you and me together." I paused, considering. "Well, except Friday night, when I have to be in bed alone early, and Saturday during the game. I love you, Mia, but I wouldn't want to have to protect you from Tennessee State's offensive line on the field."

She laughed. "True."

I held the door for both girls as we went into the lobby. Quinn glanced around with wide eyes. "Wow, this is beautiful. It makes Birch's buildings look pretty utilitarian."

"Southern colleges. Most of the stuff here is pretty old, so it tends to be a little more ornate." I led them up the steps, waving to a couple of the guys who passed us on their way down. When we reached the landing, three of my teammates were just coming through the doors.

"Taylor, you dog. Who're these lovely ladies?"

I threaded my fingers through Quinn's. "This is my girl, Quinn, and our friend, Gia. Girls, that's Buck, Kevin and Dovan. They're all running backs."

"Oh, you're *the* Quinn." Kevin grinned. "Good to meet

the chick who keeps Leo on the straight and narrow."

Quinn didn't reply, but I noticed that her cheeks went pink, and I made a mental note to thank Kevin for saying that. Yeah, it was the truth, but coming from a football player she didn't even know, I thought it probably made more of an impact.

"You all going out tonight?" Donvan leaned on the railing, the position making his insane arm muscles pop. Yeah, that wasn't an accident. These dudes were completely aware of their bodies; I knew this from locker room talk. There'd been a good-natured argument last week about which set of muscles made girls drop their panties fastest.

"Yeah. I thought we'd hit Moonie's." Thursdays were typically the team's party night, unless we were traveling on Friday for our weekend game. Post-game blow-outs were popular, too, of course. Hey, football players took advantage of any excuse to let off steam and get a little crazy.

"Cool. Maybe we'll see you there." His eyes lingered on Gia for a few minutes before he followed Kevin and Buck down the stairs.

"Oh. Baby." Gia fanned herself. "Please tell me those guys are single. And Quinn, thank you, thank you, thank you for asking me to come down here with you."

I laughed. "They're all single. But they're players, Gia. I mean that in every way possible."

She quirked an eyebrow at me as we stopped in front of my door. "You mean they're only interested in mindless, no-strings-attached sex? Sign me up."

"Gia." Quinn shook her head, rolling her eyes. "Honestly."

"So I'm not interested in a relationship. I just want to have fun for now. What's wrong with that?" Gia flipped one hand over, her clear voice carrying as I pushed open the door.

"Abso-fucking-lutely nothing." Matt stood just inside our room, leaning against my desk, his thick legs crossed at the ankle and his arms folded over his chest. "Welcome to Carolina U, sweetheart. I'm Matt, and I'm here to make your every fantasy come true."

★ Nine ★

Quinn

"Oh, my God, Quinn!" Gia grasped my arm and yelled into my ear as she leaned into the booth where I was sitting. "I can't remember ever having this much fun. Isn't it wild?"

I forced a smile and nodded. "Yeah. Wild." I glanced up at Leo, who was in the middle of an intense conversation with one of the football players—I couldn't remember this one's name. As if he felt my eyes on him, Leo tightened his arm around me and brushed his lips over the top of my head.

"You okay, Mia?"

"Better than okay." I snuggled closer.

"Do you need another drink?" He lifted the glass of melting ice in front of me and jiggled it. "I saw the waitress around here somewhere."

"I'm good for now. If I drink anymore, I'll have to go brave the rest rooms, and I saw that line earlier. No, thanks."

Leo's chest shook a little as he laughed. "You're not wrong.

But if you—oh, hey, Durham. I was beginning to think you got lost."

The guy who'd just approached our booth was as tall as Leo and built like a brick wall. His blond hair was cropped close to his head, and wide green eyes crinkled in the corners as he grinned at us.

"Nah, just got held up helping a buddy." His eyes moved to me, and his smile broadened. "You must be Quinn. I'm really glad to meet you." He nudged Leo's shoulder. "I hear about you. All the time."

Gladness swelled in my heart. It wasn't that I didn't trust Leo or his love for me, but hearing that he talked about me to his friends gave me a big happy.

And Leo seemed to agree. He lifted one big shoulder and nodded. "It's true. I have no shame. Quinn, this is Tate Durham. I told you about him this summer, remember?"

"Of course. Tate, it's really good to finally meet you."

He offered me his hand, and when I took it, he gripped my fingers. "Same here." His gaze flitted to Gia, still standing next to me, and I spied a spark of interest there.

"Tate, this is my friend Gia Capri. She goes to Birch with me, and she was sweet enough to play navigator for me today."

He shifted his attention and his hands to Gia. "Hey. Welcome to Carolina."

Gia nodded. "Thanks." She flickered a glance up and down his body. "You're a football player, too?"

Tate shifted his weight and hooked his thumbs in the belt loops at the front of his jeans. "Guilty. You a fan?"

Her brows shot up. "Of you? Seriously, dude. I don't know who you are. I didn't even hear your name."

If that put-down was meant to be a killing shot, it missed entirely. Tate only cocked his head, one side of his mouth curling into a half-smile. "I meant a fan of the game. I don't have any delusions of grandeur, sugar."

Gia's cheeks flushed. "I appreciate football as a sport, yeah. I think most of the people who play it are assholes, though." She looked at Leo and added, "With a few possible exceptions."

"Hey." Tate spread his hands in front of him. "No arguments here. No one knows better than football players what dicks we can all be." He grinned, and an adorable dimple popped up on his left cheek. "But not all of us are that way all the time."

"Yeah? In my experience, you're all nice eye-candy and decent dancing partners. You're good for fun, as far as that goes."

"And some of us might be able to take it farther than fun." Tate's gaze was level and fastened on Gia's face. "If we had the right incentives."

I glanced at the two of them: Tate with his relaxed stance and steady eyes, and Gia, who stood defiant, her hands tucked into the back pockets of her jeans, a frown on her face. Electricity buzzed between them, and they both seemed to be hyper-aware of it.

Next to me, Leo whispered, "I'm not sure whether to send them back to their corners or suggest they get a room."

I bit back a giggle. "Tate, why don't you join us here? There's space. And Gia, sit down, girl. Catch your breath. You were rocking it pretty hard out there with the guys."

"I'm not ready to sit down yet. Come dance with me." Gia

stuck out her lip and gave me her best pleading expression. "The music is smokin.'"

I shook my head. "I want to stay here with Leo. Go on, have fun. I'm enjoying watching you."

She shrugged. "Okay. I guess at least one of us should be enjoying herself."

"Watch it, chick. I'm enjoying myself just fine here, thanks."

"Whatever." She spared Leo and Tate a passing glance. "See you boys later."

I tracked her return to the middle of the jam-packed dance floor, where she was welcomed back by four massive guys whose dance moves ranged from admirable to pitiful. They were all bopping to a different beat, and I giggled.

"What's funny?" Leo's fingers tickled at my ribs, over the silky material of my shirt.

"Football players trying to dance." I gestured to the group with my chin. "Just goes to show that moves on the field don't always translate to moves on the dance floor."

"Hey, hey . . . Buck does pretty good out there." It was true; the ginger-haired halfback was doing more than just shuffling his feet. He had a few decent turns, and his arms didn't just hang at his sides, dangling there.

"Okay, I'll give you Buck. But the others?" I shook my head, closing my eyes. "Not pretty."

Tate leaned over. "Your friend holds her own." He jerked his chin toward Gia. "Dancing, I mean."

"Gia holds her own everywhere." I smiled as she executed a spin. "She's one of the strongest women I know. And she's wicked smart, too."

"Single?" Tate's voice was even, but I picked up the undertones of curiosity.

"Yup. And I'm not sure she's interested in changing that. Not right now, anyway." I tilted my head. "Of course, if the right guy were to come along and sweep her off her feet, that might all go out the window."

Tate nodded. "Good to know."

Leo cupped my face, sweeping his thumb over my cheekbones. "Is that what I did with you, Mia? Swept you off your feet?"

I turned my head to kiss his palm. "Every single day, baby."

The music changed just then, seguing from the up-tempo dance beat to a slower song that I recognized from a few years back. Leo snagged my hand.

"Come on. Let's dance."

My eyebrows shot up. "Seriously? *You* want to dance?"

"With you? Hell, yeah." He tugged me from the booth. "Anything that gives me an excuse to press your body up against mine and kiss you in the dark sounds like a winning idea to me." He grinned unapologetically at Tate. "Sorry, dude. I've got limited time with my girl, and I'm not wasting one minute."

Tate waved his hand. "I wouldn't, either. Go for it."

I let Leo drag me to the edge of the crowd, where he was as good as his word, wrapping one arm around my waist so that I was as close to him as possible. In his other hand, he held one of mine, bringing it to his lips and kissing my knuckles as we swayed.

"See? I told you. Alllll good."

I sighed and relaxed against him, laying my head over his heart and closing my eyes. "I'm half-afraid I'm dreaming. I've been wishing for this day for so long. I can't believe I'm really here."

"I know." His voice rumbled in his chest. "When I'm at practice or playing, I can focus on just that and tune everything else out. But the minute it's over, I go back to missing you like crazy." He rubbed my back with his free hand and then slid his fingers to my neck, coaxing me to turn my head. When I lifted my face to his, he lowered his mouth to mine and kissed me softly, no tongue, no pressure . . . just us, connected in every way we could be at the moment.

A few feet away from us, Gia was dancing with Kevin. They weren't holding each other like Leo held me, just fooling around as they did an exaggerated sway. Gia was laughing at something he'd said to her. He gave her a little spin, and she lost her footing, teetering off-balance. She might've landed on the floor in a heap, but suddenly, another pair of strong hands managed to catch her.

Matt stood there, his face serious, holding her. Gia straightened, and I could tell that her entire small body was tensed. She shook her head and faked a smile and laugh before she began to turn back to Kevin.

But Matt stopped her, gripping her upper arms and staring down at her as he drew her close. Gia let him hold her, barely moving in time to the music.

"Fuck." Leo grunted out the word, just loud enough for me to hear him. "What the hell's he doing?"

"Who, Matt?" I pulled away so that I could see Leo's face. "Why?" Matt had flirted with Gia like crazy back at the dorm, but he'd driven to Moonie's separately from us, and I hadn't seen much of him since we'd arrived. But now . . . he looked like a man with a plan for my friend.

Leo scowled. "You know him. He's an asshole. I love him like a brother, but he's not a good bet for any girl."

"I don't think Gia's looking for a marriage proposal. You heard what she said before. She just wants to have some fun. She works hard at school, and she came with me this weekend for a little down time."

"I know Matt. And I know girls like Gia. It's a bad combo."

I traced a line down the side of his face. "Uh huh. But we're not responsible for either of them. They're both old enough to make their own decisions." Walking my fingers around to the back of his neck, I caressed the line of short hair there. "And speaking of making decisions . . . how much longer do we have to stay here, with all these other people, when I'm fairly certain there's an empty dorm room just about ten minutes away from us?"

His eyes lit up. "Are you serious? I've only been hanging out here because I didn't want you to think I was some kind of animal who was only interested in getting you into bed."

Wrapping my arms around him, I kissed his lips, thrusting my tongue into the warmth of his mouth so that there was no doubt about my intentions.

"Take me away from all this. Now."

"Can we do this every day for the rest of our lives?"

Leo's voice was tired but sated. I lay sprawled over him, not a stitch of clothes on either of us. His hand drew lazy circles on my back, and his breath was still coming in rapid puffs that stirred my hair.

"You're sure Matt's not coming back?" I asked the question for the third time. I trusted my boyfriend, but Matt had always been unpredictable. I wouldn't put it past him to come bursting in, just to embarrass me.

"I'm sure, babe. I told you. He texted that he was taking Gia back to the motel, and then he was going to crash somewhere else tonight, with one of the guys. And Gia said the same thing, right, that he drove her back? You made sure she was okay with him?"

"Yeah." I sighed. "She said she was." I pressed my lips into Leo's chest. "And in answer to your other question, I'm on board. This. Every day. Forever."

"Excellent." He rolled over so that we lay on our sides, facing each other. "Does it make me a wuss that I'm excited to sleep all night with you in my bed and wake up in the morning without either of us having to sneak out? We can actually be like normal people, have a little morning nookie, and go out for breakfast."

"That doesn't make you a wuss. It makes you a wise man who appreciates a rare opportunity."

"That's what I thought, too." He trailed a finger down my arm. "How's it been going at school, Mia? I know we've talked and you say everything's good, but tell me really."

I feathered my fingers through his hair. "It's good. Classes aren't too bad, and professors seem okay. Life's pretty boring. I go to class, eat at the dining hall, hang out with Gia and Nate

. . . study . . . go home and see my mother a few times a week. Sometimes Mom comes over to have lunch with me or take me to dinner." I kissed his chin, bristly with scruff. "And on good days, I get to talk to my sexy boyfriend."

He chuckled. "Your sexy boyfriend pretty much lives for those calls. How about the roommate? Zelda? How's she working out?"

"Surprisingly well. I wasn't sure when we first met. Actually, I thought we were going to hate each other. We're very different. But she's more than what she appears. She's smart, even though she tries to downplay it. And she's kind of . . . prickly, I guess, when you first meet her. Defensive. My mom says Zelda has a huge chip on her shoulder."

Leo slid his knee up between my legs, pressing his muscled thigh to the part of my body still throbbing from his touch. "I'm not going to lie, babe. She sounds like she's a little challenging."

"She is. But she's also funny and kind in unexpected ways. Odd and quirky, yes, but never cruel or mean. And she's much better than Gia's roommate, Ellie." I shuddered. "That chick's a basket case. She flips out if Gia breathes too loud or texts too late. And she gets drunk every weekend and picks up strange guys. Gia's miserable with her." I spanned his broad chest with the palms of my hands. "I think you're bigger here, you know? In a good way, I mean."

"You mean all my hard work is paying off? Glad to hear it. That's really why I do it, you know—the daily practices, lifting every morning, running sprints—it's purely to make my body more attractive to you." Leo smirked.

"As long as you have those priorities lined up right." I buried my nose in his neck. "You smell so good. I need to take another one of your shirts home with me. The one you left me this summer is starting to lose your scent."

"Sure. You can go through my drawers and take your pick."

"No, I need one that you've worn and not washed." I gave him a gentle shove, rolling him to his back and balancing myself above him. "It's got to smell like you, not like some generic laundry detergent."

"Fine." He stared up at me. "God, Mia. Sometimes I forget how fucking beautiful you are. But look at you." He swept my hair back away from my face. "You make me forget to breathe."

I ventured one hand lower, between us, sliding it down the planes of his chest, over his flat stomach, to trail my fingers over a part of his body that was beginning to sit up and take notice again. Taking his cock into my grip, I moved my hand up and down once. "Maybe I can remind you to inhale and exhale again."

Draping my body over his, I began to slither down, raining small kisses over Leo as he groaned. "I think what you're doing now is more likely to stop my heart. But don't let that slow you down."

I shot him a saucy grin. "Don't worry, I won't." Lingering just south of his belly button, I ran my tongue over the ridges in his lower abs, making them jump. "I think you're more cut here, too. You been rocking the crunches, Lion?"

He huffed out a laugh. "Yeah, I've had to up my game there. But you know, no one down here calls me the Lion. I was hoping to leave that back in South Jersey."

"Okay. It's just between you and me." Stroking his engorged cock with my fingers, I lifted my eyes to his face, watching as I took just the head into my mouth. Leo arched his neck, his jaw clenching.

"Mia . . . my God."

"Hmmmm?" I slid my lips lower, taking in more of him and circling the tip with my tongue. Bobbing my head, I sucked hard and then went down even further, relaxing my throat so I didn't gag. He was throbbing heat, so hard that I wondered how it didn't hurt.

His hips began to pump against me, and I cupped his balls, fondling them, relishing his hiss of breath.

"Mia . . . babe. God, I'm close. If you want to move . . ."

I raised my mouth just long enough to speak. "I'm not going anywhere. I want you. All of you." Holding the base of his erection, I took him deep, my cheeks hollowing with the intensity of the suction.

Leo thrust upward, his fingers knotting in my hair as he roared my name, pulsing into my mouth as he gave me everything he had. I stayed with him, swallowing several times and stroking him as he came down from the crest.

"My God, Mia." He grasped me under the arms and hauled me up against him, burying his face in my neck. "You . . . you just destroy me, every time. I think I'm going to be the one to give you everything, and then you empty yourself out for me. Again." He rolled over, caging me between his arms. "I've always known I don't deserve you, but sometimes I realize how utterly unworthy of you I am. I don't know why you love me, but all I want is for you to keep doing it, forever."

I framed his face in both my hands, drowning in the soft gray of the eyes I loved. "I think that can be arranged."

★ Ten ★

Nate

Freshman Year
May

"HEY, WELLMAN. GIVE ME A HAND HERE, WILL you?"

Tuck's voice held more than a little frustration as I came into our room, drying off my hair with a towel. He was sitting on his bed, his arms braced on either side of his body so that the muscles popped out. His jaw was clenched, and he was staring at the floor, where a thick hardback book lay.

"Sure. What's up?"

A tic jumped in his cheek. "I was being stupid. Lazy. Went to grab the book on my desk without thinking about it, and it was too far out of my reach. Dropped it." He nodded to the wheelchair at the foot of the bed. "I should've gotten the chair, I guess, but . . ." He trailed off, and I heard what he didn't want to say. Whenever Tuck could ignore the chair that gave him mobility, he did.

I knew how maddening it could be, not to be able to do the simple things other people took for granted. Living with Eli Tucker for the last year had taught me to appreciate what I was capable of doing instead of brooding about what I couldn't.

Bending, I picked up the book and tossed it onto the bed. I knew from experience that it was easier not to make a big deal about any help I ever gave Tuck. He tended toward silence and occasional surliness, but he was usually pretty easy-going with me, which was amazing considering what the guy had been through. Every now and then, though, the limitations got to him, and he'd get real quiet and withdraw.

"Thanks, bro." He slid the book a little closer and flipped it open. "One more final, then I'm done."

"Yeah. I've got two more." I reached into a drawer and pulled out a T-shirt. "You excited about going home?"

He didn't answer right away. "I'll be happy to be done with classes, yeah. Going home . . . not so much." His eyebrows drew together. "Coming here gave me freedom, you know? At home, my mom hovers, and my dad worries. And tries too hard. He's always trying to come up with ways to make my life easier." Tuck gripped his thighs, still roped with muscles. "It's harder and harder for me to keep from saying that the easier life option disappeared when my spine snapped."

I winced. Years of dealing with medical procedures and hospitals hadn't made me immune to feeling squeamish about other people's injuries. "Yeah, I get that, I guess. They only want to help, but they don't understand how to do it."

"Is it the same with you?" Tuck pushed himself to sit against the pillows. "With your parents, I mean."

I shrugged. "Not really. But this has always been my life. My parents have been dealing with all my crap since I was born, so they're used to it. They know what to expect, usually, and they're pretty cool." I thought about the tight, anxious expressions I occasionally caught on my mom's face, or my dad's sometimes-forced joviality. "But it can be tough when I want to be real, and they don't. My mom and dad are the most optimistic people I know. They believe the doctors are always going to come up with a solution or a new treatment for me, and it's all going to be fine. I guess I'd rather be brutally honest. When you don't think you're going to have a lot of time left, you don't want to waste it on bullshit, right?" I remembered my talk with Quinn on the beach last summer. "You don't want to waste any of it."

Tuck nodded, slowly. We'd discussed what he called my lack of longevity, although neither of us dwelled on it, any more than we did on the hit that had taken away his ability to walk.

"So. Your girls coming over tonight?" He changed the subject in his typical fashion, and I played along as usual.

"Not sure any of them would like being called 'my' girls, but yeah. Quinn, Gia and Zelda are going to hang out. If that's okay." I was conscious of the fact that Tuck rarely left our room at night, so I tried to be considerate. It was tough for me to tackle the steps that led up to Quinn and Zelda's room, and Gia's was even further up. By default, we often met here, at my dorm, but I didn't like to take advantage of my roommate's tolerance.

I knew I was damn lucky, all in all. Tuck liked Quinn—well, who wouldn't like her?—and he had a joking, comfortable relationship with Gia, who could be, as he said, a little bit of a ball-buster.

Zelda was a different story. Oh, they seemed to be all right with each other, but there was something else there, something I didn't quite understand. He'd met all the girls at the same time, during our first week on campus. While he'd been polite and friendly to Quinn and Gia, he'd been more cautious around Zelda. I could relate a little; Zelda was over the top, sometimes. She could be loud and maybe even vulgar; Quinn said she had no filter. That didn't so much bother me, since I'd been known to be brutally honest at times, too, but Zelda talked about things that made people uncomfortable.

Still, Tuck couldn't have known that when he met her, and that had been the first time I'd seen something off. Zelda had been tense when she came into our room; I could see how wired she was. And when I'd introduced her to my roommate, she'd regarded him almost defiantly, as though she was daring him to react to her.

There had been a moment where I thought he might do just that, a fleeting sense that maybe they knew each other already. But then Tuck had only nodded, the same way he had with Quinn and Gia. And later, when I'd asked him if he'd ever met her before, he'd looked at me like I was crazy.

"How would I know her? She's not even from around here, right? Isn't that what you said?"

"Yeah, but the first day I met her, when I mentioned your name, she said something about how maybe she'd met you a while back. So I thought you might know her. Small world and all that."

Tuck hadn't looked up from his book. "Lots of people heard of me when I took that hit. It was big news in a small town, you know? And the sob-story got picked up by a few other news outlets. She might remember my name from then. Who knows, right? Doesn't matter, dude. Drop it, okay?"

I had, and when Quinn brought it up to me, I'd relayed what Tuck had said. Quinn had shrugged it off, too.

But still. There was a vibe I couldn't quite ignore.

I heard Gia's voice even before the girls knocked at the door.

"The fun has arrived, boys! Open up for party time."

I grinned in spite of myself, shaking my head. "Door's open. Come on in."

They spilled inside, the three of them, giggling. They were dressed up: Gia had on a short shimmery dress, Zelda wore something black and slinky, while Quinn looked incredible in skinny jeans and a green silky shirt. Gia staggered a little, and I didn't have to get close enough to smell her breath to know that she'd already been tossing a few back. She made a beeline for Tuck, throwing her arms around him.

"Eli Tucker! You hottie hot hottie, you. Are you ready for a good time?"

Tuck patted her back and gently pushed her away. "Hey, Gia. Looks like you started celebrating a little early, huh?"

Quinn perched on the edge of my bed and cast me a look. "She and Matt had a huge fight this morning." She kept her voice low. "I think he slept with someone else last night. At least it looks that way. It was ugly, Nate."

I rolled my eyes. "What does she expect? He's Matt

Lampert. He's been a dick since the fourth grade. And I thought they weren't serious. She always says it's casual." Gia and Matt had hooked up back in the fall, the first time Gia had gone down to Carolina with Quinn. Since then, the two had had what Gia called sex on demand. Matt seemed to run hot and cold; sometimes he was possessive and jealous of Gia . . . and then sometimes he did whatever the hell he wanted.

"Yeah." Quinn kept her eyes on Gia. "What she says and what she feels are two different things, in this case. She wants to believe it's nothing big, but I think she's in love with him. And he's breaking her heart on a daily basis."

"Fuck." I sighed.

"That's exactly what Leo says about it." Quinn rolled her shoulders. "God, I'm stiff. I spent all afternoon studying for this chem final which I'm fairly certain I'm going to bomb. I should probably pull an all-nighter, but I didn't want to dump Gia on you and Zelda."

"And for that I'm grateful." I eyed up her outfit. "So we're going out, huh? She doesn't want to just stay here?"

"Nope. She insists that we're going to Scorpio." A new club had just opened right off-campus, serving both the over- and the under-21 crowd. Since most of the area bars were pretty vigilant about not serving minors, there weren't many options when it came to going out. Scorpio was instantly popular and always crowded.

"That'll be fun." The irony dripped from my voice. I didn't like crowds on a good day, but when we also had to keep track of our drunk friend? I'd rather have stayed home to study.

Gia had given up on hanging over Tuck and was digging in her small purse. Zelda stood with her back against my closet door, her face inscrutable as she took in the scene. She was much more subdued when she came here than she was in the comfort of her own room, and I suspected Tuck had something to do with that.

"Aha!" Gia held up her hand, dropped her bag and began dancing. "I found it!" She displayed the silver tube to Quinn. "See? This is that lipstick I told you about, the one I bought in the city from that organic skin care place, 'member?"

"Yep." Quinn nodded. "Do you need help getting it on straight?"

"Nooooo . . ." Gia uncapped the lipstick. "Just a mirror."

"Open my closet." Tuck spoke patiently. "I've got one on the inside of the door, but it's low, so you'll have to bend over."

We all watched in silence as Gia traced her lips with the color, her face close to the small mirror and her ass stuck straight out.

"I can't wear lipstick." Quinn touched her own mouth with one finger. I watched in fascination, wishing it were my finger instead of hers. I'd been doing okay in the last year being only Quinn's friend and not resenting Leo, but every now and then, desire pushed through and I had thoughts I shouldn't.

"How come?" I cleared my throat and tried to focus on her words instead of her lips.

"Oh, I don't know. It always ends up on my teeth, and I feel like I look stupid."

"There's a trick to it, you know." Zelda spoke up for the first time since they'd arrived. "To make sure you don't get lipstick on your teeth."

"Oh, really?" Quinn smiled at her. "Do share, oh, makeup guru. You know I live to sit at your feet and listen to your wisdom."

Zelda's lips twitched, but she continued speaking in the same tone I'd use to talk about the weather. "It's pretty simple, but you do need another person. A guy. You put on the lipstick, and then you go down on the guy."

Quinn's eyes got big. "You, um . . . what?"

"Blow jobs are the perfect way to make sure you don't end up embarrassed later on." Zelda shrugged and smiled. "Like I said, the biggest issue is making sure you have a guy on hand who'll let you suck his cock. But I've never met a guy who'd turn down a bj." Her eyes flickered to Tuck and rested on him for a minute.

Tuck frowned, staring at her. An uncomfortable silence surrounded us, only broken when Gia capped her lipstick and smacked her lips.

"Okay, all prettified." She made a kissing sound. "Now who's going to volunteer to let me go down on him to blot my lipstick?"

I nearly fell off the bed, and on his side of the room, Tuck choked. I was pretty sure my face had gone beet-red.

Zelda laughed. "I think you're out of luck in this crowd, G. Nate's too honorable to help you out, and Tucker . . ." Tilting her head, she pursed her lips. "Tucker wants you to think he is. Of course, if the rest of us weren't here, he might take you up on it. Drunk and horny girls are his favorites."

Tuck's forehead wrinkled, and his eyes went dark. "What the hell is that supposed to mean?"

Zelda lifted one slender shoulder. "Just an observation." She pushed off the door and twisted to stretch. "Are we ready to go, bitches? Mama's got hearts to break tonight."

Since I'd become aware of the possibility of having a shortened lifespan, I'd begun setting short-term goals. At first, they were simple: I'd wanted to live long enough to be taller than my mom. To survive until I'd learned to speak Spanish and figured out calculus. To finish high school.

And now, with one year of college behind me, I felt like I could take on anything. My health was stable; it hadn't gotten any better, but it wasn't any worse, either. My parents were thrilled that the year had passed so uneventfully, and they'd even begun doing something unprecedented in our little family: they'd taken short weekend trips by themselves. A few times my mom had even made it through the weekend without calling me to check in.

I'd adjusted to sharing a room, too. Tuck and I had ended up to be pretty compatible, and a few months before the end of our freshman year, he'd glanced up from his laptop one night while we were both studying.

"Dude, you good to room together another year?"

I was relieved that he'd brought it up before I had to, but I played it off, shrugging. "Yeah, I guess. Works for me."

"Cool. Figure it's better if we stick together. You and I already know each other's habits and shit, right?"

"Yeah. Good point."

And that was that. Housing had already informed us that we'd have the same room, since the school had a limited number of accessible dorms. Familiarity and predictability were comforting to me, so I was happy about the prospect of making sophomore year a repeat of our freshman semesters.

The girls would be moving to a new dorm, one that was actually a little closer to where Tuck and I lived. They were going to have a suite, all three of them together, and I knew Quinn was excited about the prospect of sharing a regular bathroom with just two other girls, instead of dealing with a whole floor of students battling it out for the showers and toilets.

"So, Zelda, huh? You're sure you want to room with her again next year?" We were sitting on the deck at the beach house the weekend after our classes had ended, with my chair under the overhang, protected from the morning sun. Quinn sat a little in front of me in a chaise lounge, her face turned up to the light.

"Yeah, we are. Zelda's a friend now. She's got her quirks, sure, but don't we all? And she doesn't really have anyone else in her life. She tends to put people off, and I think at least a little of that is on purpose. Plus, she and Gia get along, which will be a nice change for Gia after this last year with Ellie the roommate from hell." We both shuddered, thinking of the crazy girl who'd made Gia's freshman year less than ideal.

"And the random hook-ups don't bother you?" Quinn hadn't said much to me about her roommate's extracurricular activities, but Gia hadn't been so reserved. I knew that Zelda brought guys back to the room on a regular basis, although Quinn insisted she never did it if she knew anyone else would be there. The guys talked, too; Zelda's name was unique enough that I didn't have to wonder who they were referring to when they told stories about the chick who put out like a dude did.

I'd overheard one conversation in Psych 101 between the two people sitting behind me. "It's amazing, bro. She's gorgeous, like a model or something, fucking hot—and all she wants is fucking without commitment. Matter of fact, she told me before she took me to her room that if I was going to get attached or want to call her again, I could forget it—she doesn't do complicated when it comes to sex."

Still, Zelda was always respectful to me. I wasn't sure if that was because she didn't see me as a potential sex partner, thanks to my limitations or if it was because Quinn had warned her off. Oh, she flirted a little, and she teased me, but it was never serious and never made me uncomfortable.

She didn't flirt with Tuck, either, but she definitely didn't treat him the same way that she did me. She was wary around him, as if he were a panther whose tameness she didn't quite trust. Every now and then, as on the night we'd gone to the Scorpio for the first time, Zelda would poke at Tuck, testing to see his reaction. But it never went any further than that, and Tuck always swore to me that he had no idea why she acted that way around him.

Quinn pointed her toes and stretched her legs on the lounge chair. I had to look away from the enticing length of tan skin that ran from her hips down to her feet, or I knew I'd get hard. My cock apparently hadn't yet understood the message that Quinn wasn't for us. Not in that way.

She was answering my last question, and I tried to bring my attention to what she was saying instead of concentrating on the way her shorts were riding up a little on the side of her ass.

"I don't love her hookups, but what am I going to say? She doesn't go around talking about them to Gia and me. I've heard her say shit to shock other people, but she doesn't do that with us. It's just part of who she is, and if that's how she wants to live . . ." Quinn shook her head. "That's up to her. And next year, with us being suite mates, we'll each have our own private bedroom. So what she does in there is her business, as long as she's not putting Gia or me in danger." Her eyes flashed momentarily. "Or hitting on our boyfriends."

The air changed as soon as Quinn brought up Leo, and for once, it wasn't my doing. My two best friends had survived their first year of a long-distance relationship without hitting too many bumps. There wasn't any doubt in my mind that Leo was still crazy in love with Quinn, and of course I knew she felt the same way. That didn't mean she was happy with everything that was going on, though.

We'd driven down here to the beach together the night before, and I'd noticed that Quinn had been uncharacteristically quiet. She'd talked a little about her grades, which had just been posted, and about Gia, who had gone up to New York to live with one of her older sisters for the summer. But she hadn't mentioned Leo except briefly in passing.

I rubbed the back of my neck and tried to think of a way to bring up the subject casually. But subtle had never been my thing.

"So what's going on with you and Leo?"

Quinn dropped her head back and groaned. "Oh, don't ask. I thought everything was going well, and I thought we had a plan for the summer. Then last night . . ." She massaged her temples, as though a killer headache was lurking in there.

"We had a fight. He was pissy about me taking the job down here this summer, and he said he was just going to stay in Carolina. His coach asked for some of the guys to volunteer for this football camp for underprivileged kids. He said since I wasn't going to be around anyway, he might as well do it."

I quirked an eyebrow. "I'll risk the wrath of Quinn and admit I was a little surprised you decided to work down here this year. I figured you'd want the time with Leo. I know how hard it was for you to be apart."

She grimaced. "It was my mom's idea, that we live here this summer. She met the woman who runs the local paper, told her about my interest in journalism, and one thing led to another . . . when she offered me the internship, it sounded like a good idea."

"And you thought Leo would what, just hang out here while you worked? Spend some quality time with your mom?"

"I don't know." Quinn slumped. "I guess I figured he'd get something down here, too. A job, you know. But he said that since he has to be back down at school at the end of July, no place would hire him."

"He's probably right."

"Yeah, I know. But thanks for making me feel better about it." She stuck out her tongue at me. "I think I'm mostly mad at myself and the situation, but Leo acts like I did this on purpose. Without checking with him before I made the decision."

"Did you?"

She glared at me. "Whose side are you on, anyway?"

I lifted both hands in front of me. "No one's. I'm just pointing out what seems obvious."

"Again, thanks."

I tried another tact. "What're you going to do then? How're you going to make it work?"

Quinn couldn't have looked more miserable if she'd tried. "I have no freaking idea. When we hung up last night, Leo was still really mad. And he hasn't texted me at all today."

I glanced at the sky, where the sun hadn't reached the noon-time peak. "It's still early. He's probably asleep."

"He was moving out of the dorms today, so I'm pretty sure he's up." She blew out a long breath. "I guess I should text him and apologize. Maybe we can work something out. I could go down to Carolina for a weekend, or he could come up here for a little while."

"Yeah, that sounds like a good idea." I paused a moment, thinking. "I'm not trying to insinuate anything, Quinn, but it's still really weird to me that you took the position at the newspaper without even talking to Leo. It's like you set this up to happen."

"Oh, is this wisdom from the person who aced his psych final? Are you analyzing me, Nate?" There was an edge in her teasing words that stung.

"No. I'm just saying maybe there's more going on than what it seems."

She stared at me for a few beats before she rolled her eyes. "Okay. Yes, I think you're right. Does that make you feel better?"

"Of course not. I don't want to be right. I just want you to be happy."

For several minutes, the only sound was the crashing of the waves on the beach. Quinn rolled over in her lounge chair and propped her chin on her hands so that she could see me more fully.

"I know Leo loves me. I don't have any doubt about that at all. I know he's not messing around on me. He's not sleeping with other girls or even partying with them. He's not Matt." She made a face. "But I think there's part of me that knows I don't come first. He might think I do, and he might be able to convince himself that I'm his number one priority, but in the end, football tops me."

I rubbed my knee, which was beginning to ache. "I can understand why you might feel that way. I'm not saying Leo's doing anything wrong, but it would be easy to think he's choosing the team or the sport over you. But Quinn, I think he's just doing it for you."

She huffed out another breath. "Oh, I know the line. He says he's got to work hard now so he can get drafted into the conference and then we'll be all set. He keeps telling me everything he does is for our future. I think he even believes it. But what kind of future can we have if we can't get through the present together? I drove down to Carolina four times this year. Leo didn't come up to see me even once, except when he was coming home for breaks anyway. I mean, Nate, he never even met Zelda. He didn't come up to homecoming at Birch—but I went to his, at Carolina."

"Uh huh. So what's the answer?"

Quinn laid her cheek down on the lounge. "I guess I need to talk to Leo and tell him all this, huh? Is that what you'd tell me, Dr. Wellman?"

I smirked. "Hey, I like the sound of that. You know, I've been leaning toward education, but maybe I should consider being a psychologist."

Quinn snorted. "Better work on your bedside manner first, bud. Not everyone's going to know how to take you, like I do."

I regarded her, grinning. "That's okay. Pretty sure there's a class just for learning how not to piss off your patients."

"You better take it twice, then." She rolled over, swung her legs around and dropped her feet on the deck. "All right. I'm going in to call Leo and eat some crow. Wish me luck."

I watched her go, her movements lithe and graceful as always, and wished for about the millionth time in my life that it was me who Quinn loved.

★ Eleven ★

Leo

Sophomore year
October

The Carolina sideline was relaxed. It wasn't often that this was the case, but right now, we were up by three touchdowns with a little less than four minutes left in the game. And Arkansas had just punted after another three and out that had resulted in negative yardage for them.

In other words, we were kicking some serious ass this afternoon.

To put the icing on the cake, Coach was sending in Matt as QB on this play. The last year hadn't been easy for my friend; he and the coaching staff clashed more often than not, and he chafed in the role of back-up quarterback. Thom Wilkens was still going strong, and if things continued as they were now, he'd hold onto his job up through graduation, leaving Matt only one year to lead the team, if he didn't consider playing another position. For a guy who was hoping to parlay his college career into a top draft pick, this thought was discouraging. And Matt wasn't shy about letting everyone know how he felt.

But right now, we were going out there together, the old dream team from Eatonboro High united once again. Tate came up beside me, jamming on his helmet.

"Ready to rock and roll, bro?"

I punched his arm. "You know it. Let's go in there and tie this package up in a sweet fucking bow."

As we passed him, Thom slapped our backs, yelling encouragement. We jogged onto the field, Matt glancing left and right. I'd been worried about him, but I could tell he was in the zone now, with the look in his eyes that said we were about to make magic happen.

On the first down, Matt flipped the ball to Erickson, the running back. He gained us about three yards. But on the second down, thanks to some excellent blocking from my teammates, I managed to break free just as Matt sent a gorgeous spiral pass down the field. The ball fell into my arm like a dream, and I pivoted on the ball of my foot, darted to the left, to the right and spied a gap. I slid through the opening and into the end zone to the cheers of the crowd who'd stayed to the bitter end.

Back on the sideline, the rest of the team greeted us with smacks and grunted praise. Thom stopped Matt, grinning.

"Look at you, Lampert. You made that seem easy out there."

Matt didn't answer for a minute, and I was afraid of what

he might say. But finally he only nodded. "Thanks, man. Appreciate it." He started to move away, then added, "They're pretty worn out. Their defense, I mean. That's probably why it came so fast and easy."

Matt and I got back out onto the field once more before the final whistle was blown. We didn't score again, but we did get a couple of first downs and held our own. And it didn't matter, because we'd rolled over Arkansas.

The locker room was loud and raucous. Everyone was flying high; we were sitting at 5-1, a winning record, and people were starting to sit up and take notice. Since I'd been playing pretty regularly, my name had become more recognized around the school. The campus media had done a piece on me that had been picked up by the local newspaper, and now strangers greeted me like old friends. It was wild, on a much larger scale than it had been in high school.

"Hitting Moonie's tonight, bro?" Matt stripped off his pads and jersey. "Time to celebrate."

"Nope." I was already naked and reaching for my towel, as though I could hear the ticking of a clock in my head. "I'm getting a shower, putting on my clothes and heading to the airport. Gonna surprise Quinn tonight."

He frowned. "Since when? Was this an idea that came to you while we were on the field tonight? You take a hit I didn't see out there?"

I slammed my locker. "No. I've been planning this for three weeks."

"First I've heard of it."

"Matt." I sighed, running one hand through my hair. "Listen. I didn't tell you on purpose, because you've had your head so far up your ass, I didn't know what you'd do. And if you forgot and told Gia, and she told Quinn and ruined the surprise, I'd be really pissed at you. So look at this as me protecting you from my mad, okay?"

"Dude, you are so pathetic." Matt's face darkened. "I'm not the one running off to his girlfriend instead of partying with his friends. And teammates. You want to be in this game long term, Taylor, you need to show up, and not just on the field. You got to play the capital G Game. The whole shebang. Don't bitch to me about my head being up my ass. You got no idea. No idea."

"Matt." I didn't want to engage him. For the last couple of months, he'd been like a bomb, just waiting for the right detonation. I glanced around the locker room; a few teammates were obviously listening to us, curiosity on their faces. Lowering my voice, I laid a hand on his shoulder. "Calm down. You know what I'm talking about. You're partying too much. The booze, the—the drugs, man. You're taking stupid risks, and one of these days, you're going get burned. You're going to get caught in a drug test or worse. Not to mention what you're doing with Gia."

A shadow passed over his eyes. "Gia and I are just . . . casual. You know. She understands the score. She's a free agent, and so am I."

I snorted. "You're an idiot, Matt. She's gone for you, man, and you're too blind to see it. Or maybe you don't want to see it. Whatever."

"I can't do relationship shit. You know that. I mean, look at you. All last year, you were torn up over being away from Quinn. Then you got your panties in a bunch and stayed down here moping all summer. Why the hell would I want something like that? No way, man. I like my freedom. I don't want a chick making me feel bad for doing what I need to do."

I wrapped my towel around my waist. "I never claimed Quinn and I are perfect. I'm not even saying you need a girlfriend. I'm just telling you that what you think you have with Gia isn't what she thinks you have. She might say she's fine with how you treat her, but she isn't. It's eating her alive."

"Bullshit." Matt closed his locker and pounded it with his fist.

"Yeah, well, I don't have time to argue with you about this anymore. I'll see you Tuesday." I turned and headed for the showers.

"Tuesday? You're missing class and practice?"

I tossed words over my shoulder as I walked away. "Coach and my professors approved it. I'm ahead in my classes, and I'll do extra workouts when I get back. I need to see my girl."

My flight to Philadelphia landed a little early, which I took to be a good sign. I slung my duffel over my back, hailed a cab and headed over the bridge to South Jersey. I'd considered asking one of my brothers to pick me up from the airport, but in the end, I'd only told two people outside of Coach and three professors what I was doing. If my mom found out I was coming home without actually visiting *home*, she'd have had a fit. But I wanted this trip to be all about Quinn, all about us.

The taxi dropped me off at a tall brick building on the

Birch campus. I paid the driver and stepped out, glancing around through the dusky evening and trying to be inconspicuous. Leaning against the low wall that surrounded the front courtyard, I pulled out my phone and tapped in a message.

The eagle has landed. Just outside her dorm. Update?

Within a few minutes, my phone vibrated with a text from Nate:

Q is here with me and Gia. Safe for you to go up. I'll send her back in about fifteen minutes.

I smiled. *Perfection.* When the next group of girls exited the dorm, I held the door for them, smiling as they passed before I ducked inside and jogged up the steps to the fourth floor. I found the right suite number and knocked on the door.

Since she'd met her, on their first day of freshman year, Quinn had described her new roommate to me as breathtakingly gorgeous. So when the beautiful blonde answered my knock, I wasn't surprised by her appearance.

Zelda regarded me with interest, leaning on the door jamb as an enigmatic smile played over her lips.

"So. You're the boyfriend." Her eyes wandered down my body, unabashedly checking me out, lingering over the zipper of my jeans. "Good to meet you. Finally."

I swallowed a sigh. I knew what this was all about; the fact that I hadn't come up to see my girlfriend at her school until now—midway through the fall of our sophomore year—must've looked bad to her friends.

"I'm happy to meet you at last, too, Zelda." I held out a hand. "Nate said he told you my plan. Thanks for helping."

She lifted one shoulder. "All I had to do was stay home tonight until you got here, and then find another place to sleep. Believe me, finding a warm and welcoming bed is never a problem for me."

"I'm sure." I nodded, gesturing over her shoulder. "Okay if I come in?"

She hesitated a moment before she stepped back. "Sure. Quinn's room is the second door on the right. Bathroom's on the end." She turned and picked up a small backpack from the sofa in the tiny living area. "Make yourself comfortable, I guess. Nate said she should be back here by nine."

"Got it. And don't worry. I'll just hang out in her room. I won't touch anything else."

"My door's locked, so I'm not worried. And if you get the sudden urge to poke around in Gia's room, more power to you. She's a slob. There's probably some hazardous waste in there, not to mention a lot of shit to trip over."

I laughed. "Yeah, Quinn's mentioned that Gia is a little cleaning-impaired."

"That sounds like how Quinn would put it." Zelda paused again, as though she was debating something, and then in a move too smooth to be accidental, she dropped her keys. "Oops. Guess I need these." Bending at the waist, she leaned to scoop them up, and as she did, the tank she wore gaped at the neck, giving me an eyeful of her rack.

I wasn't a saint, by any means. And like any other red-blooded male, I liked a nice pair of tits. This chick had boobs for days, and the way she was standing, I could see that she wasn't wearing a bra. Staring wouldn't have made me a perv, not when Zelda was so clearly putting herself on display.

But it would've made me a dick, because as nice as her tits

were, they weren't my girl's, and that meant I wasn't interested in them. I kept my eyes on Zelda's face, never straying south.

"It was really great to meet you, Zelda. I'm sure I'll see you again while I'm here."

If I'd expected her to be offended by my lack of reaction, I'd have been disappointed. Instead, she only smiled a little and nodded.

"I'm sure I will." She put one hand on the doorknob and stopped again, this time not looking at me as she spoke. "You know, Quinn's about the best person I've ever met. She's kind, and understanding, and she doesn't judge. I think you make her happy most of the time. But I also know you have the power to crush her. If you do that, I will cut off your dick, grind it up and feed it to dogs."

If Zelda had said those words with even the least bit of a threatening tone, it might've sounded comical. As it was, her voice was matter of fact and even, and that fact made what she said downright chilling.

I swallowed hard. "I believe you."

"Good." She left without another backward glance, and I let out a long breath of relief before I headed for Quinn's room.

I'd known Quinn since she'd slept in a toddler bed. I remembered her canopy bed with the pink ruffled bedspread, and I remembered when her walls had been covered with posters of boy bands. But at first glimpse, her college room struck me as the most quintessentially Quinn room yet.

Her bed was made up with some kind of fluffy white comforter covered with a patchwork quilt I recognized from her bedroom at home. On the wall over the bed was a large framed poster of the sun coming up over the ocean, a shot I was pretty sure she'd taken herself. Several pictures sat on the top of her dresser, including one of her father, one of me from the summer before college, and one of the three of us: Nate, Quinn and me. Off to the side sat a small wooden box, a little worn-looking where some of the varnish had rubbed off.

I knew deep down I should respect her privacy and leave it alone, but still, I flipped open the lid and examined the contents. I couldn't explain why, exactly, but over the last few months, I'd been feeling slightly removed from Quinn. We still talked every day, and she'd been down to see me at Carolina once already this semester. The sex was still smoking, but then again, that had never been an issue with the two of us. I got the sense, though, that whether or not she realized it, Quinn had cut me off from some part of her. There were thoughts she didn't share as easily as she had a year ago. She went quiet more often, as though she were grappling with stuff she wasn't willing to talk about yet.

I missed her, the open, spontaneous Quinn I'd known all of my life. I craved that connection, the one I hadn't even realized we'd had until it went away. And I had the uncomfortable sense that maybe its loss was mostly my fault. I was the one who was consumed with football; I was the one who'd gone away, even though I'd had a perfectly good reason to do it. I knew that sometimes when we talked, I was distracted, my mind on the playbook, on my class assignments and on everything else going on down in Carolina.

There were only a few small items in the wooden box: a tiny dried rosebud, a smooth white rock, almost perfectly round, and a piece of notebook paper, folded so many times that it was about the size of the pad of my thumb. I held it on the palm of my hand for a moment before I carefully unfolded it.

On the light blue lines, I recognized my own scrawl, but at first, I didn't remember writing the words.

Mia—you fell asleep and I didn't want to wake you up. I'm going in early to lift tomorrow morning, so I'll see you when you get to school. Thank you for listening to me tonight. I love you, always and always.

—L

And then the memory came back. It was during our junior year, during that brief, sweet interlude when we'd been together. My mom had been undergoing treatment for leukemia, and spring practice was just starting. I'd stayed late that night, but Quinn and I had only talked; I hadn't snuck upstairs with her as we sometimes did. She'd lay in my arms, touching my face as I poured out my worries about my mother, my frustrations about some of the guys on the team . . . and when I was finished venting, Quinn had kissed me gently and told me everything was going to be all right.

For some reason, just hearing those simple words come out of her mouth had reassured me, and we'd sat on the couch in her parents' den, just touching and murmuring the occasional word, until she'd dropped off to sleep. I'd carried her upstairs to her bed, torn a piece out of the notebook she kept on her nightstand, and scribbled the note.

Quinn had kept it, over these two and a half years, through the year when we hadn't communicated at all. I wondered what those few careless words had meant to her.

My phone buzzed, and I jumped, guilty, dropping the re-folded note back into the box. I shut the lid and pushed it back into place before I checked the phone's screen.

Congrats on the win! Just saw a clip of your TD online. Proud of you, babe.

I smiled, even as guilt panged in my chest. Quinn was so good about remembering everything going on with me, making sure to text or call me after every game when she couldn't be there. I tried to do the same, asking her how tests had gone or if one of her articles had been picked up for the school paper, but I knew that all too often I forgot.

Thanks. It was pretty much a rout. But a W is a W, right? What are you up to?

I had a pretty good idea of what she was doing, but I wanted the total surprise, so I played dumb.

I'm on my way back to my room. Tonight kind of sucked. I was over at Nate's with Gia, but she was in a rotten mood for some reason. She ended up going out with some of her party friends. Then Nate's mom called b/c his cousin is in town and she wanted him to come over for dinner. So I got ditched.

I grinned a little wider. Nate had apparently played his part perfectly. I didn't know why Gia was in a rotten mood, but I could guess it had something to do with Matt. Quinn had told me that Gia had started hanging out with a new group she'd met through a girl in her International Relations class. Since they went out to bars and parties on Greek Row more often than Quinn and Nate ever did, they'd dubbed the crowd Gia's party friends.

I'm sorry, Mia. Wish I could be there to keep you company.

It was true. Just because I was going to make that wish reality didn't make it a lie.

I know. It's okay. I'll just binge watch some Buffy and eat chips. What're you doing? Out with the guys celebrating?

I heard a noise at the main door of the suite, the jingle of keys and footsteps as the door opened and then closed. I typed back fast.

Nah, just hanging out. Decided to celebrate a little different tonight.

She was in the kitchenette; there was the sound of a cabinet opening and closing. Looking for the chips, I decided, and crossed my fingers that something would bring her to the bedroom, because I didn't want to have to sneak out and scare her.

Not that finding me in here wouldn't startle her, but still. I figured being in the bedroom was a more auspicious start to our mini-vacation, anyway. My phone vibrated again in my hand.

Oh, yeah? How's that?

Yes! She was coming down the short hall, and before I could take another breath, the door swung open and she was there, her eyes on her phone as she waited for my text response. I sat perfectly still on the edge of her bed, waiting for her to—

"AHHHHHHHH!!!!!" Her scream echoed off the walls of her room as her hand flew to her throat and she backed up against the door jamb. "Oh, my God, Leo! You scared the shit out of me? What the hell are you doing here?"

I stood up, hands on my hips. "Well, I told you I was going to celebrate a little different tonight. I thought maybe I'd do it with you." I drank her in, from the oversized hoodie that hung below her hips to the worn jeans encasing her legs. My girl was so fucking beautiful, it made my heart skip a beat.

For a nerve-wracking minute, I wasn't sure if Quinn was annoyed that I'd taken her by surprise or overcome with joy. And then she launched herself at me, wrapping her arms around my neck and hugging me tight.

"I'm so glad you're here. Thank you, thank you, thank you."

I pulled back enough to kiss her, my lips smothering the last few thank-yous. She moaned a little, opening her mouth to welcome my tongue with strokes of her own.

"How did you do this? And how long can you be here?"

I sank back onto the bed, pulling her onto my lap and holding her close. "Nate helped me. He maneuvered you over to his room and then back here at the right time. He told Zelda about it at the last minute, so she'd give us the suite to ourselves tonight. And I think he also had to tell Gia, which may be why she was so pissy with you earlier. Oh, and Tate drove me to the airport on that end."

"No one else knew?" She skimmed her fingers over my

face, her eyes devouring me as though she couldn't believe I was really there.

"I told Matt about ten minutes before I left. And Coach knew, because I had to clear missing practice Monday and Tuesday—"

"Monday and Tuesday?" Quinn was breathless, and her smile grew to light up her whole face. "You're staying here that long?"

"I have to leave Tuesday afternoon, so I can be back for a team meeting that night and practice Wednesday. I sweet-talked my professors into letting me miss a few classes, too."

"Did you happen to have the same conversation with my professors?"

I laughed softly. "Sorry, babe. But I'll be here three nights with you, sleeping in your bed—and not sleeping, I hope—and I'll keep everything warm while you're off being a good student. I know it's not perfect, but—"

"Shut up. It is *absolutely* perfect." She pressed her lips to my jaw. "It's perfect because you're here with me. You did this without me asking you to come up. You thought of it all on your own. And you came to me, to see where I'm living and going to school, and—oh! You can finally meet Zelda."

"Already did. She's the one who let me in." I toyed with a dark curl of her hair. "She seems nice."

"Nice?" Quinn rolled her eyes. "There are a lot of ways you could describe Zelda, but nice isn't usually one of them. I mean, don't get me wrong. I love her. But it's taken some doing."

"Babe? I really don't want to discuss your roommates right now. But I do want to say something else. I need to tell you I'm sorry."

"For what?" She arched her neck, wariness etched on her face. "What did you do?"

I shook my head. "Nothing. And that's the problem. I should've been up here to visit you before now. I went through our entire freshman year without seeing your college, and I justified it by saying to myself that it was just Birch, the same place we'd grown up near all our lives. But that was dumb, because it's not the college I needed to see—it was your place in it. And your people. It's ridiculous that I haven't met Zelda until now, and it's shameful that I didn't see your dorm last year. And I'm sorry, Mia. So fucking sorry for letting that happen."

She shook her head, but I saw the tears gleaming in her green eyes. "It's okay, Leo. Really. I understood."

I blew out a long breath. "I know you did, and that makes it worse. I want to say, you should've told me to get my ass up here, but honestly? You shouldn't have had to say it." I smoothed back her hair, combing my fingers through it. "And while we're on the subject, I'm sorry for last summer, too. I was an asshole. I shouldn't have stayed down in Carolina. I should've come up here and lived at the shore with you and your mom, or at least gotten a job at home, where I could've seen you every few days. I was hurt that you decided to spend the summer there, and I never stopped to think how unfair that was."

Quinn closed her eyes. "Thank you for saying that, but it was just as much my fault. I didn't talk to you before I took the internship, and I think . . . maybe it was because I knew what would happen. Nate said it was like I was testing you, making you decide when there really wasn't any right choice."

"What if I said I had an idea for next summer, one that didn't come with any hard choices?" I nuzzled her neck, murmuring close to her ear. "One that comes with so much togetherness, you'll probably get sick of me. And all the hot sex your pretty little body can handle?"

Quinn cocked her head. "I'm listening."

"The camp where I volunteered last summer? The director called me this week. He's setting up for next year, and he offered me a job."

"Okay." She frowned. "Not seeing where you're going, though."

"I talked to Coach about it, and I told him one of the issues would be having a place to live. I can't stay on campus, and I can't live in the camp housing, like I did last year. They only house volunteers. Coach has a townhouse that he and his wife rent out to students during the school year, but it always sits empty over the summer. He said I could live there, just for the cost of utilities and keeping it occupied. Maybe do a paint job and a little maintenance." I spanned her ribs with my hands so that my thumbs teased the sides of her boobs. "And you could live there with me."

Her eyes widened. "Really? I could? Your coach would be okay with that?"

"Totally. He doesn't care as long we don't trash the place or have loud parties."

"We could do that!" She grinned. "We could be together the whole summer. Just the two of us. Like . . . like playing house, in a way."

"Practicing for the future." I wriggled my eyebrows up and down suggestively. "And Coach said there are always summer jobs on campus, or even with the businesses just off campus. You could find something if you wanted, or you could just lay around all summer and write or whatever."

"That sounds like heaven. It totally makes up for last summer. And it makes me feel even worse for not coming up with a better plan last year."

"Nah, enough of that. No more sorry." I kissed her forehead and then leaned mine against hers. "Are we all done with the apologizing now, do you think? Because I think I might have mentioned we have this place to ourselves for one night. I'd like to get to the part of the program where we make up, because you and I? We've always rocked the makeup sex. And then I want to get on to the other types of sex on the menu tonight."

Quinn wriggled to sit up a little straighter, her sweet little ass grinding into my cock. "There's a menu? Oooh. What's on it? Is there dessert?"

I chuckled, grasped her hips and resettled her, this time so that she straddled my body. "There's appetizer, entrée and dessert, babe. But I have a feeling that three courses aren't going to be enough for me tonight. We might need to expand this menu a little bit."

Quinn's eyebrows rose as she lifted herself up a little and then sank down, rubbing the heat between her legs against my aching dick. Two layers of jeans separated us, but I swore I could feel her already.

"Remember that first night, in the playground?" She wound her arms around my neck, her eyes on mine, boring into my soul and completing every part of me that was wanting. "You got me off just like this, grinding me. I was so mortified because I came so fast and I'd never come in front of anyone before. Ever. And you said it was just you and me. Us. And that I should never be embarrassed by anything that happens between us."

"I remember." And remembering, my erection grew. "That was seriously so hot, babe. You just let go and trusted me, and I swore I'd never let you down." I held her chin between my fingers. "I have, though."

"This is my point." She spread her legs a little wider, letting her eyes drift halfway shut. "You said we should never be ashamed. I think that goes beyond just sex. I'm glad you said you were sorry, and I'm glad we talked. But now it's over, and we're moving on."

I framed her face with my hands and brought her lips to mine, kissing her open-mouthed and with intensity. "I like your way of moving on, Mia."

"Mmmmm." She slid back a little, stripped off her hoodie and the T-shirt beneath it in one fluid motion. I groaned at the sight of her luscious tits spilling over the lace cups of her bra. Still watching me, Quinn unhooked the bra and shook it off.

"Is this part of the makeup sex, or have we gone right into the appetizer course?"

"Didn't you hear what I said just now? We don't need makeup sex, because that's all in the past." She backed away, off my lap, reached between us and unbuttoned my jeans before she tugged down the zipper. Dropping to her knees, she gazed up at me through her eyelashes and began to ease my pants and boxers down my legs so that my cock sprang up, hard and interested. "And I've decided I'm going to choose the first item on the appetizer menu."

She bent forward so that her turgid nipples brushed over my thighs and took the head of my dick into her mouth. I sucked in a fast breath and leaned back, closing my eyes in pure unadulterated pleasure.

"Babe, you can order for me every time."

★ Twelve ★

Quinn

Summer between sophomore and junior years

"QUINN, DID YOU DO LAUNDRY LAST NIGHT? I NEED a T-shirt for today."

I rolled over in bed and groaned. "No. I was up late working on that article for class."

Leo's voice became louder as he came back into our bedroom. "Shit. I need a shirt, and I'm running late."

I opened one eye and caught sight of him running a hand through his damp hair. "Sorry. I thought you were putting a load in yesterday afternoon. You don't have anything clean to wear?"

"It's not that I don't have anything clean. I need my uniform shirt, specifically. I'll have to get one out of the dirty clothes and hope for the best." He dumped out the hamper in the middle of the floor and began sorting through it.

Guilt threaded through me. "I could toss it in the dryer

real fast. It might help."

"No, I don't have time." Leo snapped out the words. "If I get there late, I have to park way out in the far lot. And then . . ." His voice trailed off. "It's just a mess."

I heard the frustration in his voice and felt even worse. In an effort to jolly him out of his funk, I teased, "Oh, you mean you don't like the girl groupies who hang out by the entrance, just hoping for a glimpse of Leo the Lion?" I put on high-pitched tone. "'Leo! Hey, Leo? Look at me! Take a selfie with me, Leo! I love you, Leo! I want to have your babies!'"

"Stop." His face was drawn, and there was more than annoyance on it. "It's not like that's fun for me. I wish they'd all just leave me the fuck alone."

"Sorry." I'd lost count of how many times I'd said it in the few minutes I'd been awake. "I was just trying to lighten you up."

"Yeah, well, you don't have to deal with the damn press and the girls. I just want to do my job. I wish—" He growled and kicked at the pile of clothes.

"What? You wish Carolina hadn't won the championship last year? You wish you hadn't been the guy who caught the winning touchdown? You wish you weren't so hot that your picture became the most downloaded college football photo on social media?" I sat up, hunching my back over my bent knees. "Or you wish you hadn't taken the job here this summer? Or you wish you hadn't asked me to come down here and live with you? Or . . ." I swallowed over the lump in my throat. "You wish your girlfriend took better care of you? Did your laundry and cooked you decent dinners?"

"God, Quinn. Just—no." Leo straightened. "I'm not saying any of that. I just wish things were different. I never wanted all the attention, you know that. I only want to play the game." He picked up a shirt and tossed it over his shoulder. "And a fucking clean T-shirt."

"Oh!" I swung my legs over the bed. "I just remembered. You have one shirt for work that's still clean, in our suitcase. From when we went to Charleston last weekend, and we thought you'd have to go right to work from there, remember?"

His face cleared a little. "Yes! Is it in the closet still?"

I nodded. "Yeah. I forgot to move it when I was putting stuff away. Sorry." There was that word again.

"No problem." He disappeared into the closet and emerged, pulling the shirt over his head and then bent to tie his sneakers, resting his foot on the edge of the bed. "Hey, Quinn. I'm sorry I jumped on you. Things have been so crazy."

That was the understatement of the year. Or at least the summer. We'd both been so excited for this, to live together on our own for two whole months. Leo had loved volunteering the summer before, and his new job was managing all the volunteers and coordinating their work. And I'd gotten an online gig, writing for two different news blogs and their feature columns. Not everything that I produced was picked up for inclusion on the sites, but it was good for me to get both the experience and the line on my resume.

At first, everything had been exactly as I'd expected. It had been so much fun to go grocery shopping together, choosing food and planning our meals, making the bed together every morning and climbing back into it every night. The coach's townhouse wasn't anything fancy, but it was clean and well-maintained, so we had no complaints.

We'd needed this time together. The months since Leo had visited me at Birch had been filled with stress and change. Leo had been playing so well that he was consistently starting every week, which raised his visibility around campus and also brought him attention nationwide. He was flattered when it began, but as the season went on and his name was mentioned more often on the college football programs, tensions grew, both between Leo and his teammates and between us.

And then there was Matt. The more attention Leo got, the more surly and nasty Matt was. He was still second-string quarterback, and he hated that he hadn't bumped Thom Wilkens from his spot. Each week, Matt drowned his sorrows in alcohol, women and even more alarmingly, drugs and violent behavior. He'd gotten warnings from the coaching staff, and each time, he managed to pull it back together enough that things calmed down. But everyone could tell it was only a matter of time before all hell broke loose.

His relationship with Gia was in constant turmoil, too, and it felt as though we were all collateral damage. Throughout sophomore year, they'd spun wildly out of control, veering from the weekends they spent together in bed, hardly ever coming up for air, to other weeks when they screamed at each other and slept with other people. Well, to be fair, it was always Matt sleeping around; in the aftermath of their meltdowns, Gia mostly got drunk and played depressing music. Loudly.

Leo hated what was happening with his friend, but like the rest of us, he was powerless to stop him. I knew, too, that he felt guilty about his own success, as if that were somehow a slap in the face to Matt.

But this summer was going to be different. The first few weeks were perfect; Matt had moved back to South Jersey for the summer, where he was living with his grandparents again. This was part of the plan put into place by the university, in exchange for Matt being able to return to school—and the football team—in the fall. He had to toe the proverbial line, take summer classes at Birch and attend substance abuse therapy sessions. Leo and I both had our doubts about how effective this plan was—Matt's grandparents had never been the most hands-on adults, even when he was younger—but for now at least, Matt wasn't our problem.

And then about three weeks after we'd moved into the townhouse, the Lionesses were born.

It had all started on a slow week in the sports world. A journalist with a small Southern news organization, looking for a story, had decided to do a piece on the up-and-coming college players ahead of the season. Something about Leo had intrigued her, and she'd done a little more digging into his past. The spin she gave his pre-college life got her article picked up beyond her own publication, but it was the picture of Leo after the championship game that made the whole story go viral.

Leo went from being a vaguely familiar name among those who followed college ball to being a face recognizable all over the country. Two of the national morning shows talked about him during their pop culture segments, both mentioning his mother's battle with leukemia and his old high school nickname—the Lion.

The next day, a group popped up on social media. The Lionesses were made up almost entirely of girls, and their sole reason for existence was the adoration of my boyfriend.

That was fun for me.

Although the Lionesses' membership stretched from coast to coast, there was a devoted cluster right here near Carolina University, made up of girls who lived locally and those who happened to be staying on campus over the summer. Leo and I weren't exactly hiding, and the story about him had mentioned his job at the camp—*This talented young man isn't taking his summer off for fun and sun—instead, he's working at a football camp for underprivileged children, teaching a whole new generation the love of the game that has sustained him through hard times.* Even so, neither of us expected the Lionesses to turn up every morning at the entrance to Camp Bryant.

The first few days, we'd both laughed at it. Leo had taken pictures of the crowd with his phone, sending them to me with a caption that read, *Jealous, babe?*

I wasn't. I knew how much Leo loved me, and those girls meant nothing to us. Leo learned to get to work early enough to score a spot in the lot closest to the back entrance of the camp, and we waited for it all to die down.

But it didn't die down. Instead, there were more pictures, more stories and more exposure. Leo began to dread the daily gauntlet he had to run to get to work, and we both had to shut down our social media accounts.

Things got even worse when one of the crazier Lionesses surreptitiously followed Leo home one afternoon. By the next day, when I went out to make an early-morning coffee run, there were twenty girls camped outside our door. To say that they were all dismayed to see me would be more than accurate. The original article that had lit this firestorm hadn't mentioned that the sexy Lion had a girlfriend, and so the chicks outside immediately jumped to the conclusion that I was just a piece of tail. They'd booed me and jeered, and I'd had a sudden flashback to high school, when I'd had the audacity to date the football star.

As it became more apparent that I wasn't just some random hook-up, the verbal and virtual assaults intensified. Messages popped up on my phone, calling me every vile name in the book. Unattractive and unpleasant pictures of me were floated around the web. Even though I no longer even glanced at my social media accounts, it was impossible to ignore what was going on. I was afraid to go out, afraid someone would know me as the Lion's girlfriend.

Now, with his clean T-shirt stretched over his broad chest and his sneakers tied, Leo straightened. He regarded me with a frown, and I wondered if my expression reflected my mixed feelings about our perfect summer.

"I know things have been . . . different than we thought." I spoke slowly. "And if we're talking about wishes, I wish that story had never been written. I hate that you have to deal with those crazy girls. But it's got to end soon, right? I mean, doesn't everyone say the public has a short attention span? Something big will happen, and you'll be yesterday's news."

Leo shrugged. "I keep hoping. But I'm not so much worried about me as I am about you. When was the last time you were out of the house?"

I grimaced. "Um . . . three days ago? When we went to pick up the pizza?"

"Mia." He sighed. "The townhouse complex security is

keeping everyone away from the front door. No one's going to bother you again when you go out. There are no girls sitting out there now, waiting to pounce on me. Or you. It's safe."

"I know." I lay back on the pillow, staring up at the ceiling. "They're not at the door. But they're still out there, Leo. When I stop at the grocery store, it feels like people are staring. And I can't even go online anymore, except for work. The things people write about me . . ." I closed my eyes. "It's so ugly."

"I know, babe. But it's going to die down. Like you said, attention spans are short. Pretty soon, someone will do something stupid, and everyone will forget about both of us." He leaned over me and kissed my forehead. "Love you, Mia. I'll see you this afternoon." Pausing just before the doorway, he glanced back at me over his shoulder. "Oh, and I'll do some laundry when I get home. You . . . go out today. Somewhere. Anywhere. Get a mani-pedi or whatever it is girls like to do."

I shook my head. "It's no fun without girlfriends. I'll tell you what. I'll stay home today, clean the house, do the laundry, and then when you come home, we'll go out to eat. Okay?"

Leo sighed. "Fine. Whatever you want to do."

"So aren't you going stir-crazy?" Zelda sounded curious and mildly amused as I updated her on the latest Lioness craziness.

"Surprisingly, no. I don't mind being here, as long as I have something to do." Holding the phone between my shoulder and ear, I pulled a pile of wet laundry from the washer and dropped it into the dryer. "I'm not sure I'm cut out to be a housewife, but I really don't have anything to complain about. I can write whenever I want, and three of my articles have been picked up so far. No classes, no homework, and tons of privacy."

"And quality time with Leo the Lion? That's got to be an added benefit."

"Of course." I answered quickly, and I knew Zelda probably picked that up.

"So everything's fine and dandy with you two? Sunshine, rainbows and sparkles?" She was teasing, but I knew enough of Zelda now to realize that her snark hid real concern. She just didn't want anyone to realize that she actually had feelings.

"Mostly." I hesitated. "I love Leo, Zelda. You know that. He loves me. We're meant to be together. This is just a . . . bumpy time. Everyone goes through them." I cleared my throat. "Speaking of which . . . how is everything going with our favorite dysfunctional couple?"

"Oh, God." This time, Zelda's exasperation was genuine. "They're driving me crazy, Quinn. I swear, I'll never forgive you for abandoning me to her this summer."

"Hey, hey. I didn't abandon you. You and Gia are adults, and you both made the decision to stay on campus together. How're your classes going?"

"Mine are great. As for Gia's . . . I couldn't swear to it, but I'd say probably not so wonderful."

"I was afraid of that. Things are still rough with Matt?"

"They're driving me fucking insane, if that's what you mean. If they're not having loud and obnoxious sex, they're having loud and obnoxious fights. I'm not sure which are more annoying." She paused, and I heard a rattle on the other side of the phone.

"What're you doing?" I closed the dryer and started it up, stepping away from it so I could hear Zelda.

"Uh, I'm cooking." Her voice held a faint tinge of . . . I couldn't read it. Embarrassment?

"Cooking? For you and Gia? Well, aren't you a good roommate?" I flopped onto the sofa. "You never cooked for me."

"No, doll, I'm not cooking for Gia. I have a . . . date. I guess. Sort of."

If she had told me that she was a spy who was cooking for the head of the CIA, I wouldn't have been more surprised. Zelda was predictable only in her cynicism about romance and relationships. She had regular sex with an abundance of men, and she liked men, but she didn't trust them.

"Uh . . . okay. Can I ask the name of this date?"

"You can ask, but I'm not going to tell. This is way outside my comfort zone, Quinn. It's probably not going to amount to anything. If I'm wrong and it does . . . then you and I can talk. I'll tell you all the down and dirties. But until then—if there is a then—I'm going to play it close to my chest."

When I didn't respond right away, she hurried to continue. "It's not that I don't trust you, Quinn. I just don't trust me. I'm going out on a limb here, and I'm actually scared shitless."

"Zelda." I crossed my legs at the knee and kicked one foot in the air. "I'm not insulted that you want to be, um, discreet. It's your business. But don't be scared, okay? You are the most incredible woman I know. You're beautiful, you're funny and you're smart. Any guy would be lucky to date you. So don't mess this up just because you think you're not the relationship type, okay?"

Something sizzled on Zelda's side of the phone. "I appreciate everything you said, Quinn. I don't necessarily agree with you, but still, I'm grateful. I can only promise to do my best."

"Good. Have fun, and don't think I'm going to forget this. When I get home next month, you are so cooking for me."

She laughed. "You got it, doll. We'll be in our new apartment with a real kitchen, not this lame ass kitchenette. So I'll make you something special to celebrate moving in, okay?"

"It's a date." I giggled at my own joke. "Have fun tonight, Zelda. Don't do anything I wouldn't do."

"Oh, don't say that." She groaned. "The girl who's been in love with the same dude since they were eight? You're my boundary? I'm so thoroughly fucked."

"That dude just came in the front door." I waggled my fingers at Leo. "I promised him a night out, so I better get my ass in gear. Or he might trade me in for a Lioness."

"Never going to happen, doll. That guy's got it bad for you and only you."

"Yep, and same goes on my end." I scooched so that my head hung off the front of the sofa while my legs were propped on the back and made a face at my boyfriend. He rolled his eyes at me. "Have fun tonight, Zelda. Love you."

"Love you right back. And I'll try."

I disconnected the call and tossed my phone onto the cushion next to me. "Hey, lover. How was your day?"

"Hot. Long. Mildly irritating." He braced his hands on either side of my head, caging me in as he kissed my lips. "But getting better now."

"Want to take this upstairs and see if it gets even better?" I linked my hands behind his head, holding on.

"I'd love that, but I promised to take you out tonight. And let's face it, if we go upstairs and get into bed, we'll end up ordering food to be delivered and you'll go another day without leaving the house."

"Is that a bad thing?" I narrowed my eyes.

"It is, yes. So I'll make you a deal." Pushing himself up, Leo slid one arm beneath my knees and the other under my head, lifting me against his chest. "I'll carry you upstairs, we'll get a shower together—no nookie, just showering—and then we'll go out to eat. And *then* after dinner, we'll come home and finish whatever it is we start in the shower. Deal?"

"Delayed gratification? Hmm. I guess I can get behind that. Okay, babe." I thumped him on the back. "Onward and upward."

"This is the best pasta I've had south of Philadelphia." I laid down my fork and sighed. "And the company's not bad either."

Leo flashed me a smile, but there was something under it, something not quite complete. All night, his laughter hadn't seemed to reach his eyes, and he'd been preoccupied.

"All right." I rested my elbows on the table and leaned my chin in my hands. "Tell me what's going on. You've been giving me lip service all night. Did I not live up to your shower expectations?"

This time, real heat flared in his eyes. "Hardly. As a matter of fact, you exceeded them. I'm lucky I can sit still here with the boner you gave me."

"Hmm. Okay then, what is it? Don't forget, Leo, I've known you forever. You can't hide this shit from me."

He fiddled with his knife where it lay alongside his plate. "I got a call today from a guy who works for *Football Sunday*."

"What's that?" I frowned.

"It's an online sports magazine. I think it still has a monthly print component. Anyway, they want to do an article on me. He called it a spread."

My stomach dropped. "Uh huh. And . . .?"

"And Coach says he thinks I should do it. So do the PR people at the university. It'll bring a lot of attention to the college and hopefully some donations to the sports program."

"Haven't you done enough this year to help them out there? I thought we were trying to get things to calm down, right? We don't need to get everyone all riled up again. God, Leo, it'll never end if you do this."

"The article from before wasn't sanctioned by the university. They didn't interview me, they didn't talk to anyone official, but this time, they will. There'll be boundaries. The head of public relations from the college will have final approval. That's part of the deal."

I pushed away my plate, since my appetite had evaporated. "Do you seriously want to do this, Leo? Does it sound like a good idea?"

"I don't fucking know, Quinn. God, I'm torn all the time. All the damn time. What Coach says, what the school wants, what my team needs, what you want . . . I can't make everyone happy. It's fucking frustrating." He balled up his cloth napkin and threw it onto his plate. "I bring you down here so we can finally be together, and you're basically a prisoner in the townhouse. But I don't know what to do."

The waiter came over to pick up the paid check, and we lapsed into silence until he'd moved away.

"And now . . . the PR guy told me to be careful about what I say and do when I'm out in public. Now that people know who I am, I represent the whole fucking college, apparently. No drinking, no partying. Which is fine, but it's got me second-guessing everything I say or do. That waiter. Is he going to post on social media that I didn't tip him well enough? I hate it."

Leo's voice had risen, and I glanced around the restaurant. "Let's go home. I just—I want to get out of here."

"Fine." He pushed back his chair and stood aside, letting me pass first. I kept my head down and hurried out, waiting to feel Leo's hand on the small of my back the way he always touched me as we walked together. But when I glanced back, his face was stormy and his hands were clenched in fists at his sides.

We were both silent all the way back to the townhouse. Leo unlocked the front door, and we walked inside. I felt wooden and uncomfortable, and for the first time this summer, the townhouse didn't feel like home.

"There's one more thing, Quinn." Leo spoke from behind me, as though he couldn't bear to face me. "I asked the PR people if we could include you in the article. I thought some nice pictures of the two of us together, and maybe something about how we grew up together . . . but apparently *Football*

Sunday doesn't want to talk about me having a girlfriend. They said it doesn't fit the image they want to project of me."

My throat was tight, and my mouth was dry. I stood in the semi-darkness of our living room, and I didn't know what to say.

Finally, I croaked out words. "And you're all right with all this, Leo? You feel good about this?"

"Fuck, no, I don't. Are you crazy? But what am I going to do? Remember I'm at Carolina on a full-ride, Quinn. Football is paying for my education. I have to play by their rules until I graduate."

I nodded. "Okay. So . . . what? I hide out while they're here taking pictures and interviewing you? You want me to just stay upstairs?"

Leo came closer to me, still standing at my back. "No. I mean, I don't know . . ." He sighed, and I felt his breath stirring the hair on my neck. "Can we talk about this tomorrow? Figure it out then? I'm fried, and I'm mad and I'm just done tonight. I want to go to bed."

"Sure." I swallowed. "Yes. Let's do that."

Upstairs, we undressed in silence. I went into the bathroom to wash my face, and when I came out to climb into bed, Leo took my place. I slid beneath the sheets and lay on my side, my eyes closed, listening to the sounds of him brushing his teeth. I'd gotten used to it over these weeks, the subtle nuances of living with someone. We'd slept together for over a year now, and we'd spent a few days at a time with each other, but there was something different about actually living under the same roof. I knew his rhythms, his bedtime habits and then how he woke up in the mornings. They had become familiar to me, and I loved that.

After a few minutes, Leo came back into the bedroom. He switched off the overhead light and felt his way through the dark to the bed. I felt the sheets shift as he got under them, adjusted his pillow and sighed into the darkness. I didn't know I was going to say anything until my voice pierced the quiet.

"The first time we slept together . . . really slept together, in the same bed, not just for sex . . . it wasn't at the hotel, because we didn't sleep much that night. But when I stayed over at your house the first time, when your parents were away, I was terrified. I was scared I was going to talk in my sleep, or drool, or snore—something embarrassing. I was so nervous, I thought I'd never actually nod off, but I did. And when I woke up, you had your arms around me, and I realized I'd never slept so soundly in my life."

I drew in a ragged breath, and to my shock, sobs wracked my body. Tears I hadn't known were imminent slid down my cheeks and soaked the pillow. All the tension from this summer, this uncomfortable distance between Leo and me and every bit of uncertainty poured out. As always happened now, whenever something set me off, grief over missing my dad struck, too, making everything somehow worse.

Next to me, Leo made a noise deep in his throat and gathered me close, pulling my back against his chest, wrapping his arms around my waist and burying his face in my neck.

"It's okay, Mia." He murmured soft words into my ear. "It's okay, baby. It's going to be all right. I promise."

But we both knew he was making promises neither of us could trust.

The next morning, I woke up with gritty, swollen eyes, a pounding head and a sense of doom I couldn't shake.

Leo was already awake, sitting on the edge of the bed, his clean T-shirt in his hands. He stared down at it, turning the gray cotton over in his hands.

I pushed my back against the pillow, sitting up and wrapping my arms around my knees. "What time is it?"

"Just after seven." He stretched the shirt wide, the way he always did right before he pulled it over his head. I watched the interplay of muscles on his back, tempted to trace the ridges and ropes.

"Leo." I took a deep breath. "I think . . . I think we need to take a break. I'm going to head back up to New Jersey. I should spend some time with my mom anyway, before classes start again."

"What the hell are you talking about?" Leo turned around, his eyebrows drawn together. "Quinn, what are you saying?"

"Everything is so screwed up." I flexed my feet, intent on the movement of the sheet over them. "What they want from you at the school, and what you're being pushed to do . . . me being here complicates all that. I don't want to make all of it harder on you. So I'll just go home, and then, we can see."

"We can see? We can see what, exactly?" He sounded angry, but I heard the fear and pain underneath.

"Leo, it's all timing. Right now, the team and the school are asking so much of you. What you said last night is true.

You need this education, and that comes with a price tag. If you have to play by their rules, then that's what you're going to do. And if they don't want you to have a girlfriend, we already know what's going to end up happening."

"They didn't say I couldn't have a girlfriend. They just said the magazine doesn't want to play up that angle."

I shook my head. "You're quibbling, Leo. They want to do a story on Leo Taylor, the hot and sexy *single* football player, the one all the girls want to dream could be theirs. I don't fit into that scenario. And the last thing I want to do is skulk around, hiding our relationship. You know me, Leo. I couldn't live that way."

"You're making this more than it is, Quinn. It's one story. They'll come over here one day, or maybe they won't even come over. Maybe I'll meet them at the college, and then it's done. We've got three more weeks together before I have to move back on campus when practices begin, and once that happens, you'll be at Birch. We're separated most of the time anyway. And then how hard is it to just lay low for another two years, until I can graduate? After that, we make our own rules, babe. We write our own ticket."

"You're fooling yourself if you think that's true. There's always going to be someone telling you what they want you to be. You don't think whatever team you sign with will have a take on this?"

"It won't matter then." He was stubborn. I could see it in the set of his mouth. But I knew that deep down, he already realized that I was right. He was fighting both me and himself, trying to make something true into a lie.

"Leo, I can't take this anymore. I just can't. I love you. I know you love me. That's not even in question. But what people have said about me, what they're still saying about me—it's horrible. After this article comes out, it's only going to get worse. I can't deal with it."

He dropped his head into his hands. "I can't control that. People are fucking idiots, Quinn. They're going to say whatever they want. So just don't look at the social media shit. Ignore it, and they'll stop paying attention after a while."

"Maybe, or maybe not." I reached for his hands and clutched them in my own. They were icy cold. "I'm not suggesting that we . . . that things go back to what they were before. I can't lose you as my friend. Not again. Let's just look at this as a little breathing room, okay? If things cool down, like you think they will, maybe . . . we can try again. But right now, I want to go home. I want to be with my mom. I need some space to think it all over."

"Quinn, I don't want anybody else. You know that. It's you, Quinn. It's always been you, and it's always going to be you, forever. Don't destroy us over this."

"Just a break." I repeated the words. "Just a break."

Leo pulled me against him, and once again, his face was burrowed in my hair. "I don't want you to leave."

"If it wasn't now, it would be in a few weeks. We're just moving things up a little." I stroked his back. "Tell me you understand, Leo. Tell me you're okay with this."

He lifted tormented eyes to mine. "I'm never going to be okay with you leaving me or with us being apart, in any way." He drew in a deep breath. "But . . . yeah, I understand. You've been stuck in the house, afraid to go out, and I know all of this puts you in a terrible position, too."

A small trickle of relief mingled with a stream of regret. "It does. I don't want to mess up anything for you. I never want to stand in the way of your dreams or your future."

"Mia Quinn." He held my face between his two hands. "You are my dream and my future. Don't ever forget that."

I'm one of them. The thought drifted unbidden and unwelcome into my mind, but I didn't say it aloud. Leo would only deny it, and that was not an argument I cared to have today.

"Tell me this is temporary." He leaned back, searching my face. "Just until you feel a little steadier and the fucking media stuff goes away. Right?"

I nodded, but I couldn't say the words. I couldn't tell him what he wanted to hear, out of fear I might say what he wasn't ready to accept.

But I knew the truth.

Football Sunday

If you haven't heard the name Leo Taylor, you must have been living under a rock. The rising junior at Carolina University has, in the last year, become the most watched and the most popular college football player in the nation.

Taylor's story is that of a typical American boy. The youngest of three boys, his parents are middle-class residents of a small town in Southern New Jersey. Their two oldest boys, Simon and Daniel, played basketball, but the baby of the family, Leo, found his real love in the game of football.

Taylor led his Eatonboro High team to the state championship two years in a row. His high school coaches call him a born leader, someone who inspired the other players to give their best every game. His best friend Matt Lampert was the team's quarterback, and they were both recruited by Carolina.

But there the similarities end. While Taylor's gone from victory to victory in his college career, Lampert's languished on the sideline. With Carolina QB Thomas Wilkens playing at the top of his game, sources say Lampert has refused to consider a different position, and his extracurricular activities have made the coaching staff reluctant to deal with him.

Back in high school, Leo Taylor was dubbed the Lion, for both his name and for his habit of roaring after a TD catch. Recently, that name has followed him to Carolina, where a growing group of fans has dubbed itself the Lionesses. The Lionesses attend every game, and their presence on social media has become massive. Each week, the group holds a contest to see who can capture a new picture of Taylor.

Teammates say Taylor doesn't enjoy his new fame, but between his face and body that drives women wild and his continued prowess on the field, it doesn't seem that this Lion will be extinct any time soon.

And ladies . . . sources tell us Leo Taylor is single. Roar, indeed.

★ Thirteen ★

Nate

Junior Year
Fall

ONE THING MOST KIDS WHO ARE SICK A LOT HAVE IN common is that we don't take for granted long stretches of health. For the first seventeen years of my life, a regular hospital stint was part of life, just as much as my birthday was—only less predictable about when it would fall. I'd gone almost four remarkable years without a serious illness, from the autumn of my junior year in high school to late summer before my junior year in college, but I never got used to it. Every time I had a tickle in my throat or an odd pain in my legs, I waited for the inevitable.

When it finally came, the timing wasn't as bad as it could have been. In early August before our third year of college began, I woke up at home and realized I was running a fever. Before the end of the day, I was in the hospital, and by the next day, I was in the ICU.

Quinn had come home early from her summer with Leo. She'd told me a little about what everything had been like down there, and how it had happened that she and Leo were, as she termed it, taking a break. I'd waited for her to shut down again, as she had that first time, back in high school, but she hadn't.

"It was my decision, Nate," she assured me. "It was something I had to do. Not forever, but for now. And I'm really okay."

So she was home when I got sick, and as always, she came to sit next to me at the hospital, holding my hand and doing everything she could to keep me going, whether it was with cajoling, threats or teasing. She made me laugh, and she kept my mother company during the long hours of waiting.

I was just beginning to feel more human on my first day out of intensive care. My nurse had promised to help me take a shower, and we were joking about making that happen when Dr. Randall, my long-time coordinating physician, strolled into my room.

"I figured I'd be seeing you sooner or later." I nodded to him. "This has got to be some kind of record for me, right? Almost four years without a hospital stay. If anyone's counting."

"We are, and it is." Dr. Randall sat down on the edge of my bed. "The fact that you've been so well overall and off antibiotics for so long is probably one of the reasons you responded so quickly to treatment this time."

I grinned. "So we'll aim for a longer break next time, huh? This was almost four years. I think I could make six my goal."

I expected Dr. Randall to laugh and agree, but instead

he frowned. “I wish I could encourage you to commit to that goal, Nate, but you know our deal.”

“Yeah.” Years before, when I was younger, I’d promised that I’d always be completely honest with the good doctor about my symptoms and feelings. In return, he’d promised full disclosure when it came to the progression of my disease and my overall prognosis. “So . . . the news isn’t good?”

He pursed his lips. “It’s not bad, but some of your test results have been more consistent with an indication of disease progression than with stability.”

“Which means in English . . . it looks like it’s beginning to gain on me.”

“It looks like we need to keep our eyes on things.” Dr. Randall corrected me gently. “I’m not telling you to write your will, Nate. I’m just saying we need to test more frequently, and you’re going to have to watch your activity and your diet, as well as your exposure to illness. You might have to slow down a little. Got it?”

“Yeah. I understand.”

“Good.” He tapped the side my bed. “We’ll be in touch.”

I returned to school with renewed purpose that year. Tuck and I moved into an apartment on the first floor of the Birch upperclassman apartment building, both of us happy to be out of the same room we’d shared for the first two years of college. None of our parents were particularly thrilled that we’d be more on our own, but Tuck and I had pushed the issue until they all agreed.

My favorite part of living in the apartments was being so close to Quinn. She shared a three-bedroom unit with Gia and Zelda on the third floor, a mere elevator-ride away. As a result, we all spent more time together that year, either in the girls' room or in ours.

We were all hanging out on the third floor one Saturday in October, watching the Carolina game on the TV in the girls' living room. Quinn leaned forward, her eyes trained on the screen. The volume was cranked up so we could hear every word the announcer said.

"Taylor's having quite the year, isn't he?" One of the men in a loud checked sports coat intoned those words over the sounds of the crowd.

"It's an interesting story. Coach Demby brought in these two players from the same school in South Jersey, and the differences in them are fascinating. Taylor's been starting for about a year now, and he's kind of become the most eligible bachelor in college football today, thanks to some well-placed media coverage." There was a dry note in the other commentator's voice. Apparently not everyone appreciated the articles about Leo that had been popping up everywhere.

"Unfortunately, it hasn't been such an easy road for his buddy, Matt Lampert. Lampert came into this team as a quarterback, when Carolina already had a young QB. He's come in late in a few games, but he hasn't started yet. It's an awkward situation, because Wilkinson is healthy and on fire, while this other talented young man sits around twiddling his thumbs."

"True. And he's not just twiddling his thumbs, either, or at least that's what we hear. Lampert's got quite the reputation for his partying, and he's been getting into some trouble off the field. Shame when you see these talented young players squander their abilities in destructive behavior. But it seems to be happening more and more often these days."

"Oh, for the love of God. Would he just shut up?" Gia threw a pillow at the television. "You know, if they'd just leave Matt alone, maybe he'd have a chance to turn things around. What do they expect from him? He doesn't feel like he's part of the team. He feels like he's an also-ran, while Leo can't do anything wrong. He's the golden boy."

Quinn sighed. "It's not Leo's fault, Gia. He didn't ask for the attention. It's just how everything shook out with the positions they play." She twisted a strand of her hair around her finger. "Matt knew when he decided to go to Carolina that Wilkens was going to be there as quarterback for the next three years. He was banking on an injury or Wilkens going into the NFL early, and now that neither is happening, he's sulking like a little kid."

Gia stood up. "Quinn, I don't get why you're defending Leo. He left you behind fast enough when the college told him he needed to be a swinging single."

"That's not how it was." Quinn's cheeks flushed. "I'm the one who told Leo we needed to take a break. I'm the one who couldn't deal with all the press. It's not his fault."

"Still. Homecoming's next week. Did Leo ask you to come down? You went last year and freshman year."

"No." Her reply was short and clipped. "He didn't, and even if he did, I wouldn't be going. You don't think the media would be all over that?" She took a deep breath and slumped back on the couch. "Besides. We're not together like that anymore. We're just friends. For now. Again. Still. Whatever."

"Uh huh." Zelda spoke up from the corner where she'd been reading. "That must be why you've been dating so much, Quinn. You know, out every night, partying, sleeping with every guy you meet . . . all of that is because you and Leo aren't together anymore. Just friends."

"She doesn't date or party." I couldn't be quiet any longer. "And she sure as hell isn't sleeping around."

"Like me, you mean, Nate?" Zelda tossed her book onto the coffee table. "Don't worry, hon. I was just teasing Quinn. We all know she's not a super slut like I am."

"Chill, Zelda. Nate didn't mean anything. And Nate, Zelda was just being sarcastic. Christ, what's wrong with everyone today?" Tuck scowled at all of us. "I'm the surly one, remember? I'm the only guy entitled to be pissy and moody here, watching a football game. From my fucking wheelchair. Taylor's a gifted player, sure, but he doesn't have the moves I did. And Matt Lampert's wasting the chance I'd kill to have. So if I'm not sitting here moaning and bitching, the rest of you sure as hell shouldn't be. Got it?"

We all froze, afraid to look at each other. And then Gia snickered, Quinn started to giggle, and finally we were all roaring. Zelda stood up and stretched her back, still laughing.

"Come on, Eli. I'm hungry for chocolate ice cream, and I don't want to go alone. Let me take you and your fucking wheelchair away from the annoying football game."

Tuck looked at her, his face inscrutable, and then he nodded. "Yeah, good idea. Catch you guys later. Try not to brawl while we're gone."

Once the door had closed behind them. Gia and Quinn

hooted. "Did you hear that? She called him Eli. And how he looked at her! Who do they think they're fooling?"

I frowned. "What do you mean?"

Quinn shook her head. "Zelda and Tuck. Gia and I are almost a hundred percent sure they're secretly seeing each other."

"Why would it be a secret?" I didn't understand subterfuge and intrigue.

"God only knows." Quinn lifted one shoulder. "Zelda is so paranoid about dating and about anyone thinking she actually has feelings. I think she's just scared shitless."

"Huh." I hadn't thought about it much, but now that I did, Tuck had been acting strangely. Maybe he was seeing someone. And it was definitely possible that it was Zelda, though I'd never thought they even liked each other.

Gia stood up from the sofa and stretched. "All right, kidlets. The game's over, and once again my kinda-sorta boyfriend slash fuck buddy didn't get any field time. This means he's going to need some serious TLC in the form of hot phone sex from yours truly. If you hear moans coming from my bedroom, pay no attention at all."

"Eww and TMI." Quinn wrinkled her nose. "Tell Matt I said hello."

Once she'd disappeared behind her bedroom door, Quinn glanced at me. "And then there were two. What's on your agenda for tonight, Nate?"

"Oh, I don't know. I guess dinner and catching up on some reading."

She sighed. "Yeah, me too. We're a couple of wild ones, aren't we?"

I smiled at her. "I don't know. I like our lives. I've never been much a party animal, anyway."

Quinn laughed. "Yes, I'm aware of that."

"But speaking of parties . . ." I leaned back in the chair, rubbing my palms on the thighs of my jeans. "Homecoming for us is in three weeks. I haven't gone before now, because . . . well, you were with Leo. But would you go with me? As my date?"

Quinn's mouth dropped open a little. "Oh, Nate. I don't know. I wasn't planning on going to homecoming at all."

"But now you can. With me." I licked my lips. "Quinn, you know how I feel about you. I understand about everything with you and Leo, and I know it's been hard for you. But maybe if you give dating me a try . . . you might like it. Maybe it'll be better than you think it will be."

"I'm sure it would be wonderful, because you're wonderful. But I'm not sure I'm ready to move on yet, Nate. Leo and I . . . we haven't made any decisions. We're still in this weird holding pattern."

"But it's just me. He won't mind that."

Quinn cocked her head. "You just said you wanted me to try dating you. And trust me, Nate, Leo's fully aware of how you feel about me. He's going to mind."

"Come on, Quinn. Please." I didn't want to play this card, but I could hear Dr. Randall's voice in the back of my mind, along with a ticking clock. "I want to experience homecoming. I want to have a real college experience. And I won't be comfortable doing it with anyone but you."

For a few beats, she didn't answer. Finally, she dropped her head back onto the sofa. "Okay. Okay! Fine. I'll go, but I'm not going to promise to enjoy myself."

"Just put on a dress and let me take you. I'll take care of the rest."

I'd never been to a dance before. In high school, I hadn't been interested in anyone but Quinn, and she'd either been hung up on Leo, dating Leo or trying to get over Leo. I was excited about homecoming for more than one reason.

As it turned out, the dance part wasn't very exciting. It was held at a hotel just outside of town, in a non-descript room that reminded me more of setting for a business meeting than for a dance. The music was loud, the food was bland and there were far too many drunk people.

But I didn't care, because Quinn was with me, and she was beautiful.

She wore a short black dress with high heels that made her legs look endless, and her hair fell over her shoulders in a cascade. She smiled at me like I was the only guy in the room, and she danced with me to a slow song, her arms twined around my neck.

"Quinn," I murmured in her ear. "Thank you being my date tonight. We've never danced before."

She pulled back a little to see my face. "We haven't. You're pretty smooth on your feet, Nate Wellman."

I laughed. "Only when that means I can shift my weight and shuffle. I'm a champ at that. I guess I missed my calling all these years."

"Maybe." With a sigh, Quinn laid her head against me. "And you smell good, too."

"Thanks." I mentally thanked my mom for giving me a bottle of cologne and insisting I'd need it at some point.

We danced in comfortable silence for a few minutes, before I got up the nerve to ask her what I'd been wanting to ask all night. "Quinn, could I kiss you? Just once, please?"

She lifted her chin and stared up into my eyes. I couldn't read her expression, but after a moment, she framed my face with her hands, stood on her toes and touched her lips to mine.

I'd been dreaming about kissing Quinn for more years than I could remember. The feeling of her mouth on me was better than anything I could've imagined, and I couldn't stop myself from threading my fingers through her hair, angling her head to give me better access and coaxing open her lips.

She didn't respond at first, but when her lips parted, I deepened the kiss, feeling my heart pound against hers as my body responded. We stood there on the dance floor, perfectly still, as my tongue made tentative strokes against Quinn's.

When she drew back a little, I leaned my forehead against hers. "Quinn, I know things between us aren't . . . the same. I know you're still figuring things out. But I love you. I always have, and I always will. You're the only girl I have ever wanted. I want you to know that."

Her eyes clouded, and she sighed, laying her head on my chest again. "I do know it, Nate."

"Could we try? I've never had a girlfriend. I don't know what it's like. And I'm not asking you to sleep with me." She stiffened, and I hurried to go on. "I just want to be able to kiss you now and then. To hold your hand. Take you out to dinner or watch a movie."

"We do all that already." She spoke against the lapel of my jacket.

"Not the kissing and the hand holding." I rubbed her back, daring to let my fingers venture onto the bare skin revealed by the deep V of the dress. "I don't know how much longer I'm going to have this chance, Quinn. What if we just tried it . . . and if it doesn't work out, or if you end up back with Leo, then I'll understand."

"Nate, I love you too much to ask you to be my fall back guy until the time is right for me to be with Leo again. That's not fair to you."

"It is if that's what I want. And I do." I brushed a kiss over her temple. "I'll be your fall back, Quinn. I'll be your in-between. Your rebound. I just want to be with you for now." *Because now is the only time I have.* I didn't speak the words out loud, but I heard them in my head. "You don't have to say yes right now. Just . . . don't say no."

The music ended, and a new, faster song began to play. Quinn covered my hands, still at her waist, with her own and stepped back. She looked at me for a long moment before she squeezed my hands and nodded.

"Okay."

★ Fourteen ★

Quinn

Senior Year
Spring

I WASN'T SURE EXACTLY HOW IT HAD HAPPENED, BUT BY the beginning of senior year, it seemed that Nate and I were in a relationship.

It began at the homecoming dance, and then things happened slowly and gradually from there. Nate held my hand as we walked to class. He kissed me good-night when he left my apartment at night. His kisses weren't long or involved, and they didn't feel like they were leading anywhere more complicated, but still, I was uneasy. I tried to ignore all that, until one day, when I was meeting him at the student union after a class, I heard Nate talking to someone I didn't know.

"Yeah, I'm just waiting for my girlfriend, and then we're going to the movies."

For a brief second, I actually thought, *Nate has a girl-*

friend? And then I realized he was talking about me.

"Honestly, Quinn? You and Nate have been dating since last fall." Zelda shook her head at me as she dried a pan. "You're just the last one to notice."

"And maybe you didn't notice because of all the sex you're *not* having," Gia put in helpfully. "Which, I have to say . . .why not? Nate is totally a hottie. You know I'd have done him, back before I was all into self-destructive jerks who like to torture me."

"It's not like that." I handed Zelda another dish to dry. "We're just like we've always been. Except he kisses me. And apparently calls me his girlfriend."

"Is he a good kisser?" Gia leaned her hips against the counter. "I always thought he would be. You know, that intensity and attention. Like, you'd feel like the only girl in the world."

"Yes." I rinsed off a plate. "He's actually a really good kisser. But don't you think it doesn't matter how good someone is, if he's not the right one? It's like pesto. You could eat the best pesto in the world, but if you're not really a fan, it's not going to do anything for you."

"True." Zelda picked up her wine glass and drained it. "But you know, if you keep an open mind, you get to enjoy a lot more pesto. And sometimes it's okay even if it's not the best pesto. Sometimes you just need pesto, regardless of the quality." She sighed. "Eating the best pesto all the time is pretty amazing. But the sampler platter wasn't half bad, either."

I raised one eyebrow. "Why do I get the feeling we're not taking about pesto anymore? When did this conversation veer into sex?"

"Honey, it's always about sex." Gia leered at me. "Besides, we were talking about you and Nate, and when you turned into you-and-Nate. And why you're not having pesto. I mean, sex."

"He hasn't pushed. He hasn't even mentioned it." I shrugged. "We don't talk about that stuff. Leo and I, we talked about everything." I remembered, with vivid clarity, the night we'd slept together for the first time. I could see us in my mind's eyes, sitting in my car outside the hotel, talking about what we were going to do.

"Speaking of Leo . . ." Zelda crossed her arms over her chest and smirked at me. "How's everything going there? And how does he feel about you and Nate?"

"I haven't seen him since Christmas break." I wrapped my arms around my waist, staving off the pain that came whenever I thought of him. "I haven't said anything about Nate and me. Mostly, because I didn't know there was anything to really say about us. Leo and I talked over break, but it's always the same. We go round and round, with Leo trying to convince me things can change and me believing they can't. It's the same situation. And now that they won the championship again, it's gotten even worse. He has agents talking to him, and they're working on where he's going to end up in the draft." I slid a glance Gia's way.

Her expression was grim. "I'm not sure what's worse: Leo being too popular to be with you, or Matt getting kicked off the team altogether, thanks to his inability to kick the booze and drugs. Oh, and of course, the fact that he can't keep his dick in his pants."

I slung an arm over her shoulder and side-hugged her.

"I'm sorry, Gia. I wish Matt had been able to pull it together. He could've had a good senior year . . . or if he'd been willing to switch positions, like Coach Demby suggested, he could've played more. He might be in the draft, too."

"Yes, but that would be logical." Gia's voice was just a little bitter. "And apparently, it's Matt's way or no way at all."

On the counter, my phone began to ring. Frowning, I answered it. "Nate? What's up?"

There was a rasp on the other end of the line. "Quinn. Need help." His breathing was heavy and labored. "Get my mom. I need to go to the hospital."

"Nate?" I called his name in alarm, but there was no answer. "Shit!" I cut off the call and scrolled for Sheri's contact info. As I waited for her to answer, I grabbed my purse and a jacket, yelling to the girls. "Nate's sick. Zelda, can you drive? We need to get him to the hospital."

"And here we are again." Sheri grimaced. "Sitting in this damn hospital. Again. Waiting for news."

"It was so scary. I've never been there when he first got sick, you know?" I shuddered. "Sheri, I was terrified."

"You did fine, kiddo." She patted my hand. "You called me, and you got him to the hospital. The rest is up to the doctors." She closed her eyes. "And Nate."

I watched his chest rise and fall over the gentle hiss of the oxygen. "I've been worried about him for the last few months. He's seemed . . . like he's slowing down. I notice he's avoiding crowds. Sleeping more." I raised my eyes to hers. "What's going on, Sheri?"

She swallowed and bit her lip. "When Nate got sick at the end of the summer before last, Dr. Randall let us know that he was running out of options. It's okay as long as he stays healthy, but we knew then that we were dealing with the clock running out." She squeezed my hand. "Since Nate was born, Quinn, we've known he was facing what the doctors called a limited lifetime expectation. We've learned to appreciate and enjoy each day." Tears swam in her eyes. "But I've been dreading this all along—when the doctors say there's nothing left for them to do."

"There's got to be something. He's been doing so well lately. Aren't there more doctors? Better hospitals?"

She shook her head. "Nate's old enough to know what he wants and what he doesn't want, Quinn. He doesn't want to waste his life chasing medical options. He wants to enjoy the time he has." She raised one eyebrow at me. "Especially now. I can't remember him ever being happier than he has this last year, and I know that's you. So thank you."

I felt vaguely uncomfortable. "Nate's always been a priority to me, Sheri. I wish . . ." I wished I could love him like he loved me. I wished I could give him what he really wanted—to be the girlfriend he deserved.

"We talked about this years ago, Quinn. Remember? I know how you feel about Nate, and I know how you feel about Leo." She smiled. "Things aren't easy for you, are they, sweetie? But you're doing right by my boy, and no matter what, I respect that. Nate's not stupid. He knows that Leo has your heart. But you've made room for him, too, and you're giving him something Mark and I never could—a taste of a normal life. So please don't feel guilty about conflicted feelings."

I grasped her hand tightly. "I just want Nate to be okay. I want more time with him, you know?"

Sheri sighed. "Oh, honey. I do know. Believe me, I do."

Nate's recovery was slower this time. He spent a week in ICU, a week during which I hardly slept and missed every class. Once they moved him to a regular room, he was in the hospital for another ten days, fighting off further infection and recovering.

On the day Nate was released, Sheri texted me at noon to let me know she'd brought him home. He was going to spend at least two weeks at home, where Sheri and Mark could monitor his meds and take him to follow up appointments with the doctor.

As soon as classes ended, I drove to the Wellmans' house, giving a quick knock as I opened the front door.

"Is there an escapee from the hospital around here?" I called, stepping into the living room.

"God, yes." Nate lay on the couch, covered with a quilt. "And I don't plan on going back any time soon. Want to be my partner in crime?"

I grinned. "Always. Always have been, always will be." I pulled a footstool over next to the sofa and leaned up to kiss his cheek. "Nice and cool, by the way. Feels like ninety-eight point six to me."

"Should be, after all the shit they've been pumping into me the last two weeks." He caught my hand and tugged me close. "Hey. I've been stuck in the hospital with no privacy. Don't you think I deserve more than a kiss on the cheek?"

I forced a smile. "Of course." I touched his lips with mine, planning to keep it light, but Nate gripped the back of my neck and deepened the kiss, opening his mouth, making the caress intimate and passionate.

"That's better." He grinned and released me. I noticed that his cheeks were a little more flushed, and his chest rose and fell rapidly.

"I'm so glad you're home. Now you need to take it easy and get better, so you can come back to school. Tuck's been even more grumpy with you gone. He said to tell you to get your ass back there fast, or he'll replace you, and I quote, with another needy nerd."

"Hmph." Nate's eyes drifted shut, but he was still smiling. "Tell him I'll be back to annoy him soon, and he'll be wishing I'd stayed gone."

"I'll pass on the message." I watched his face closely. "You look tired. I just wanted to stop by to see for myself that you were home. I better let you rest now."

"Don't leave yet." He threaded his fingers through mine, opening his eyes a little. "I need to talk to you, Quinn. It's important."

"You need to take it easy." I squeezed his hand. "We can talk later, Nate. I'm not going anywhere. And neither are you."

He managed a weak smile. "Wish I could agree with you. But you know me, Quinn. No filter. No small talk. And I want to tell you something now. I need to do it today. It can't wait."

I frowned as I sat down again next to the sofa. "Okay. I'm here. You tell me what you need to, but then you sleep some, okay? You need your rest to recover."

"Fine." He settled himself more comfortably and looked down at my long slim fingers folded against the back of his hand. "I love the feel of your hand in mine. I always have, since we were little."

My stomach rolled. There was something in his voice that scared the shit out of me. "So what's happening, Nate? What's so important that you have to get it out now?"

"Dr. Randall talked to me just before he let me go." Nate played with a long thread on the edge of the blanket that covered him. "He said there's no doubt my disease is progressing."

This wasn't completely unexpected, since Sheri had said something along these lines during our talk in the hospital. My eyebrows drew together as I focused on what it really meant. "Okay. Well—what are they going to do? A new protocol? Do you need to take a leave from school?"

He shook his head slowly. "There isn't anything else new on the horizon. Not at the moment, anyway. From this point on, they're going to focus on maintaining."

I knew, logically, what Nate was trying to say. But I couldn't believe it, not really. I didn't want to accept it. "Maintain. All right, well, that's doable, isn't it? Keep taking your meds, and then you'll be ready when the next new treatment comes along."

"Quinn." He was looking at me steadily, patiently. "That's not what's going to happen. I've known for the past year that the symptoms were getting worse, even though I hoped—but the doctors can see the decline on a cellular level." He paused, and I could tell he was struggling with his next words. "I don't know the exact timeline, but I know what the end result is going to be. My body is shutting down, and . . . I'm going to die."

I thought I was going to be sick. My throat burned and my middle clenched. "Don't say that, Nate. Just . . . don't."

"I have to say it. We've got to be honest with ourselves and with each other, because if we don't, we're just wasting time. I'm not going to do that when every minute is precious."

"Okay." I nodded and sucked in a deep breath, trying to steady myself. "Okay. What . . . how long?"

"I don't know for sure. Maybe six months, possibly a little longer."

The tears I'd been battling filled my eyes. "Nate, I can't do this. I can't lose you. You're my best friend, and I can't . . ." The band around my chest constricted until I couldn't breathe or talk.

"You can. I need you, Quinn. And I'm going to need your help. And . . . something else, too." For the first time since I'd come into the room, he looked unsure and nervous, his face losing its resolve.

I held his hand in both of mine and lifted it to my lips, kissing the knuckles. "Anything. You know that. Anything at all."

He gave a shaky laugh. "Don't say that before you hear what I want. Don't promise something you might not be able to deliver."

"Unless you're going to ask me to put a pillow over your face, you can pretty much count on me coming through for you. When have I ever let you down?"

"Never." He answered quickly, staring deep into my eyes.

"You've never let me down, Quinn, not in almost twenty-two years of friendship. And God, I've been a demanding friend. When I look back, I can see how selfish I've been. I always wanted you, and only you, and you gave me anything I wanted, even when it wasn't in your best interest."

A sob stuck in my throat. "No. You were never—"

"Quinn, don't try to whitewash our history. You sat next to me on the playground every day for years, when I know you wanted to be out playing with the other kids. With the normal kids. You chose me over Leo when we were younger, even when I knew you wanted to be with him. And I was such a jerk, I let you make that choice, and I told myself it was okay. Nothing in my life was fair. I hated not being able to run and play kickball or just be fucking typical, but I thought having you made up for that. I guess maybe I felt entitled to your time and attention."

"I never resented giving it to you."

Nate smiled. "I know. That's what makes this both easier and harder. Easier, because you've never made me feel bad for needing you, and harder because I know this last thing I'm going to ask of you is probably the most selfish thing I've ever done."

I tilted my head, narrowing my eyes. "You're scaring me now. Just tell me what you need, and if it's in my power, I'll do it."

He sat up a little straighter, and his face flushed. "I wish I could do this differently. God, I wish I could do just one thing like regular people do." He took a deep breath, his chest rising and falling with the the effort. "Okay. For someone whose days are numbered, I'm doing a lot of stalling." He licked his lips, pressed them together for a second, and then lifted his gaze to meet mine.

"I want you to marry me, Quinn."

If I were honest, I'd expected something along these lines. Part of me had sensed that maybe he was going to ask me to love him—really love him, be his official girlfriend, to sleep with him—for whatever time he had left. But hearing him say those words made me dizzy.

Before I could reply, he hurried on. "It's all I've ever wanted. I want to be married to you, and if we had the luxury of time, I'd keep . . . wooing you, I guess, as long as it took until you really loved me, too. Until you wanted to marry me as much as I want you. We'd do things the normal way. But we don't. *I* don't. I can't wait for you to fall in love with me for real. So I'm doing the most selfish thing I've ever done and playing the dying friend card."

"Nate." I couldn't say more than his name.

"I want you with me for as long as I have. And I want the gratification of being able to call you my wife. I want to give my parents the memory of a wedding. They haven't had anything like the typical experience with me as their kid, but this I can give them, if you help me. I already talked to them about this. They were surprised . . . but they'll go along with whatever we decide."

Everything was swirling around in my head. And I could only think of Leo. When I'd pictured someone proposing to me, it had always been Leo. I could see him, in my mind's eye, kneeling before me, my hand in his, and I could feel the excitement and love we'd feel, standing on the edge of the rest of our lives together.

But instead, I was sitting next to my other best friend, the one who probably had less than a year to live. And he was asking me to give him a portion of my own life. How could I deny him this? How could I say no to him, when this was all he was asking of me?

"Look at it this way." He was still speaking, but his eyes had dropped to fasten on our still-joined hands. "It's a limited time marriage. I promise you, Quinn, I'm not going to be around to celebrate our golden anniversary. Most likely I won't make it to our first one." He leaned in, looking at me again. "But I promise that for as long as I do have, everything in my life will be focused on making you as happy as I can. You'll have my heart and soul for as long as it's mine to give."

I bit my lip and tried to catch my breath. I knew I had to give him an answer, but my voice wouldn't work.

"Quinn. Please. Just say yes."

Vulnerability and uncertainty battled on his face, and in a mad rush of memory, I saw everything Nate had been to me. I remembered the awkward toddler, learning to maneuver the walker that Leo and I didn't need. I saw his lurching swagger when he was finally able to manage walking on his own. I saw the boy who saved me a swing every day, so the two of us could sit on the sidelines of the playground, and the teenager whose love for me had been steady and real for as long as I had lived.

All of that gave me the strength I needed to utter one word.

"Yes."

★ Fifteen ★

Leo

Senior Year
April

I HADN'T HAD A HANGOVER LIKE THIS FOR A LONG, LONG time. My head was pounding, and my mouth was like a roll of cotton. For a long disoriented moment, I couldn't remember where I was or why I was awake. One hand groped out, reaching for Quinn, before my traitorous mind remembered the truth.

She's not in your bed. She hasn't been in your bed for over a year. And she's fucking marrying someone else.

The pain stabbed again, just as sharp and fresh as it had the first time I'd heard the news. Quinn had made sure it came from her, and she'd actually called me, explaining what was going on. I'd run through the gamut of emotion from grief over Nate's news to anger over what he was asking of Quinn to hurt over the fact that she'd agreed.

Quinn was engaged to Nate. They were getting married in two months. I didn't have to do much mental arithmetic, because the countdown ticked away in my brain on a daily basis.

On the bedside table next to me, my phone sounded, and I realized that was what had awakened me. Its insistent ring and vibration paused and then started up again. Clearly someone was trying to get through to me and wasn't going to give up.

I frowned as I focused my bleary eyes on the screen and answered. "Gia? What's up?" I didn't hear from her very often, and worry for Quinn and for Nate threaded through me.

"Leo, do you know where Matt is?" I heard the concern in her voice. "He's not with you, is he?"

"Ah . . ." I rubbed my neck and tried to think. "I don't know if he's home. He didn't go out with us last night, and I just woke up. What's going on?"

"He tried to call me last night. Like, a lot. Ten times, maybe more. I lost my phone, thought I'd left it in someone's car, and then I just found it this morning in my other bag—God, that doesn't matter. He left one message, and I couldn't figure out what he was trying to say." She sniffled, and I heard her take a long breath. "Leo, I'm worried about him."

"Yeah." I raked one hand over my hair. The truth was, we were all worried about Matt, even more than normal. Since he'd been kicked off the team last fall, he'd gradually stopped going to classes, and there was no way he was going to graduate next month. His grandfather had called me occasionally, asking if there was anything we could do to help get Matt back on track. I'd refrained, barely, from telling the man that his concern was too little, too late. If his grandparents had cared back in high school, we might not be watching him spiral now.

And then two weeks ago, Gia had come down for an unexpected visit. I'd had to sit in my bedroom in misery, listening as she told Matt that they were over, for good.

"I can't do this anymore." Her voice had been filled with such anguish that it brought tears to my eyes. "Matt, I love you. I've loved you for four years, but God, you destroy me. Loving you has made me happier than anything else, ever, but it's also almost killed me. I want to believe you can turn things around, but I don't think you can do it while I'm part of your life. Or maybe I'm not strong enough to give you what you need to get better."

"Gia, no." Matt had actually begged her, which was out of character for him. "Please. Just give me another chance. I'm pulling it together, baby. I'm going to stop drinking, and I was thinking . . . I could go finish up school at Birch, with you. I can make it happen, baby."

"How many fucking times have you promised me everything was going to get better, Matt? How many fucking times have you broken my heart? You think I don't know you're still dicking around? You think I don't see the pictures, hear the stories? No, Matt. I'm done. I'm sorry, but it's over."

It had all gone downhill from there, with Matt shouting obscenities at Gia until she finally fled the apartment, sobbing.

"Was this the first time you've heard from him since . . . since you were here?" Matt hadn't mentioned her name once since that night.

"Yeah. He texted me once, but it didn't mean anything. That's why I was freaking out this morning, when I saw all his calls. Can you check and see if he's in his bedroom?"

"Ah, sure." I stood up, giving my head a minute to stop spinning before I opened my bedroom door and walked the few steps to Matt's. "Hold on, Gia."

I knocked on the door, not too hard at first, and then with increasing volume. When I didn't hear anything from inside the room, I opened it and looked inside.

Matt's bed was empty, which didn't surprise me, but what was odd was that the bed was made. His room was neat, as though he'd done his sort-of annual cleaning last night. Matter of fact, I was pretty sure I'd never seen Matt's room look so good.

I lifted the phone to my ear again. "No, he's not here, Gia. I'm sorry."

She blew out a long breath. "Shit. Okay. You said he didn't go out with you last night. Where was he?"

I cast my mind back. "Uh, he was here. I went out with some guys from the team, though, and you know he won't hang with them anymore. Tate drove us. Matt said . . ." *What the hell had he said?* "He said he needed a little downtime, and he'd see me later." Now it began to come back to me, and with the memory came an overwhelming sense of foreboding. "Gia. When I left, Matt hugged me. He told me not to worry about him, just to go have a good time." Why hadn't I picked up right then that something was off? Matt never said shit like that. Why had I been so wrapped up in my own misery that I'd missed my friend's odd words?

"My God. Leo, you've got to find him. Where would he go?"

"I have no idea. He doesn't have any other friends down

here anymore, not that I know of. He almost never leaves the apartment, unless he's going to a bar or the liquor store or—"

"Or to score drugs or women, right? I'm not stupid, Leo, and you don't have to protect me from Matt. Not now."

I opened my mouth to answer her, but before I could, the doorbell rang. Relief flooded through me.

"Gia, that's probably him at the door. He's always forgetting his damn keys. Let me talk to him, and then I'll call you back and let you know what's going on."

"No." She was adamant. "Don't you dare hang up this phone, Leo. I want to hear now."

"Fine." I unlocked the door and swung it open. "Dude, you are in so much . . ." My voice trailed off at the sight of Coach on the other side. "Gia, it's not Matt."

"Leo, son." Coach's face was somber, and if I didn't know any better, I'd think his eyes were red. "I need to come in and talk to you."

"Yeah, okay." I stepped back and covered the mouthpiece of the phone, holding it up. "Matt's girlfriend—well, his ex-girlfriend, I guess—is trying to find him. Let me just tell her that I'll call her back."

Coach was never known for hiding his emotions, and this morning wasn't any exception. I saw the expression on his face when I said Matt's name, and suddenly, I knew. I just knew.

"Gia. Hold on a second." I lowered the phone from my ear, but I didn't hang up. "Tell me. Just tell me. Please."

His mouth shook. "God, Taylor, I fucking hate this. Fucking hate this shit. Okay." He rubbed a hand over his mouth. "Got a call this morning from the cops in town. They'd been at a motel . . . someone from the housekeeping staff found him.

Found Matt. He'd left a note, and he'd asked them to call me, not you." His face crumbled. "The fucker didn't want you to find out from the police. Goddamn. He knew I'd come to you."

"What did he do?" I couldn't speak above a whisper.

"Pills. He took a shit load of pills, the cops think probably last night. By the time the housekeeper found him, he was . . . he was long gone, son. Cold. Nothing they could do."

"Did they try? Did they even fucking try to bring him back?" I was shouting. "Or did they throw him away, write him off like everyone else fucking did?"

"Leo, it was too late. He's dead. Matt . . . he was a tortured soul, son. We did everything we could to help him, but sometimes—"

"No, we fucking did *not.*" I was wild now, ranting. "It was just easier to cut him, to toss him off the team, to say he was a loser, a fuck-up and no one even tried—"

A noise from the phone next to me caught my attention. I'd forgotten about Gia for a minute, but now I heard her cries. With a shaking hand, I raised the phone again.

"Gia. He's gone. He fucking committed suicide."

On the other end, she was emitting a sound I hadn't heard for a long time. Not since the morning after Quinn's father had been killed. The keening, anguished noise ripped out what was left of my heart.

"Leo?" As if I had summoned her by my thoughts, Quinn's voice floated over the phone. "God, is it true? Matt?"

"Yeah." A sob wracked me. "Tell Gia . . . tell her I'm going to take care of everything. Tell her I'm bringing Matt home."

Matt Lampert had never been much of a planner, but he'd managed his suicide with a precision that would've changed his life, had he applied it there. He'd cleaned his room, as I'd noticed, and when I opened his closet, I'd found his clothes bagged. In his duffel bag were all the personal items that might mean something to me, to his grandparents and to Gia.

At the motel room where he'd ended his life, the police had found only two notes. The first was the one Coach had referenced, a polite missive requesting that the authorities notify Coach Demby, who would then know how to proceed.

The second note was a piece of paper with Gia's name written on top, and it had only two words on it.

I'm sorry.

The coach had offered to help me with anything I needed, but I tried to do everything myself. I owed that much to Matt. I called his grandparents and broke the news, and with their guidance, I made arrangements for Matt's body to be cremated locally.

And then I brought him home.

Matt's memorial service took place on a beautiful April morning, one of those days with clear blue skies, bright sunshine and soft breezes. His grandparents were members of the Episcopal church in town, so that was where they held the service. The sanctuary wasn't big enough to hold everyone who came, so they had to broadcast the priest's words outside, where the overflow sat on folding chairs on the church lawn.

I sat in the front row next to Gia. Her face was pale, and her eyes were hollow. Quinn had whispered to me earlier that Gia was on some kind of medicine to keep her calm, because she'd been hysterical for hours. She looked a little like a zombie, and every time we had to change position—there was a lot of kneeling, standing and sitting in the funeral liturgy—her eyes darted to me in panic, mutely asking me what she was supposed to do next.

As if I was supposed to know.

Matt's grandparents sat closest to the aisle. They were stoic, although his grandmother dabbed at her eyes now and then.

Quinn sat on Gia's other side, holding her hand tightly. When I'd seen her a few days before, she'd hugged me tight, and holding her was the first good thing I'd done in over a week. I hadn't wanted to let her go, but I was conscious of our new situation. The girl I held wasn't mine anymore. She belonged to Nate, and the small gold ring on her left hand reminded me of that fact.

The service ended, and we all shuffled out of the church. Classmates from high school whom I hadn't seen in almost four years grabbed my arm and embraced me, weeping softly. I heard murmurs among a few teachers who'd come about waste of potential, and I wanted to smack each and every one of them.

Of course Matt had wasted his potential, but he'd begun down that trail long before he'd taken that fatal dose of pills. It had started back in high school, maybe even earlier. And none of the people who were crying or talking had done a damn thing to stop him.

Just beyond the boundary of the church's grass, the police were holding back a small knot of reporters who were covering the tragedy that was Matt Lampert's life and death. My lip curled in derision. Fucking vultures.

"Can I catch a ride over to the Lamperts' house with you and Gia?" Quinn laid her hand on my arm. "I don't want to be by myself right now."

"Sure." I cleared my throat. "Surprised Nate didn't come."

Quinn's eyes shuttered. "He can't be in crowds. His immune system is so damaged right now that he could pick up anything."

I nodded. "I'm sorry. I can't quite wrap my mind around the fact that our friends are dying off when we're only twenty-two."

She winced, and I felt like shit for what I'd said.

"Come on. My car's over here. Let's go."

I hadn't been back in Eatonboro at this time of year for a long time. We drove the short distance from the church to Matt's grandparents' house in a silence that was only broken by Quinn's soft assurances to Gia, who stared unseeing out the window.

The huge house was already filled with people when we arrived, and I realized a good many of them hadn't bothered to come to the church. That pissed me off; they didn't care enough to pay their respects to Matt's memory, but they were willing to kiss up to his wealthy and influential grandparents.

Fucking idiots.

Quinn and I settled Gia on a chair in the study, where it was quiet. She leaned against the side of it, sighed and closed her eyes. Within a few moments, I could tell she was out.

"The meds make her sleepy." Quinn rubbed her hands together, her forehead furrowed as she watched her friend. "I think I'll just stay in here and keep my eye on her. If she wakes up and doesn't know where she is, she'll freak out."

I sat down next to Quinn. "I'll keep you company."

She smiled. "You don't have to. There are probably a lot of people who want to catch up with you. I saw your parents were at the church, too. That was nice of them to come."

"They loved Matt. I think my mom feels bad that she wasn't more proactive in his life when we were younger. She didn't want to interfere with his grandparents, but God. No one did. If someone had, maybe we wouldn't be here today."

"Matt made his own choices, Leo." Quinn's voice was weary. "You were a wonderful friend to him, always. And he had this enormous potential, so much going for him, but he took a different path. No one is to blame for that."

"I know that in the rational part of my brain. But then there's that voice that keeps telling me there was more I could've done. Why did I go out that night? I needed to blow off steam, and I was . . ." My eyes slid to Quinn's left hand. "Still dealing with a lot of my own shit. But I should've realized he needed me. I let him slide down, and I just shook my head and thought, *that's Matt*."

"He didn't make it easy to help him. Please, Leo. Don't take the blame for this, okay? Don't let it drag you down, too. Matt wouldn't want that. You've got so much coming up—the draft is in ten days, and your whole future is wide open. Don't lose sight of that."

I laughed, but there wasn't a speck of humor in it. "My future, huh? It doesn't feel that bright and shiny, Mia." I used her special name for the first time since the day she'd left me in Carolina. "All I ever wanted was to play football and be with you. One I'm going to get, but it came at the expense of losing the other."

She closed her eyes and leaned her head against the back of her chair. "Leo, please don't. We've been over this so many times. I can be your friend, but that's all. I can't, and I won't, compete with football, and I can't deal with the stress of being the Lion's girlfriend. I still get the occasional hate message, you know? And I know I can't handle it."

I reached into her lap and gripped both of her hands in mine. "It doesn't have to be that way, Mia. I'm about to graduate. I'm going to sign with—well, I'm not going to say and jinx it, but after the draft, things are going to change. You wouldn't be the Lion's girlfriend. You'd be my wife."

Her eyes flew open, and she stared at me, surprise and pain mingled there. "Leo, don't. Please don't. You know I can't. I promised Nate, and I won't go back on that. I can't."

"Quinn, you're making a huge mistake. You don't love him. Not like you love me. You and Nate don't have what we do. We're meant to be, babe. We've always said it, and we've always known it. What the hell happened?"

"Life happened, Leo. And football happened. I never said that I don't love you. You know I do. You know this kills me, too. But this . . . being married to me . . . it's all Nate wants. It's his last wish, really. Am I going to deny him that, when it's in my power to say yes?"

"So you'll ruin your life to make his dream come true?" I hunched over, lowering my voice. "Quinn, did you ever think, what're you going to do if Nate doesn't die? What if you're stuck in this marriage?"

Her eyes flared. "That's a horrible thing to say, Leo."

"It may be, but it's true. Isn't that what Nate always says? Don't waste time not telling the truth. Well, there's my truth, Quinn. I think you're making the biggest fucking mistake of your life. And it is *killing* me."

She sighed. "I know that. I would give anything for you not to be hurting, Leo. But I can't give Nate what he needs without taking away what you want. I wish I could make you both happy, but it seems like that's always been an impossibility. And right now, Nate needs me more than you do. You have your friends, football and years of life ahead of you. Nate has me, and that's it."

I snorted. "Nothing's promised us, is it? You think I have years of life ahead, but who's to say I don't get hit by a bus tomorrow?"

"Shut up." Quinn spoke through clenched teeth. "Leo, how can you say that? Do you not see that I'm going through hell, too? Can't you give me a little fucking break, and maybe try not to make this harder on me than it already is?"

"I'm sorry." In the face of her anguish, my own anger retreated. "Mia, I'm sorry. I'm just torn up over all of this. You and Nate. Matt. Why do things have to be like this?"

"Because life's not fair, Leo. It never was, and it never will be. We take the good things and give thanks, and we help each other through the shitty stuff. That's all we can do." She looked so sad, so tired, that I only wanted to pull her into my arms and hold her. Offer her comfort and maybe a little distraction.

"Mia." I touched her face, gladness swelling in my heart when she leaned into my hand, turning so that her lips pressed my palm. "Come with me. I know this house. There're rooms—I know where the bedrooms are. No one will notice. I need you, Mia. I need you so much."

For a second, I thought she might actually agree, and then she shook her head. "Leo, are you insane? We're at a funeral. I'm not sneaking upstairs with you for sex. Not to mention the fact that you and I aren't together anymore, and I'm engaged to someone else. To Nate."

"But can he give you what I can, Mia?" I dropped to my knees in front of her, bracketing her ribs with my hands. "When he kisses you, does your heart speed up? When he touches you here . . ." I palmed her tit, smiling a little when her mouth fell open. "Does it send a spark right down to your center? And when you hear him say your name, does your pussy get wet?"

"Stop, Leo." She pushed against my shoulder, but her hand didn't use any real pressure, and there was still indecision in her voice. I capitalized on that, raising up and kissing her, open-mouthed, pouring all of my longing and pain into that connection.

"No." She twisted away, and tears filled her eyes. "Please, Leo. Don't do this. I can't tell you no. If you . . . if you keep pushing, I'm going to give in. I'll let you take me up there to an empty bedroom and fuck me silly. I'll let you do anything you want to me. I can't tell you no. But please. It'll destroy me, after. I won't be able to live with myself. Please don't ask me to do that."

She was tearing me up, ripping out my heart, and I couldn't do it. I sat back on my haunches and gazed up into her tormented eyes.

"Okay. All right, baby. I'm sorry." I held her hands. "But just so you know. I wasn't asking you to go upstairs so I could fuck you. I want to make love to you, the way I always did. The way we always did. It was never just sex with us, Mia. It was always love. Every single time."

She nodded. "I know."

Because I was a fucking masochist, I asked the question I dreaded. "Does he . . . have you and Nate . . . do you . . . sleep together?"

Pain and embarrassment crossed her face. "You shouldn't ask that, Leo. And I sure as hell shouldn't answer it." When I didn't say anything, she rolled her eyes. "No, okay? No. We're not having sex. Nate can't, uh—it's a side effect of the disease and the treatments. I mean, I can touch him, but he can't maintain . . ." Quinn's face was bright red. "I don't want to talk about this. It's not fair to Nate."

"All right. Sorry." But I really wasn't, because knowing Nate wasn't having sex with Quinn was the best news I'd had in months. I knew for a fact that I was the only guy Quinn had ever been with. The idea of anyone else making love to her, even Nate, when she was going to be his wife, absolutely killed me. I felt bad for Nate, of course, but at the same time, I was fucking relieved for myself.

"Leo, you're going to come, right? To the wedding?" She bit the side of her lip. "I really want you there, but I understand if you don't want to."

I forced a smile. "If you want me to be there, and if Nate's okay with it, of course I'll be at your wedding." I stood up, releasing her hands. "Anything for you, Quinn. Remember that. Anything for you. No matter what."

Yeah. Like I'd said. Fucking masochist.

★ Sixteen ★

Nate

Senior Year
May

My wedding day dawned clear and warm. I was awake as the sun rose over the ocean, sitting up in bed to watch the colors spread over the blue water and shoot rays of gold onto the sand. Today was the happiest day of my life, and I wasn't going to miss a single minute of it.

My mother had worried that having both graduation and the wedding in the same week would be too much for me, but I knew that nothing was going to stand in the way of me marrying Quinn. I briefly considered not walking at that ceremony, just sitting in the audience to cheer for Quinn, Gia, Tuck and Zelda, but it was important to my parents that I walked onto the stage to receive my diploma. I wanted to give them every memory I could, because I knew they were going to need those someday soon.

We'd driven down to the shore the day after graduation, and I'd settled into the same bedroom where I always slept. Quinn popped in now and then, bringing me updates about how preparations were progressing. I could hear voices rising and falling, and I knew Carrie and my mom were cooking, but I stayed put in bed, resting so that I was sure to be strong enough for the big day.

Of course, not everyone was as blissful as I was. Carrie walked around with a tight smile on her face, and I'd noticed she couldn't quite look me in the eye. Quinn had told me that her mother was less than happy about our decision. I understood that, but I didn't have time to worry about it. I knew Carrie was trying to understand, out of her love for both my parents and me, but seeing her only daughter marry a man whose death sentence hung heavy on his head couldn't have been easy.

And then there was Gia, who had turned into a nearly-silent shadow of her former self in the weeks after Matt's suicide. She never smiled or reacted. She showed up where she had to, and she responded to questions when she was forced to do so. But beyond that, she was almost a zombie. I knew Quinn was worried about her, and I missed her bouncy laughter.

We weren't doing a rehearsal or anything else that might wear me out prematurely. The ceremony was going to take place in the living room, with just our families and close friends present. Gia and Zelda were both maids of honor for Quinn, and I'd asked Tuck to be my best man.

"Hey, sure. Just don't ask me to stand up for you." He'd winked at me, smirking, and I smiled back, thinking that Eli

Tucker sure did seem happier these days. I was pretty sure I knew why, too.

Leo would be there, as well. I'd asked Quinn if she thought his feelings would be hurt if I didn't have him as my best man, and an odd expression had crossed her face.

"No, I think he'll understand."

We didn't talk about Leo much anymore. I wasn't stupid; I was fully aware that Quinn still loved him. I knew they were still in love. If I were an unselfish guy, the type who only wanted to see his best friends be happy, I'd have released Quinn from her engagement to me and told them both that seeing them together would be enough for me. But I wasn't that guy, and honestly, I wasn't certain they were capable of being happy together. I wasn't convinced that Leo understood yet what Quinn needed.

But he was enough of a friend to be in the room when his two best friends tied the knot, no matter how he really felt about it, and I had to respect him for that. He's been drafted by the Richmond Rebels in the first round back in April, and I knew he was excited to play for them. His graduation had been three days before ours, so he'd made it up in time to cheer the four of us across the stage.

Everyone had plans for the future, it seemed. Leo had football, Tuck was going into teaching, Zelda had gotten a job with a non-profit farm-to-table group, Gia was going to grad school and Quinn had been offered a position with an on-line news agency. She'd be able to work from home, which was a relief. The only one of us who didn't have a job or a plan was me; my only focus would be living as long as I could and making Quinn happy.

My dad came into my room around nine the morning of the wedding, carrying my suit. "Hey, hey, I thought I was going to have to wake you up. You ready for some breakfast, bud? Mom's making up a tray."

I swung my legs over the side of the bed. "I can come out and eat with everyone else. She doesn't have to bring it to me."

"Nope. All the women folk say you need to stay put, so you don't see the bride before it's time. Bad luck and all that, you know."

I snorted. "Dad, all due respect, I don't think luck has anything to do with this whole deal. Unless it's in making sure I stay alive through the ceremony."

My father frowned. "Are you feeling that bad, Nate?"

"No." I shook my head. "I was making a joke. Sorry. Dark humor."

"Oh, yeah. Ha." He sat down on the edge of the bed with me. "You're sure you want to go through with this, right? I mean, there's no shame in changing your mind."

"Dad." I leveled a glance at him. "This is the one and only thing in my life that I'm sure about. I want to live the last part of my life as Quinn's husband. I haven't made much of my twenty-two years, but if I can say Quinn Russell was my wife, I'll die a happy man. I know that doesn't make sense to anyone else. But it does to me, and it does to Quinn."

"I understand, Nate. I'm just checking." He paused. "Leo got here last night."

"Ah." Something ugly twisted in my gut that had nothing to do with my disease. I didn't want to think the worst of the two people closest to me, but . . . "Did they . . . was Quinn . . ."

"She behaved exactly as you'd expect a girl getting married the next day to behave. She was happy to see him, and Lisa and Joe, too. But she didn't go off alone with him, if that's what you're wondering. She slept in her room, with Gia and Zelda."

"It's okay, Dad. I trust Quinn. I was just. . ." I shrugged. "Curious, I guess. It's hard being stuck in here and just hearing everything going on out there."

"No one's making you stay in bed. You can come out any time you want." He grinned. "Except now, of course. Now you're a prisoner until it's time to say I do."

"I wanted to save all my energy. I didn't want anything to possibly go wrong with today."

"I get it." My father gazed over my shoulder, out the window. "I wanted to talk to you about tonight, Nate. About your wedding night."

"Uh huh. I think I've got that covered, Dad. But thanks."

"Have you and Quinn talked? Does she know about your limitations?"

I fucking hated that word. *Limitations.* "Yes, Dad, she knows. She knows that I'm physically unable to have penetrative sexual intercourse." My voice held a tinge of derisive mocking.

"But you know, son, you can still . . . bring each other pleasure."

"Dad." I laid a hand on his arm. "I know. I did research, and I talked to Dr. Randall. I know what I'm doing."

He nodded. "Okay. Well, then, I've done my fatherly duty. I'm going to go get on my suit, and then I'll be back in a little while to help you with anything you might need. If you do need anything."

"Thanks, Dad." I closed my hand around his arm to keep him from moving away. "Really. I appreciate everything you and Mom have done, and I appreciate you understanding why I need to do this. Thank you, for just—everything."

His throat worked, and his lips pressed together. "Nate, I hope you know we'd do anything to make you happy. Anything. You're our son, and we—" He shook his head again.

"I know that, Dad. I know."

At high noon on the Saturday after we'd graduated from college, I saw my every dream come true when I married Quinn Russell.

The ceremony was brief but filled with meaning. I hardly heard a word of it, because I couldn't take my eyes off my beautiful bride.

Quinn wore a short light pink sundress, with flowers in her hair. Her eyes were clear and steady, and when the minister pronounced us man and wife, she kissed me with warmth.

We celebrated afterwards with barbecued chicken and a variety of cold summer salads, because those were my favorites. Carrie had made a cake, and Quinn and I sliced it together before we fed each other the first bite.

My father lifted a glass of champagne and made a toast, and we all got tears in our eyes when he mentioned Bill, and how much we missed him. It made me wonder if Quinn would have married me, if her father were still alive; would Bill have understood? Or would he have talked her out of it?

And then it was my turn to speak. "I told my dad earlier how much I appreciate what he and my mom have done to get me to this day. That goes for all of you. For all the really crappy stuff that I've had to deal with in my life, I've been blessed by having all of you as my family. We don't all share blood, but we share a bond that goes even deeper, and that has made every day of my life better. Fuller.

"Today has been perfect for me, because marrying Quinn is all I've ever wanted. I know you don't all understand the whys of that, but you're here anyway." My eyes traveled over every face, resting briefly on Leo's. He returned my gaze, and there was no acrimony or accusation there. Only a sort of sad resignation. "That means a lot. You know I don't like to fudge on the truth. And the truth is, before the year is out, you'll probably all be gathered again, this time to say good-bye to me. What sucks is that I won't be able to be there, to hear all the sweet things you're all going to say."

Across the room, my mom gave a half-sob, half-laugh, and my father pulled her against his side.

"So I look at today as not only my wedding day, but as our last big celebration. Being here with all of you is almost the best thing ever." I lifted Quinn's hand to my lips. "But the absolute best part of today is that now I can call this beautiful woman, the best person I've ever known in all my life, mine. My wife."

There was a smattering of applause, and I kissed Quinn. Just because I could.

I lay in bed at the end of my most perfect day ever, staring out the window at the stars that dotted the black velvet of the sky. I was tired, but not exhausted; I was glad that I'd paced myself all day.

I was even happier about that when Quinn came into our room. She wore a long white nightgown, with her hair in a dark cloud around her face. The lights were out in the bedroom, but my eyes were used to the dark, and I could see her clearly.

"Hi." She sat down on the edge of the bed.

"Hey." I shifted over, flipping back the sheets. "Slide under."

She slipped her feet beneath the covers and settled back. I put my arm around her, pulling her against my chest. Her hair tickled my nose, and I breathed in her tantalizing scent.

"You know we don't have to do anything tonight, right? We can just sleep." Her voice sounded muffled. "I know you must be tired."

"Not *that* tired." I swallowed hard and skimmed the back of my fingers down her arm, stopping when my arm brushed over her breasts. Her nipple reacted, coming to a hard point, and I felt myself harden.

What I wouldn't have given to roll over her body and make love to her fully, to sink myself into her softness and be one with her. I felt so omnipotent today, so fully myself, that I was tempted to try. What stopped me was the fear that it wouldn't work, that I'd be so mortified, I'd ruin tonight for us.

So I didn't even think about it. Instead, I cupped her boob and circled the nipple with my thumb. She was holding herself very still, and I couldn't tell what she was thinking.

"If I do anything wrong, just tell me. I only want to make you feel good." I shifted a little, my heart thudding as I lowered my mouth to suck her nipple into my mouth, soaking the cotton of her nightie as I did. Quinn sucked in a quick breath, but she didn't pull away.

"Nate." She whispered my name. "Can I touch you? Is that okay?"

I nodded. "I'm not sure I'll last long, but yeah. Please."

Quinn brushed her hand down over my stomach, pausing at the waistband of my boxers. Her fingers shook a little as she moved her hand underneath, and I held my breath. When her fingers closed over my cock, it was the most incredible feeling I'd ever had. My hips began to pump of their own accord, everything in the world diminishing to a narrow tunnel. My balls tightened and then everything exploded as I cried out her name.

In some important ways, I was a normal twenty-two-year old male. Over the years, I'd jerked off plenty . . . usually to thoughts of the woman whose hand was now stroking me down. But having her bring me to climax, even when it had taken mere seconds, was mind-boggling. I wanted that every day, for the rest of my life.

And I wanted to do the same thing for her.

"Quinn, let me make you feel good." It was hard for me to hold myself over her, but I could lay next to her and touch her. "Please. Let me do this. Let me be your husband in this way, at least."

She seemed to draw back a little, and then, finally she nodded. "Okay."

I wasn't smooth. I didn't have finesse. Quinn—my wife—

was the first girl I'd touched like this. My hands trembled as I shoved up her nightgown, exposing her boobs, but I fastened my lips around one nipple while my fingers played with the other. I couldn't tell whether or not Quinn liked that, but I took my time, and in a few minutes, her breathing changed and she began to shift her hips restlessly.

Keeping my mouth on one breast, I crept my hand down, lower, until my fingers rested just over her core. I knew I needed to be mindful of how I touched her here; not too hard or too light. I tried to remember what I'd read online and the pictures I'd seen.

When I ventured one finger over her folds, Quinn drew in a deep breath. She wasn't slick, the way I had read she would be if she was really turned on. But that was okay. I knew what to do next.

I found the small knob right where the internet had said it would be, and I pressed it lightly. "Quinn. I know this isn't what you're used to. I know you've been . . . I know you have experience. If you need to think about . . . if you want to picture Leo, I understand. If you need to think about him, do it. I just want you to feel good. It's still going to be me touching you."

A sob broke from her throat, but I kept touching her. I kept moving my finger over her clit and then, as she began to respond, I replaced my finger with my thumb and thrust two fingers into her.

Quinn arched, one hand gripping my wrist as though to hold me in place. Her mouth opened, her eyes screwed shut and she gave a short, loud cry as her channel convulsed around my fingers. It was the single most amazing thing I'd ever experienced in my life, feeling her orgasm and knowing I'd done it. I'd brought her pleasure, even if it wasn't the traditional kind of wedding-night consummation.

After a few seconds, she pushed my hand, rolling a little away from me. I lay next to her as her breathing slowly returned to normal.

"Quinn . . . that was beautiful. Thank you so much." I kissed her neck and then her lips, softly. "Thank you for . . . everything."

She laid one palm alongside my cheek. "I love you, Nate."

"I love you, too, Quinn. Thank you for marrying me."

Settling on my back, I kept her close to me, reveling in the wonder of falling asleep with my wife in my arms.

She was all I had ever wanted, and she was mine. For as long as I lived.

Quinn

As soon as I knew Nate was asleep, I slipped out of bed, moving slowly and carefully across the room to where my robe hung on a hook behind the door. I pulled it on and turned the door knob, padding down the hallway to the living room, where the French doors opened onto the deck.

Everyone had gone home after the wedding, leaving Nate and me to enjoy the house for our wedding night and the rest of the week. Nate couldn't really travel, so this was our honeymoon. I was glad; I loved this house, and being at the beach was a balm to my stormy soul. Still, it felt strange to be here without my mom. The past few months had been rocky for us; she'd made no secret of the fact that she didn't agree with my decision to marry Nate. Eventually, she'd gone along with it, out of love for all of us, but I knew she was worried about the future. My future.

The night air on the deck was chilly, damp with the salty ocean scent. The beach was empty and silent aside from the rhythmic crashing of the waves.

I sat down on the step that led to the beach, curling my toes over the wooden step below me, wrapping my arms around my middle. I felt empty, hollow and numb.

My body was still thrumming with the aftermath of my orgasm. I hadn't expected to be able to come, not with Nate touching me. I loved him, I had always loved him, but I had never desired him. I'd never wanted him the way I wanted Leo with every beat of my heart.

To my shame, I'd had to think about Leo while Nate's hands were on me. I'd imagined Leo's face, how he looked when he made love to me, the way his eyes went soft when he thrust into me. It was only with the memory of his body inside mine that I'd been able to climax.

What I couldn't let myself remember was Leo's face today. I'd realized pretty quickly how cruel I'd been to ask him to be there. He had kept his distance, both last night and today, rarely getting close enough to touch me and never speaking to me alone. I'd played along, understanding that he needed that separation to stay sane.

But I'd made the mistake of glancing at Leo during the

ceremony, and the pain I'd seen in his eyes as Nate had recited his vows nearly broke me. When it was my turn to repeat after the minister, I couldn't help staring at Leo as I said the words meant for Nate.

"To have and to hold, from this day forward, forsaking all others . . ." And that was the phrase that jerked me back to the moment. *Forsaking all others*. That was what I'd done. I'd forsaken Leo in favor of Nate and what he needed. I had a good rationale for doing it, but all the excuses in the world wouldn't change the hurt it caused Leo.

I looked down at my hands, at the slender gold band on my left hand. I was married now, married to a man who I loved but wasn't in love with, a man who wanted me more than anyone else in the world. A man who would be dead within the year.

Sitting alone, with only the waves and stars to keep me company, I laid my head on my folded arms and sobbed.

Not Quite the End . . .

Yet.

Book #3

Coming in September

★ Epilogue ★

"DON'T YOU THINK YOU'VE HAD ENOUGH?"

Eli Tuckerton, one-time star receiver for Gatbury High's football team, a guy I'd once loved to watch play the game, looked up at me from his wheelchair. In his eyes, I saw compassion, sympathy and understanding.

I fucking hated that.

"No, as a matter of fact, I don't." I slammed back the rest of my boilermaker and signaled to the bartender. "And I'm pretty sure I just met you yesterday, dude. Which means you're not even a little qualified to tell me what to do."

"I've known you for two years. Does that give me the right to say you need to slow down?" Standing next to the wheelchair, one hand resting on its back, Zelda cocked her head at me. Her blonde hair was twisted up, exposing the slim column of her neck, and I thought distractedly that this chick was extremely fuckable. Maybe she'd be just what I needed to take my mind off my problems. Maybe she could do what this booze wasn't and make me forget Quinn.

I was about to open my mouth to make a suggestion to

that effect when Tuck slid one arm around her waist. I didn't miss the way his hand curved over the slope of her ass, even though he was pretty subtle about it. *Damn.* Apparently the delectable Zelda was off-limits. I wasn't the type of guy to snake a girl who was clearly taken.

"No." I finally answered her question. "It doesn't. None of you are my mother, my father, or even my one of my older brothers." I picked up the shot the bartender had just delivered and dumped into the new beer. "And you're sure as hell not my girlfriend or my wife."

*Wife.*The sting was still there. Well, it was more than a sting. It was like a stab. A painful, throbbing stab with a knife that had been coated with poison. Yep, that about covered it.

Satisfied with my inner-analogy, I took a long drink and wiped my mouth.

"Leo." Gia turned at last from the stool next to mine. Her eyes were tired, as they always seemed to be these days. "Come on. You know that's not the answer to anything. I get that you're hurting. It sucks."

I gave a bark of humorless laughter. "Sucks. Yeah, you could say that." A lump rose in my throat, and I blinked away suspicious moisture in my eyes. "As a great man we both once knew used to say, this day sucks big giant T-rex balls."

A ghost of a smile flitted across Gia's face. "That's right. He'd say that."

"God, Gia. I miss him so fucking much."

She closed her eyes. "I know. I know you do. Sometimes I think you and I are the only ones who will remember him, in the end. To everyone else, he'll just be a footnote or some kind of cautionary tale for college football players who go astray.

Who will know who Matt Lampert really was?"

I reached up onto the bar and took her hand, squeezing it. "We will. I promise."

One side of her mouth curved up a little, but it wasn't really a smile. "Meanwhile, you really have had a lot to drink. Maybe we should go up to our rooms." The four of us had decided to stay at a hotel in Ocean City tonight so that we didn't have to drive home. It had sounded like a good idea at the time, but now I was wishing I'd driven back to the airport and caught the first place to Richmond. Anything to get away from New Jersey.

"Go ahead if you want. I'm not ready yet." I gulped the beer again.

She sighed and leaned her head on her chin. "Fine." Glancing back at Zelda and Tuck, she added, "If you want to go up, or wherever, I'll keep my eye on Leo."

Zelda shook her head. "I'm not leaving you two. But let's move to a table, okay? It's too hard for Eli to get up onto a bar stool, and I want to sit down."

That was a compromise I could make. We settled ourselves at a nearby booth, with Gia sitting next to me and Tuck transferring himself deftly from the chair to the vinyl bench. Zelda scooted in next to him.

For the first few minutes, we were all silent, and then Zelda ventured to speak. "It was a nice ceremony, at least. I mean . . . for what it was."

Gia nodded. "I guess."

"What the fuck, you guys? That was some kind of messed-up shit." Tuck shook his head. "I love Nate like a brother. We were roommates for four years, and I hate that he's—that his time is running out. But come on. What he did to Quinn, asking her to marry him now, that was just wrong. She's miserable. Anyone could see it."

The idea of Quinn being unhappy should've given me a perverse thrill. She was the one who'd said yes to Nate's ridiculous proposal. She was the one who'd ripped apart what we'd shared and was now married to another man. But I couldn't find it in me to be glad that she was suffering.

I'd kept my distance the night before, greeting her casually and then making it a point to stay as far away as I possibly could. The last time we'd talked alone had been the day of Matt's funeral, when I'd tried to proposition her upstairs to a bedroom, and there was a definite possibility that I'd try that again, given the chance. While that might make me feel better for the short term, it wasn't the answer either of us needed.

Today, during the ceremony, she'd stared into my eyes as she'd made her vows. I'd wanted to scream. I'd wanted to jump up and object, only the minister never paused for anyone to say why these two should not be joined together. I had a shit ton of reasons, but apparently no one cared.

Afterwards, when everyone was kissing the bride, I'd taken my turn, drawing her into my arms like old times and touching her smooth, cool cheek with my lips. I'd intended to leave it at that, stepping back away from Quinn, but she'd clung to my shoulders for an extra moment, moving her mouth to just below my ear.

"I'm sorry, Leo. I'm so sorry."

After that, I'd had to get away. Each minute under the same roof with them was excruciating, and when at last everyone had begun to clear away, I'd rounded up Gia, Zelda and Tuck and insisted it was time for us to take off.

"What are you going to do, Leo?" Zelda pinned me with a stare now. "Do you . . . will you wait for her? Or what?"

The 'or what' option seemed to be the most attractive at the moment. I had a feeling that choice covered another boilermaker.

"I'm going to get on a plane tomorrow morning and fly back to Richmond. I'm going to do everything I can to make it on this team, to be who they need. To play the game." I fiddled with the paper coaster under my mug. "And I'm going to do everything in my power to forget all about her. She's made her choice. I need to move on."

Gia sighed. "Do you really think that's possible, Leo?"

I shrugged and leveled a gaze at her, one that was meant to convey more than one meaning.

"I'm going to do my damnedest to find out."

Don't miss
Days of You and Me
Coming September 27, 2016

And please consider leaving a review for this book at your favorite book vendor!

★ Acknowledgements ★

This book was not easy to write. I knew it going in, but still . . . the painful parts were harder than I anticipated. I don't set out to write books with angst and sad stuff, but that is in the nature of this story. Leo, Quinn and Nate haven't had a smooth road, and this was perhaps their bumpiest section yet. Perhaps.

Thank you, as always, to the wonderful team of people who make my books possible: cover designer Robin Ludwig of Covers by Robin made this beautiful cover and Stacey Blake of Champagne Formats made the inside just as pretty. My fabulous promotion helpers, Maria Clark, Jen Rattie and Mandie Stevens, make every day a little brighter. And Olivia Hardin keeps me as sane as it gets—and makes me beautiful trailers, too!

Huge thanks (and a few extra boxes of tissues) to my beta team: Kara Schilling, Krissy Smith, Marla Wenger, Dawn Line and Julianna Santiago. You ladies rock beyond the telling. Big loves and hugs all around.

All of my Temptresses have been wildly supportive of the Keeping Score Trilogy, and I am so grateful. I couldn't do what I do without their support.

Book 3 is coming in September, so hang tight. And in case you didn't pick it up, there will be two spin-offs (at least) from this trilogy: *Your Wildest Dreams* and *Not Broken Anymore* will be released in 2017. Can you guess which characters will be featured?

On a more serious note, football is something that has always been a big part of my life—as a fan. I have special love for college football (Go Army!), and it's always a treat to see these young men with amazing talent live lives of responsibility and consciousness off the field, giving back where and when they can. It's also heartbreaking to see some of the players take a different road, one that may lead to dark places. I didn't know Matt Lampert's future or fate at the beginning of *Hanging By A Moment*, and I was saddened by it. Unfortunately, his story is all too realistic. It is my hope and prayer that the young men currently struggling with the side effects of fame and success would find a better answer—and a happier ending—than Matt did.

Suicide prevention is a cause dear to my heart. If you or anyone you know needs help, please check out To Write Love On Her Arms (https://twloha.com/). The website includes help lines, emergency text help, and much, much more. Remember: Hope is real. Help is real. Your story is important. Don't end it before its time.

And with that, I send you all oodles of love for reading, for your sweet messages of support and for reviews. You are important to me. Never forget that.

A sneak peek excerpt of *Days of You and Me*

The front door was open, so I knocked on the screen door, peering into the living room and calling. "Hello? Anyone home?'

"Come on in, Leo."

I almost didn't recognize Nate's voice, but as I stepped inside, catching the screen door so that it didn't slam, I saw him lying on the sofa. His hips and legs were covered with a knit afghan, and several pillows were at his back. He was thinner than ever, if that was even possible.

"Hey." I stood awkwardly, unsure of what to do next. "Uh, did I wake you up?"

"Nah." Nate shook his head, but he looked exhausted as he blinked, and I wondered if he was having trouble sleeping. "Sit down, okay? So I don't have to break my neck staring up at you."

I perched on the edge of the chair nearest the sofa. "This better?"

He nodded. "Much, thanks." His eyes darted around the room, as though he was looking for his next line. "Thanks for coming up, Leo. It means a lot."

"Sure." I glanced around my shoulder. "Is, uh . . . is anyone else at home?"

A faint smile played about his lips. "No. Quinn had a meeting in the city for work, and I convinced my mom to go with her. I'm okay by myself for short stretches, and my mother needed the break." He hastened to add, "They both do."

"So what do you need, Nate? What did you ask me to come up?"

He frowned, staring out the window at the ocean. "I want to talk to you about Quinn, Leo. Specifically, about what's going to happen when I'm not here anymore."

Annoyance flared in my chest. "Oh, you want my word that I won't make any moves? You want Quinn to stay a widow for the rest of her life, with no other prospects for marriage and a family?"

Nate sighed. "No, of course not. And I'm not asking for your word about anything. I just want to give you some advice." He paused, his lips pursing as he searched for the right words.

"I'm going to help you to get Quinn back. This time forever."

Hanging By A Moment Play List

Guardian Alanis Morissette

Love the One You're With Crosby, Stills and Nash

Stressed Out Twenty One Pilots

Lucky Jason Mraz

Why Don't You Love Me New Hollow

Falling Slowly Steve Kazee

I Can't Make You Love Me Bonnie Raitt

Apocalypse Jackie Evancho

Hanging By A Moment Lifehouse

To see other play lists and keep up with new ones, follow me on Spotify (https://open.spotify.com/user/1230830566)!

★ About the Author ★

Photo by Heather Batchelder

Tawdra Kandle writes romance, in just about all its forms. She loves unlikely pairings, strong women, sexy guys, hot love scenes and just enough conflict to make it interesting. Her books run from YA paranormal romance through NA paranormal and contemporary romance to adult contemporary and paramystery romance. She lives in central Florida with a husband, kids, sweet pup and too many cats. And yeah, she rocks purple hair.

Follow Tawdra on Facebook, Twitter, Instagram, Pinterest and sign up for her newsletter so you never miss a trick.

If you love Tawdra's books, become a Naughty Temptress! Join the group for sneak peeks, advanced reader copies of future books, and other fun.

Printed in the USA
CPSIA information can be obtained
at www.ICGtesting.com
JSHW031710140824
68134JS00038B/3622